A LONG,
LONG SLEEP

A LONG, LONG SLEEP

ANNA SHEEHAN

GOLLANCZ
LONDON

The right of Anna Sheehan to be identified as the author
of this work has been asserted by her in accordance with the
Copyright, Designs and Patents Act 1988.

First published in Great Britain in 2011 by Gollancz
An imprint of the Orion Publishing Group
Orion House, 5 Upper St Martin's Lane, London WC2H 9EA
An Hachette UK Company

A CIP catalogue record for this book is available
from the British Library

ISBN 978 0 575 10471 6 (Cased)
ISBN 978 0 575 10472 3 (Trade Paperback)

1 3 5 7 9 10 8 6 4 2

Printed in Great Britain by Clays Ltd, St Ives plc

The Orion Publishing Group's policy is to use papers
that are natural, renewable and recyclable products and made
from wood grown in sustainable forests. The logging and
manufacturing processes are expected to conform to the
environmental regulations of the country of origin.

www.orionbooks.co.uk

— *For Drew,*
because he was my only
and this was my first ———

A long, long sleep, a famous sleep
That makes no show for dawn
By stretch of limb or stir of lid,—
An independent one.

*W*as ever idleness like this?
Within a hut of stone
To bask the centuries away
Nor once look up for noon?

—EMILY DICKINSON

—chapter 1—

I'd try to hold on to my stass dreams as long as I could. It's a game I would play, struggling to keep track of those misty images that were always so easily lost. I'd try to keep myself in stasis, keep my heart beating too slow to feel, refuse to wake up my lungs. Once or twice I managed to hold on so long that Mom panicked and turned on the resuscitator.

So when the electric-blue seascape I was trying to hold on to was interrupted, not by a hand but by the feeling of lips on mine, I was startled. I sucked in a breath through my nose and sat bolt upright, knocking my head against my would-be rescuer.

I couldn't see. Everything was dim and painful, as if I had just opened my eyes into a bright light after days in the dark. An unfamiliar voice shouted unfamiliar words: "Holy coit, you *are* alive!"

I felt utterly lost. All I could do was grope for what I knew. "Where's Mom?" My voice wasn't mine; it sounded like a croak. I tried to take stock of my condition. My muscles ached, and my lungs seemed filled with fluid. I coughed, trying to force air into the dormant passages. I tried to get to my feet. Piercing pains like knives shot through my legs and arms where I tried to lift myself. My very bones ached. I slid back down into the smooth, soft cushion of the stass tube.

"Whoa!"

My rescuer leaped toward me as I fell. Warm hands grabbed at me, and my muscles screamed with stiffness. "Don't touch me!" I gasped. I didn't understand why I was in such pain.

He let me go, but the pain didn't diminish. "Coit, you scared me." The voice sounded overly excited. "You weren't breathing there—I was afraid I'd botched the system and exed you."

I barely understood half of what he was saying. "How long?" I whispered.

"You only seemed dead for a minute," he said as if to reassure me.

I'd meant how long had I been in stasis, but I abandoned that line of thought. It didn't matter. I told myself that every time I woke up. It didn't matter. "Who are you?" I asked instead.

"My name's Brendan. I live in suite five. Do you know where you are?"

I frowned, or would have had my head not begun to ache. Suite five housed an elderly couple and their collection of tropical fish. At least that's who had lived there the last time I'd been awake, but I had no idea how long I'd been stassed. "Unicorn Estates, of course. What are you doing here? Did you just move here?"

There was a long silence. "No, we've lived here all my life." He sounded frightened now.

I blinked and directed my bleary eyes toward where I was sure he was. Brendan was a dark shadow, a blurry silhouette of a man. A young man, from his voice. I was confused. "Why did you wake me up?"

He started, as if surprised. "You wanted to stay in stasis?"

"No, I mean, why did *you* wake me up? Where's Mom?"

There was a long silence. "Um . . ." He took a deep breath. "I don't know where your mom is. Do . . . do you know who you are?"

"Of course I do!" I said, but my voice was still shaky and hoarse. I coughed again, fighting the stass fatigue.

"Well, I don't. I'm Brendan, and you are?"

"Rosalinda Samantha Fitzroy," I said precisely. I was annoyed. Who was this boy? I'd never had to tell anyone who I was before.

He took a step backward and then vanished out of sight. Alarmed, I tried to force myself back into a sitting position. My arms screamed, and my back seemed almost too weak to hold me up. Whatever strength my initial surprise had lent me, it was gone now. I pulled myself upright on the edges of the stass tube and tried to find my shadow man.

He was on the floor, less of a shadow now that I was sitting upright. He'd stumbled. His eyes were two white smudges in a dark circle of a head, opened wide to stare at me.

"What?" I croaked.

He scrambled backward, crablike, until he found purchase

on a box and hauled himself back to his feet. A box? Where the hell was I? This was definitely not my own comfortable closet, carpeted in rose pink, with all the latest fashions neatly on their hangers. This was vast, echoing and cluttered at once, like a storehouse. Tall shelves full of dark shapes towered over our heads. "Did you say Fitzroy?" Brendan asked. "Rosalinda Fitzroy?"

"Yes," I said. "What of it?"

"I need to go get some help." He turned his back to go.

"No!" I yelled, or as close to a yell as my stagnant lungs and my parched throat could. I didn't know why I'd cried out at first. Stass chemicals did a number on your emotional state, so sometimes it was hard to put a finger on how you were feeling. After a moment I realized I was terrified. Everything was wrong, nothing was what I expected, and I had a feeling that something truly terrible had happened.

He turned back to me. "I'll be right back."

"Don't!" I breathed. "Don't leave me alone here! I want my mom! What's going on? Where's Xavier?"

There was a moment of hesitant confusion, and then I felt his hand on my shoulder. This time it was gentle, and my muscles didn't scream so loudly. "It's okay. Really. Just . . . I can't do this alone."

"Do what alone? Tell me what's going on! Where's my mom?"

"Miss . . . ah . . . Fitzroy . . ."

"Rose," I said automatically.

"Rose," he repeated. "I came down here just . . . exploring.

I didn't know this place existed. I stumbled on your stass tube and accidentally started the revive sequence. No one has been in this corner of the subbasement since the Dark Times."

"Dark times?" I asked.

"The Dark Times?" he said as if it should be obvious. "When the . . . Oh, God." His voice fell to a horrified whisper. "That was sixty-some years ago."

"I'm sorry . . ." I whispered, unable to grasp what he was saying. "Sixty . . . y-years?"

"Yeah," Brendan said quietly. "And . . . if you're really Rosalinda Fitzroy . . ." Whatever more he had to say would have to wait. The ocean from my dream returned in the form of a roaring surf, which blocked all sound and stopped my breath. Sixty years. Mom and Daddy, dead. Åsa, dead. Xavier . . . my Xavier . . .

I think I screamed. The last thing I felt as the shadows overcame my vision completely was Brendan's strong arms catching me as I fell.

—chapter 2—

I woke in strange surroundings with strange voices at my feet. I lay on my back, reclined rather than flat. Cool fabric under my fingers. A familiar smell—antiseptic and illness. Hospitals always smelled the same. Used to holding on to my stass dreams, I kept my eyes closed and my breathing even.

"What does the doctor say?" The voice was male, wavery with age. He sounded concerned.

"They're having trouble figuring out who to give that information to." That was a woman, brusque and kind, a voice I immediately liked.

Another voice cut her off. "Me, of course." This one was strong and imperious, used to being obeyed. "Who else?"

"She has no family." That was the older male.

"She has UniCorp, and that means me," said the younger one. "Imagine waking up to discover she's the sole surviving heiress to an interplanetary empire!"

"We aren't an empire" was the older man's gruff reply. "Honestly, Reggie, I think you have delusions of grandeur."

"Well, who do you think should be responsible, then? You?" There was no response, so the younger man continued. "This is mostly your fault, anyway. This would be so much easier if you'd left well enough alone. If you'd let me sign her over to the social services anonymously, it wouldn't even be in question. It's not as if anyone would believe her story." He sighed. "I don't know why we even had to tell the board, or the state. We could have given her a new identity. I doubt her memory's very strong."

"Because that wouldn't be *right*," said the older man, with a bite to his words that kept even the imperious one from arguing.

"All of this is moot," said the woman. "Dad, Reggie, calm down, both of you. The judge will be here in a moment. I think your proposal will be accepted, Reggie. No one disputes that you're the president of UniCorp."

I opened my eyes at that. "*Daddy*'s president of UniCorp," I croaked.

The three people at the foot of my hospital bed jumped. The woman came toward me. She was Eurasian, slender, and well groomed, though her clothes seemed casual. The two men wore business suits, but the cut had changed from what I was used to. I couldn't make out their features, as my eyesight was still blurry. The younger man looked like a blur of gold, while the older one no more than a blur of white, with a dark suit beneath it.

A finger tapped on the glass wall of my hospital room. A blurred figure fidgeted in the hallway. "The judge is here," said the younger of the two men. "I'm on it. Ronny, Annie, I'll leave this to you." He gestured at me as he left. Apparently the judge was the important one, and I was nothing more than a "this."

"Who are you?" I asked the two who were left.

"We work for UniCorp, dear," said the woman, while the man turned away from me. "My name is Roseanna Sabah, but you can call me Annie. This is my father, Ron. I'm Brendan's mother. You remember Brendan?"

Brendan. My shadow man. "The one who woke me up?"

"Yes." Mrs. Sabah smiled. "He found you yesterday. You've been in stasis for so long, we had to bring you to the hospital."

Something clutched at the back of my throat, something dark and terrified. "So it's true, what he said?" I croaked. "Sixty years?"

"Sixty-two," said the old man from the back of the room. His words fell like lead weights.

"And my mother and my father . . . and everyone I knew . . ." My vision disappeared completely as I started to cry. I tried to force the tears back, as Mom had taught me, but I couldn't. The tears ran down into my mouth. They tasted strange, oversalinated and thick.

"I'm afraid so, dear," said the woman. "Mark and Jacqueline Fitzroy died in a helicopter crash while you were still in stasis. But you are alive, and we're all going to see that you're well taken care of."

"How?" I managed to whisper.

"I'm afraid your parents died without making a will," said the woman. "By default, their company went to their shareholders and the board of directors. However, now that you're back with us, all their assets revert to you."

"Are you telling me . . . I own UniCorp now?"

"No," the old man snapped brusquely. For some reason, his voice frightened me. "Unfortunately, UniCorp owns you. At least until you come of age."

"Dad, don't frighten the girl."

"She should know where she stands!" He was almost yelling now.

The woman pulled away from my bedside. "Until you can control yourself, Dad, you should stand outside!" she hissed. "I'm sorry your company is in shambles, but that's no call—"

"It was never my company," growled the old man. "It was Fitzroy's. And now it's Guillory's. Give this speech to him!" He took a deep breath and turned away. "But you're right. You should be the one to talk to her. I have some things to take care of."

He strode out the door. Mrs. Sabah came back to my bedside. "Sorry about that," she said.

"It's all right," I lied. Now that the stass chemicals had faded further, my fear bubbled beneath my voice.

"I should let you sleep," Mrs. Sabah said, touching my hand gently. "Don't worry about anything. Right now all you should think about is getting better. We can deal with everything else when you're stronger. I'll be back in the morning. Bren would like to see you're okay, too, if that's all right."

I nodded for her, even though it hurt my neck.

"Get some rest, dear. Don't worry. We'll sort everything out."

Six days later, I was perched before the backdrop of Unicorn Estates while at least a hundred reporters snapped pictures of the miraculous Sleeping Beauty. Or so they called me. I didn't feel very beautiful.

Despite six days in the hospital, plus twenty-four hours of primping and preening, health monitors, vitality injections, and a thousand other ministrations to which I had been subjected, my hair was still lank and brittle, my skin sallow and sensitive, and my bones protruded so much I looked like a skeleton in a bag. My eyes were weak, my breath was shallow, and I felt ill when I tried to eat. I felt like an old woman. Technically, I was one.

More than eighty years old at the age of sixteen. I'd never spent so long in stasis. No one ever had. Even the astronauts and colonists on their way to the outer planets were revived every month, to prevent stass fatigue.

Mr. Guillory spoke now at the podium, back straight, gold-tinted hair immaculate. Mr. Guillory—"Call me Reggie!"—was apparently my designated executor. Since I had no living relatives, he was the one responsible for finding me a guardian and a home. He was in his late fifties, and though I knew he deserved my respect, I was hard-pressed to like him. His light-brown eyes didn't seem to look directly at me when he spoke to me, and he seemed to me like an expensive golden statue. Something about him frightened me, but he also reminded me of Daddy, so I was very polite to him.

"UniCorp is thrilled to have discovered young Rosalinda," Guillory said. "When Mark and Jacqueline Fitzroy died without an heir, it was a great tragedy. To have their issue returned to us is a joy beyond imagining."

One of the reporters shouted out a question. "What about the rumor that you tried to have knowledge of her discovery suppressed?"

Guillory didn't even flinch. "Six days ago, Rosalinda was suffering extreme stass fatigue and was subjected to a severe shock. We thought it would be best for her to spend a few days acclimating to her situation before the press descended and scrutinized her every move. We never intended to suppress the truth beyond what we thought was best for Rosalinda's mental and physical health."

"So what is the state of the UniCorp organization, and what will be the future of the corporation's assets?"

"Rosalinda is, of course, the sole heir to the finances of her parents' immediate holdings. However, until she reaches the age of ascension, her finances are to be held in trust by our company. A lawyer has been appointed to her through UniCorp, and she will be taken care of to the best of everyone's ability."

The reporter's face was deeply skeptical. She tried to follow up. "But what about ownership of the company itself?"

Actually, even I didn't know the answer to this question, and I watched the back of Guillory's head with interest. But the reporter was ignored as Guillory pointed to someone else.

"How is it that Rosalinda was left in stasis in the first place?"

Guillory sidestepped. "As you know, the Fitzroys were financial giants of their time. With their considerable assets, the Fitzroys purchased the stass tube for their family's personal use long before the Dark Times. It is presumed that it was lost during the unrest that followed. Next?"

"Rosalinda is underage," someone called out. "Who is going to care for her?"

"Rosalinda's lawyers have already found a suitable foster family. The family that resided in her old apartment has generously agreed to move to a comparable apartment nearby, so Rosalinda will be able to return to the home she knew before. The foster family has been thoroughly vetted and is beyond all reproach. Next?"

"How was she discovered? The rumors are garbled."

Guillory smiled. "For that I'll turn you over to my young friend Brendan Sabah, who made the startling discovery. He is the son of one of our most prominent executives, and a remarkable young man. Bren, if you would step up to the microphone?"

I studied Bren as he approached the podium. He exuded confidence, not a tremor of stage fright. Little, it seemed, ever fazed Bren. I'd learned a bit more about him during my week in the hospital. He was my age, athletic in a streamlined way, and he moved like a panther. Mrs. Sabah told me he played competitive tennis. His dark skin came from his father, who had emigrated up to ComUnity from off the Ivory Coast. He looked more like a holostar or a fairy-tale prince than a high-school student.

"My parents bought Unicorn Estates six months ago, when it came up for sale, and I started poking around to help," Bren told them. "It turns out there were a lot of rooms and storage facilities that no one knew about. A set of biometric cards was handed over with the deed. Some of those old cards opened the storage rooms in the subbasement, and it was in one of those rooms that I found Rose's stass tube."

"What did you do when you first realized there was a girl inside?"

"I didn't know it was a stass tube right away," Bren said. His eyes glinted in the light of the flashbulbs. He'd picked up his mother's stunning eyes, which shone hazel-green in his dark face. "It was covered in dust, but a light was still flashing on it. I tried to wipe off the light to see what it was, but it turned out the light was a button, and when I pressed it, I had started the revive sequence."

"So the tube opened, and you found Rosalinda?"

Bren shrugged. He seemed a little uncomfortable. "Yeah."

I knew why he seemed uncomfortable. When he'd seen that I wasn't waking up, he'd been afraid he'd botched the revive sequence, which was why he'd started rescue breaths, and I think he was a little embarrassed to discover they weren't necessary.

"When did you first realize who Rosalinda was?"

"She told me," Bren said. "My granddad had the hospital confirm it."

At this point, Guillory stepped forward and nudged Bren out of the way. "Bren contacted his grandfather, one of our top CEOs, and he brought the matter to my attention. Are there any more questions?"

A reporter's hand shot up. "I have a question for Rosalinda!"

Guillory turned to me and gestured for me to stand up. I flung Bren a panicked look. His face softened sympathetically. "Go on," he mouthed.

I took a deep breath. I wasn't one for cameras. Even the idea that they had been recording me sitting behind Guillory had frightened me. I didn't want to go up there, but everyone expected it of me. . . . My mother's voice echoed in my memory. *It doesn't always matter what you want, dear. Sometimes you have to do what others expect of you.* I didn't have to like it. I just had to do it. I made myself rise from my chair.

More cameras flashed as I stood. I swallowed. One step. Two steps. Three. And then I was at the podium, and Guillory's firm hand kept me from backing away.

"Miss Fitzroy, how does it feel to wake up in a new century?"

I swallowed again. I was in constant pain, weak as a kitten, and perpetually exhausted, but I didn't think that was what she meant. In truth, I didn't know how I felt. And I didn't want to know. Between the shock and the pain and the stass chemicals, my emotions seemed distant, like they didn't belong to me. "It's good to be back," I said, handing them their sound bite. Cameras flashed. It was a lie, but that didn't matter. That was all they wanted to hear.

. . .

He was covered in dust, but that didn't affect him. He was past noticing such things. Then the name passed through the net and tickled his programming. "Rosalinda Fitzroy."

Electrodes fired that had long been dormant. Systems slipped into active mode. He accessed the file that had triggered the response program.

This world was shocked last week at the discovery of the daughter of Mark and Jacqueline Fitzroy, the founders of the interplanetary corporation UniCorp. Apparently kept in stasis for more than sixty years, Rosalinda Fitzroy was found beneath Unicorn Estates. Today we see Rosalinda for the first time as UniCorp . . .

His programming scanned the file. If it had only been the name, he would have let himself go dormant again. But then the voiceprint confirmed a match.

"It's good to be back."

TARGET IDENTIFIED: ROSALINDA SAMANTHA FITZROY.

Once, his response would have been instant. Now his processors were wearing down. Slowly, after an eternity of seconds, his primary directive flickered into awareness.

DIRECTIVE: RETURN TARGET TO PRINCIPAL.

His directive active, he implemented a net search for the principal.

SCANNING . . . SCANNING . . . SCANNING . . . SCANNING . . .

It took a good twenty-four hours before his programming came up with the result.

PRINCIPAL UNAVAILABLE.

His programming wandered around for another eternity,

and it was some minutes before it finally found its secondary directive.

SECONDARY DIRECTIVE: TERMINATE TARGET.

That was a difficult one. Pathways that had never before been implemented were suddenly called into action. The recovery pathways of his primary directive were always on the alert, but this secondary directive had never been necessary before. He put the secondary directive on standby, awaiting a second scan. The principal might become available by the time the target was acquired.

Only then did his system begin the required status check.

STATUS REPORT: .03 PERCENT EFFICIENCY, LOW POWER, STANDBY MODE.

The report recommended a refit, and after some painful moments of wandering, his central information processor agreed. The recharge cable was already connected to his heart, but it took him more than five hours to turn it on.

RECHARGING. 100 PERCENT EFFICIENCY PREDICTED IN 687.4 HOURS.

The fact that it would take him nearly a month to achieve a reliable efficiency rating did not bother him in the least. Time meant nothing to him.

Systems whirred. Nanobots powered up one by one and scurried around his systems, cleaning his veins of detritus, lubricating his joints. His vision cleared as the nanos swarmed over his eyeballs, removing a heavy layer of dust.

As he awaited the completion of his recharge, he performed another scan for the principal, a scan he would perform again and again before his directive was carried out. The secondary directive was not his main program. If he had had feelings, he would have said that termination made him uncomfortable.

But he had no feelings. All he had were updates.

STANDBY RECHARGE.

STANDBY . . .

STANDBY . . .

STANDBY . . .

—chapter 3—

The next month was a bit of a blur. It was all too big, too dark, too terrible. I'd been ripped from my own time, and my world had died around me. Nothing belonged to me. Not the world, not my life, not even my own feelings.

My new parents were not really mine. Barry and Patty Pipher, a pair of accountants from Uni Florida, had been called in by Guillory. Their work had been reassigned to ComUnity, and I was a replacement for their two children, who were, apparently, off at college now. Not that I ever met them. The Piphers didn't even put up photos of them. For all that the Piphers were my new parents, children didn't seem to be a top priority for them. Barry was friendly but distracted, seemingly unwilling to think about anything but work. He smiled easily, at everything, but it always seemed like habit more than actual pleasure. Patty was frighteningly prim, even more straitlaced than my mother had been, with skin that looked like it had been airbrushed and hair that seemed molded out of plastic. She made me feel about twelve.

My home was not my home. Unicorn Estates hadn't changed much, of course. Some things keep plodding along in their prescribed patterns for decades, and Unicorn Estates was like that. But Unicorn had never felt like it belonged to me. It wasn't the kind of place that "belonged" to anyone.

By definition, Unicorn Estates was a condominium building, but such a one that would make regular condos weep. My parents had it built when I was seven, just after the UniCorp Building had been established and the town of ComUnity was beginning to spring up around it. In truth it was less of a condo complex than a vast mansion that housed many large and spacious apartments.

The population boom in my childhood had made owning one's own mansion prohibitive. Space was guarded zealously by the governments. But the wealthy still wanted their mansions, so while each apartment was self-contained, every amenity—fine chefs, indoor and outdoor swimming pools, hot tubs, saunas, billiards, ballrooms, stables and tennis courts, a gymnasium, private theaters, everything—could be had at Unicorn, without the bother of having to maintain it. Bren's parents ran it now. Before I was stassed, my mother had managed it, while Daddy spent his time with UniCorp. It was all very familiar to me.

Even though I was in my old apartment, it didn't feel the same. Barry and Patty hadn't seen any reason to redecorate, but the apartment had changed owners many times since my mother's hand had arranged the furnishings. Mom had favored pastels and off-whites, leaving my home something of a blank canvas on which I could paint whatever I wanted to see. Now most of the apartment had been washed with earth tones, the formal crisp edges rounded into something quieter, homier. I did like the previous occupants' taste in artwork. Whoever they were, their taste favored large surrealistic Dalí-style landscapes and small striking portraits of historical figures, like Nehru and van Gogh. It reminded me of some of my own work. I liked it, but it didn't feel like the same place I had lived with my mother and father.

The first time I walked into my room, though, I nearly burst into tears. If my life was going to be different, if my world was going to be dead, I wanted *everything* to have changed. Maybe I could slough off whatever or whoever I had been before and become someone completely new. Or that's what I'd been telling myself.

But when Barry and Patty had opened the door to what had once been my room, I was shocked into a life I'd been carefully shutting out. Suddenly I was forced to remember who I was. And it hurt.

My room was the same. Almost exactly. I wondered if they'd found a photo of it in some computer archive, because it was nearly identical to what it had been sixty years ago. There were subtle differences — the patterns on the rug had changed, the furniture was a slightly different shape — but the bed in the corner had a rosebud coverlet, just as mine had had. There was even a print from Monet's water lilies sequence, though it was different from the one I'd had before.

It actually hurt to see it, to stand on my rose-pink carpeting, looking up at Monet's lilies, and know that when I turned around, it wouldn't be Mom or Daddy or Xavier standing behind me, but Patty and Barry and Guillory, all watching me like I was some nature program.

Then the sun slid through the clouds, and my eyes caught on one subtle but fabulous difference, something that had not been in my room before. In the window hung a tear-shaped prism. It caught the late-afternoon light and shattered it across the room into a thousand tiny rainbows. My tears died before they were born. I went to the prism and touched it, letting the rainbows dance around me.

The pain faded a bit. Someone had hung this for *me*, only for me. I suspected Mrs. Sabah. It seemed as real as a kiss. This room wasn't just some exhumed corpse of my old life. It was a gift. From Guillory or Mrs. Sabah or even the decorators, I didn't care. It was kindly meant. Which meant . . . what? That I wasn't alone?

There was another gift across the hall, something I had never expected. A dream of another life come true in this one.

It was a studio.

Not just any studio. A full, complete artist's studio, with an art sink and cups full of paintbrushes. A bookshelf stood at the ready, packed floor to ceiling with art books. Books on technique, on style, on history, from ancient Egyptian sculpture to

Neo-Dadaism. A drying rack for paintings, followed by the strict geometric lines of a cutting shelf, for matting or collage, and tools for stretching my own canvases. The drawers beneath the windows held multicolored chalks, charcoal and blending tools, a vast array of untouched colored pencils, and ream upon ream of paper, from blacks for my chalks to rough watercolor blocks. An entire spectrum of tubes of watercolors. A smattering of little pots of acrylic. Best of all, a whole big drawer of oil paints, bright and new and untouched, just waiting for my hands. Another drawer held more brushes and paint knives and palettes and everything I could possibly have desired.

I could make masterpieces in this room. There were two easels and a drafting table, with a light fixture for night work. Behind them, against the wall, a vast tank of tropical fish brought the colors of the paints to vivid life. It was a dream. A vision. The heart of every secret wish, the one thing I'd known I could never have. Even looking at it, my whole dark, fathomless future seemed a little brighter.

Things were hardest when I thought about my old life. How Mom used to take me to lunch, how Daddy would tousle my hair as he passed me on the way to his study—the same room that now held my studio. I missed Åsa, who would make me Earl Grey tea and drop terse one-word compliments in her smooth Swedish accent on my latest paintings or my most recent test scores.

And I missed Xavier with a constant drone of pain, like the sound of the ocean, occasionally washing over me to leave me drowning. I didn't know how I was supposed to get through without him. Deep down, I knew I could have endured losing Mom and Daddy and the world I was born into if I could just have Xavier back, the way he always had been.

I'd tried typing his name into the net while I was still in the hospital, just to see if by some miracle he could still be alive. Not that I knew what I'd do if he was. But I wasn't surprised when the name didn't come back in the current population files. After all, if Xavier had still been alive, he'd have taken me out of stasis decades ago. I didn't dig any further back; I didn't want to know how he'd died. I didn't want to know any more details about how Mom and Daddy died, either. They'd probably all died during those Dark Times that I still hadn't caught up on. If I didn't know how it happened, it was like they were still alive, if only in my head.

Losing all of them hurt, but my love for Xavier was still as sharp and agonizing as a blade, and I was sliced on it. Of course, my friendship with Xavier had always been a problem sharp enough to wound. Even when he was a child, he could tear at my heart.

There was one time back when he was five and I'd just come out of a stint of a few months. I couldn't have been much more than ten. I came out to the gardens. Xavier and his mom were outside—his mother working on some project, him playing with a pile of sticks. It was awfully bright outside, and I'd only just gotten out of my stass tube. My eyes weren't quite up to it. I was considering going back inside when I was bowled over by two-and-a-half feet of irrepressible energy.

"Rose!"

I blinked at the tornado of blond hair and freckles that had been the toddler I'd been playing with before I went into stasis. "Xavy?"

"Rose, Rose, Rose, Rose, Rose!" Xavier began dancing around me, singing my name over and over. "Rose, Rose, Rose!"

Mrs. Zellwegger looked up from the picnic table, where she was working on a portable screen. "Looks like you have a fan," she said absently, before she turned back to her work.

Xavier was so big I was surprised he even remembered me. "Look at you," I said down to the little boy. "You've grown so tall."

"I'm five years old now," he said proudly.

"Really?" I had no idea how long I'd been in stasis this time, but I knew Xavier had been four the last time I played with him. He'd been only half-articulate before, his conversation difficult to understand and wandering off on tangents that I couldn't follow. I'd played with him much the same way as I would have a dog, hiding behind trees and romping on the grass.

"I had a birthday in June, and now I'm five years old, and I'm going to school in the September!"

"Are you?" I asked.

"Look what I got! Look what I got!" he demanded, pulling on my arm. I followed, amused, as Xavier led me across the lawn to a small pile of toys under a tree. "I got it for my birthday. It's a treasure box." Nestled in the grass was a toy pirate chest made of plastine-infused wood, with a skull for a keyhole. He opened it up and started plying me with treasures.

Xavier had put all his most precious items in this box, and now he set me on the ground and started piling them all in my lap, showing off his new alphabet computer game box and his monster doll with "Five sharp teeth! Five, like me." And here was a box of crayons, and some kind of funny-shaped stick, and a feather, and his mother's old cell, broken, but he could pretend, and a toy fish, and, "Rose? Why are you crying?"

I blinked. "I'm not really crying," I told him, wiping at my watering eyes. "The sun's just really bright for me. My eyes hurt a little; it makes them watery."

Xavier's excited face turned serious, and he stared at me for a long moment. He frowned. "Here," he said. He dug in the bottom of his treasure box and pulled out a pair of toy sunglasses. "Keep them." They were made of plastic, and at least two sizes too small to fit on my face, but he handed them to me with such earnestness that I couldn't refuse them. With difficulty, I pulled them over my eyes. They didn't reach near my ears and hung wide on my temples, sticking to my head like a mild vise, but it was a very sweet gesture. "Thank you, Xavy."

"Rose?" he asked, all earnestness. "Where were you?"

I shook my head. "It's hard to explain. I went to sleep for a little while, but I'm awake now."

"Can't you come live with me?" he asked. "You can sleep in my room."

I smiled. "I have my own room."

"But then I could wake you up and you wouldn't sleep so long and you wouldn't miss my birthday."

"I'm sorry I missed your birthday," I said. "I won't be going to sleep like that for a while."

"Promise?"

"I promise."

Xavier pulled the toys off my lap and then took their place. His little arm sneaked around my waist, and he buried his head in my shoulder. "Don't ever go to sleep again, Rose," he said. "Stay with me forever and ever and ever."

"Absolutely," I told him, nuzzling his soft child's face. "Forever and ever."

I'd been a child myself, and I didn't understand how deeply I'd been lying to him. Now I'd been asleep for sixty-two years, and I'd missed every one of Xavier's birthdays.

Barry and Patty barely saw me those first few weeks. I wasn't really there. My world dwindled to my bed and my studio. I sketched remembered faces—especially Xavier's—and painted intricate landscapes. The stass fatigue made me slow, and I tired easily, but I realized quickly that my skills had actually improved as I'd slept. My artwork was the only thing I cared about. I showed up to meals when Barry and Patty asked me, and trotted off to buy underwear when Patty told me, and put away my laundry, because that was what was expected. And when Barry told me that I had an appointment with a psychologist, I dutifully climbed into the limoskiff and let him take me to a professional office in town.

"This first is just an informal session," said my psychologist after I'd sat down on the comfortable sofa. "Just so we can get to know each other a bit. Have your foster parents told you anything about me?"

I shook my head. "No," I said. "I was just told I had an appointment."

"Ah." Dr. Bija turned to her notescreen and touched it a few times. I was still trying to get the hang of my own notescreen. I knew touch-screen computers fairly well, but these flexible handheld things that pretended to be notebooks were new to me. It was nice that you could toss them around the room, accidentally sit on them, pile them under real books, and still use them to access the net and take all your school notes on, but they weren't really notebooks. Not as far as I was concerned.

My psychologist was in her midforties, with rich black hair graying around the temples, her skin a warm brown. She was wearing a smart linen pantsuit. Her name was Mina Bija. "Mee-na Bee-ja," as Barry had sounded out for me. He had dropped me off at one of the hundreds of buildings that had sprung up in ComUnity in the sixty years I'd been in stass. I didn't want a psychologist, but Barry assured me it was just so that I would be sure to assimilate. I rather thought Guillory wanted to spy on me, but it wasn't my place to argue the point.

"So you're Rosalinda. Do you prefer to be called Rose or something else?"

"Rose is good," I said, surprised she'd asked. Guillory still called me by the full Rosalinda, as if I were in some kind of trouble.

"Feel free to call me Mina," Dr. Bija said. "Your case was referred to me by Mr. Guillory, yes?"

"I think so."

"Of course, I saw you in the news about a month ago. Have you ever seen a psychologist before?"

I shook my head. "No. I have a physical therapist I'm going to, but never a psychologist."

"So I'm your first, eh?" she asked. She grinned with something of a self-deprecating air, which helped me drop my guard a bit. "Well, just so we have everything out of the way, you should know that I do work for UniCorp, here out of Uni Prep." I looked around her office again. I hadn't realized we were in my new school. "I understand you are to begin attending here soon?"

"Monday," I said.

"So soon? That must be scary."

I shrugged. "No scarier than everything else."

Her face turned concerned. "Yes, you've been through quite a shock."

I squirmed uncomfortably. "I'm not sure I really want to talk about that."

"Of course. Let's talk about school. How do you feel about being enrolled at Uni Prep? Do you think you're ready to go back to school?"

I shook my head. "I don't know. I guess."

"Not worried at all?" Mina pressed. "You have sixty years of technology and history to catch up on."

"I doubt I'll notice a difference," I said ruefully.

"Oh, really? I hope you do find it easy to assimilate. It would make things much more pleasant for you."

"That wasn't what I meant," I said. "It's just . . . I was never very good at school. I can't imagine it could be much worse, even with all the new stuff." I looked down at my knees. They were clad in Uni Prep's gray linen school uniform. I had a choice of skirts in the Uni plaid of green, blue, and gold, or the same gray or dark-green linen as the uniform jackets. Guillory had arranged for several changes of the entire spectrum of Uni Prep selections to be delivered to me at Unicorn. I was actually relieved. It meant I didn't have to go shopping for clothes. Patty had taken me to get some nightclothes and undergarments, and I'd found it a nightmare. I was used to fashions changing, but not at all used to choosing what I was going to wear. I wished Uni Prep had regulation pajamas.

"You don't do well in school?" Mina asked.

I shook my head. "Never have."

She frowned. "You do realize that Uni Prep strives for excellence in all fields."

"You think I should ask to be sent somewhere else?" I asked, somewhat afraid she'd say yes. Her primary loyalty had to be toward the school, after all. I didn't want to go somewhere else. For one thing, I'd have to give up the comforting uniform. For another, Uni Prep felt like an extension of my parents' protection, the closest thing I had to the kind of life they'd have given me if they were still alive. I didn't want to leave that behind.

"No," she said, "but I think we should have a talk with your school counselor, maybe arrange for some tutors."

Now it was my turn to frown. "Aren't you the school counselor?"

"No," Mina said. "I'm the resident psychologist. The school counselor's records are the school's records. Mine are private. I work through the school so there is easy access for the boarders. Many of them are away from home for the first time and need support. But I also have clients outside of the school and outside of ComUnity."

I did feel better. "I'd work with tutors. But it might not help—I'm not very smart," I admitted. "I used to try, but it never worked, so I don't bother much anymore."

"This is before you were in the hospital?"

"Before I was stassed," I clarified, wondering why she'd avoided the word. "Sometimes I'd get so far behind that we all just gave up and I'd start fresh in a new school."

I couldn't read the look on Mina's face, but she hesitated a moment before she asked, "And would that help?"

No one had ever asked that before. "Not really," I admitted.

Mina was okay, but I didn't feel quite right talking to her. I dodged most of the rest of her questions. She was part of this world, and I didn't fit properly into it. I was a child out of time. Nothing seemed to make sense. I didn't know how to program the holoview, and I couldn't even figure out how to work the stove. Which was ironic, since the stove and the refrigerator were a UniCorp's subsidiary's specialty, with their tiny NEoFusion™ labels stamped on the front.

The all-but-everlasting NeoFusion power source had been UniCorp's master patent, the first step that had made the rest of the interplanetary corporation possible. Before I'd been put into stasis, it was only used for expensive, important devices, like central power plants, as well as interplanetary shuttles and the rare self-contained units, such as my stass tube. Now, apparently, the same NeoFusion batteries that powered my tube were everywhere. Unfortunately, so were the subtle, heat-activated SubTouch™ controls, which reacted before I'd even touched them. In theory, they prevented infection, something people seemed much more worried about after those Dark Times. In reality, I couldn't get the stove to work, and then I nearly burned down the condo.

All I wanted to do was fall into my drawings. I most assuredly didn't want to go to school.

But what choice did I have, trapped in a world that wasn't mine, with my life belonging to everyone else? Eat dinner, talk to a psychologist, prepare for class. I did whatever they asked of me. It was all I could think of to do.

—chapter 4—

The building was tall, frowning and ancient in style—jagged-stone construction, arched windows and high gables. It was the House of Usher, the home of the undead, a dark, dreary dungeon of a place. And it was my school.

Uni Prep was considered the best school in the solar system. Most of the upper echelons of the colonies sent their children to be educated there. The day students, such as myself and Bren, were the cherished young citizens of ComUnity itself.

I'd seen it before, of course—Dr. Bija's office was around the west wing—but I hadn't been through the imposing front entrance. The whole place had been built in a style known as Gothic Revivalist, built in the years after what Bren called the Dark Times. Uni Prep looked like a massive mausoleum, with some entirely incongruous chunky bits of modern artwork around the moldings that reminded me of fungus. I half expected Nosferatu to leap out of the nearest exit and go for my throat. People must have been really depressed during those Dark Times.

I dragged myself up the dungeon stairs and across the entry foyer to the central quad, where Bren had half promised to meet me. The interior of the school was pleasant enough, I supposed. The arched windows did, in fact, let in the sun. There were dozens of students milling about here and there, folded notescreens under their arms, laughing and smiling as if they weren't living in a crypt. But the cadence and accent of their speech was slightly different, and I kept hearing things that made no sense. "Noid, that's so sky!" "You're such a burning sped!" "I comm, already!"

I shuddered.

"Welcome to Uni Prep," Bren said from behind me. I whirled. I felt so relieved to see him I could have cried. "Sorry, this is it," he said, gesturing sadly at the quad. The quad was a sort of cement pit in the center of the school that pretended to have something to do with a garden and so had several exhausted trees swaying gloomily in pots. Bren began pointing things out to me so quickly that I could barely keep my balance. "Down that way are the grav-courts for interplanet games. They have the weights for Mars, Luna, Titan, Callisto, and Europa. See that group of girls over there?" He pointed to a handful of girls who looked as squat and square and sturdy as tortoises, yet who moved as gracefully as dancers. "That's the Uni volleyball team. They think they're so sky. They're mostly boarders, and they're thick as thieves. Get one of them angry, and you'll get exed in your next phys ed class, and probably have most of your homework hacked."

He turned me in another direction. "Over there are the scholarship students." A tight knot of students chatted beneath one of the hapless trees. They looked like a perfectly ordinary group of kids to me. "They mostly stick together for protection. They're pretty harmless and they're all okay individually, but don't be seen with them as a group or you'll be branded forever. You'll never see the end of it. I comm, it burns, but that's the way it is."

He pointed out the narrow entryway of the quad at a pair of buildings that flanked the back of the school like bodyguards. Also like bodyguards, they were squat and bulky compared to the Gothic Revivalist majesty of the school proper, though I could see the hand of the same dismal architect. "Those are the dorms for the boarders. Insane security. Everyone's scanned the moment they get in, and they're very strict about girls and boys. Make sure you have a boarder with you, or you're likely to get a reprimand. There's a bit of a rivalry between boarders and day kids. Nothing to worry about, but there's been some vandalism, so don't let people think you're up to the same thing."

He glanced over the rest of the quad. "Can't see anything else you need to watch out for. You comm everything?" I guessed he meant *Do you understand?,* but I hadn't picked up the new slang. I managed a nod, which seemed to work. "I have to get to class. Do you have your schedule yet?"

"No," I said. He had gone through everything so quickly and so dizzyingly that I began to suspect he wanted to get rid of me. The thought made me sad. Bren was the closest thing I had to a friend in this insane new world. "Do you know where the office is?" I asked.

He pointed at an imposing door behind me. "Through those doors and to your right. You need me to show you?"

I smiled. Even if he was doing it under some kind of duress, he was taking very good care of me. "No. I think I can manage. Don't be late."

"Okay. I'll see you at lunch."

I let loose a relieved, and somewhat shaky, sigh. "Thanks." Whenever I started a new school, it was always hell trying to figure out where to sit at lunch. But if Bren was looking after me, I knew it would all be all right.

To my surprise, Mr. Guillory was waiting for me in the office. "Ah! Rosalinda, I was just talking to your school counselor here, just to make sure you're to be in all the right classes. We're putting you into sophomore history because they're about to start the turn of the century, which is about where you . . . ah . . . left off. I thought it would be good for you to catch up on some of what you've missed."

I swallowed. I wasn't actually sure I wanted to know what I missed. "Thank you, Mr. Guillory."

"Please, call me Reggie," he said again. "Now, I trust that you should be able to take up where you left off in math, English, and Chinese, yes? I found your . . . ah . . . most recent school records in the city archives. You were taking Chinese, weren't you?"

My parents had thought my learning Chinese would be

good for me, as it had been the second most used commercial language after English. They'd signed me up for Mandarin in every school I went to. I hadn't been very good at it. "Yes, thank you."

"We were discussing about what sciences to put you in. Is social psychology all right, coupled with elementary astrophysics?"

There was such a thing as "elementary" astrophysics? "That will be fine," I said, collecting the paper copy of the schedule, even though I knew it would also be downloaded onto my notescreen.

"I thought astrophysics would be useful for you, considering the interplanetary empire you'll be inheriting, eh?" Guillory and the counselor laughed, and I forced out a laugh to be gracious.

"I'll show you to your first class," Guillory said, and took my shoulder in one golden hand before he snatched the schedule out of my grip. "Social psych. I think that's right down here."

Most students were hurrying through the halls, afraid they'd be late for class, but when they caught a glimpse of me walking with Mr. Guillory, everyone seemed to hit a brick wall. If they had any doubts about who I was, Guillory's presence quashed them. I created a sea of stillness everywhere I went, with all eyes fixated on me. I could hear people muttering behind me. "Is that the Sleeping Beauty?" "Noid, she doesn't look so beautiful!" "I heard she stassed herself because she wanted to preserve her longevity." "I think she's a fake. UniCorp just wants a figurehead." "Look at her with Guillory, sucking up."

"Already a sped puppet." I kept my head down, refusing to meet the eyes of any of the people staring at me. Any hope I had of fitting in had been quashed by Guillory's bold appearance. He, of course, strode through, oblivious.

"Here we are," said Mr. Guillory. "Would you like me to talk to your teacher and find you a seat?"

"No, that's quite all right—" I began, but Mr. Guillory strode right up to the teacher, his golden skin all but glittering with efficiency.

"This is Rosalinda Fitzroy. I trust that you've been briefed as to her treatment?" he said, not nearly quietly enough.

I blushed bright red and tried to hide it beneath my hair. I wished I were not blond and fair and so quick to turn as red as the rose I was named for. My skin was practically translucent. Daddy always called me his "little rose." The students who were already seated stared at me, some in wonder, some with unabashed curiosity, a few with blatant loathing. I wished I could disappear.

Mr. Guillory finally departed (taking the copy of my schedule with him), and I tried to make sense of the class. If they had asked me, I would have told them to give me all remedial freshman classes and then ply me with a dozen tutors. But that would have been too much trouble. If Dr. Bija had spoken to the school counselor, as she had suggested, her recommendations had been completely ignored. After a little while I gave up and started sketching a landscape on my notescreen. It was one of my stass dreams, all twisted tree-scapes and melting horizons. But the notescreen just wasn't a sketchbook. Though I could pull up palettes with a thousand and one shades of color, it didn't feel like real artwork to me.

As the tone sounded for the end of class, I dutifully copied down the homework assignment, but I knew I wouldn't get very far with it.

In English we were supposed to be studying turn-of-the-century authors, which Mr. Guillory had thought would be old-school for me. I didn't have the heart to tell the teacher that I'd never even heard of half the authors or that I hadn't read a single book on the syllabus. The authors they thought were classics must have been utterly obscure when they first came out.

As far as Chinese went, it was all Greek to me.

I had phys ed right before lunch and was horrified to discover we were doing a track unit. I ran approximately twenty yards before the coach put me on the sidelines. I was panting and shaking and I would have thrown up, but I had eaten so little that all I did was retch ineffectively. Stass fatigue still impeded most of my motor functions. The coach said he'd try to arrange a pass on my phys ed credits for this term. "That's . . . not . . . necessary. . . ." I panted.

"It is," he said. "Mr. Guillory's orders. I'm to make sure you're well cared for."

I was most chagrined to discover that after Mr. Guillory had left me in my social psych class, he had traveled to each of my teachers in turn, interrupting their classes, to inform them of the special treatment I merited. If most of the school hadn't already been resentful toward me, they certainly were now. I'd ask Dr. Bija if she could arrange for my physical therapy sessions to be counted toward my gym credits. I could do some of the exercises the doctors had set for me while everyone else ran laps or shot baskets.

When I was finally released, I fled to the cafeteria, hoping to find Bren. But the crush of bodies defeated me. Finding one beautiful boy in a school of two thousand wealthy members of the elite was next to impossible. I stood in line and carefully collected the standard meal.

People had been parting around me like Moses and the Red Sea for most of the day, with expressions ranging from selfish curiosity to outright loathing, and I'd gotten used to being the elephant in the room that everyone looked at but no one spoke to. But when I stepped away from the line, I was immediately accosted by a well-dressed boy who looked like an Asian version of Mr. Guillory.

"So, you're the Sleeping Beauty," he smarmed. "I'm Soun Ling. Pleased to meet you." His tone suggested that the opposite were true. Still, he stuck out a soft hand for me to shake. I couldn't figure out how to touch him without dropping either my tray or my notescreen, so I left his hand hanging in the air. He ignored this slight. "Would you care to sit with us?"

A handful of the kids behind him, male and female, snickered. I wasn't sure what they were laughing at, but they made me uncomfortable. I'd been the new girl in school enough times to know full well that things could get very unpleasant very quickly if you allied yourself with the wrong group of people. Either you alienated others or, more often, ended up the butt of some horrible conspiracy. That was why I had treasured my friendship with Xavier so dearly. I wasn't sure why, but I knew without a doubt that Soun Ling was the wrong person to have my name attached to. I stood helpless, wondering how to extricate myself from this predicament without making an enemy of Soun, or anyone else.

"Rose!"

The name cut through the bustle of the cafeteria, and my head turned toward the lifeline. Bren's hand shot up over the heads of the other students, and I sighed with relief. "My friend is waiting for me," I said. I wasn't sure if Bren actually counted as a friend, but it was close enough.

Soun Ling's eyes looked daggers at Bren. "Already sucking up to the CEOs, eh? I should have known." He turned his back on me.

I swallowed, relieved but still nervous. What had he meant?

Bren had saved a seat across the table from himself. When I approached the table, he pulled his notescreen off the spot and nodded at the empty chair. "Thanks," I said, sliding into the seat.

"Don't mench." He pointed at some of the people around the table. "This is Molly, Anastasia, Jamal, Wilhelm, Nabiki, and Otto. Everyone, this is Rose."

The others looked at me blankly, as if they had no idea why Bren had dragged me over but weren't going to argue with what he thought best. "Hi," they all said, almost in unison, then seemed to forget I was there as they turned back to one another. I hoped I wasn't supposed to remember all of their names. They were a rainbow of diversity, but their hairstyles looked uniformly expensive, and the cells around their necks were universally top-of-the-line. Their notescreens were all top-notch, too—I recognized the same logo as on my own wildly expensive screen.

I sat quietly at the table, nursing my food. I still couldn't eat much without feeling sick to my stomach. The doctor told me it might be some years before I could eat normally. The others chatted on, making jokes and teasing one another. Usually when I was at a school for the first time, people asked me questions, and I answered. But this time all the questions had been asked by the reporters, and they'd heard the answers on the news. They didn't seem to have anything to say to me, and I didn't know what to say to them.

After I had nibbled for a while in silence, Bren cleared his throat. "So how's the day going?"

I shrugged. "Okay."

"I saw you get set on by the jackals."

"Jackals?"

"Yeah, Soun and his cronies. Bunch of burning speds. Their parents are wannabe rich. They like to hook up with the real rich kids and milk them for presents. Sorry, I should have warned you about them this morning."

"It's okay," I whispered.

"No, I thought you'd be safe. We aren't in their grade. I underestimated your fame."

I shook my head. "I'm not famous."

"I didn't say you were an idol or anything, but absolutely everyone knows who you are."

I sighed, unable to look at my barely touched tray any longer. I felt nauseated. "Bren? Soun said to me . . . that I was already sucking up to the CEOs. What did that mean?"

Bren grinned, self-deprecatingly. "That's just what *they* call us. It's because of our families. My grandfather's just one rung down the ladder from Guillory. Executive CEO, not quite chairman, but really powerful. My dad's on the board, about four steps down from that, and Mom's head of research for the Central Graphics Department." He started nodding to the other kids around the table. I noticed most of them had stopped talking the moment Bren opened his mouth. It reminded me a bit of the way people deferred to Daddy at company picnics. I wondered if Bren knew how powerful he was, or if he was oblivious. "Nabiki's dad is the leader and creator of the Neuro-Linguistic Research Department."

"My mom is vice president of Research, Development, and Human Factors," said one of the boys, a tall Nordic blond with a thick German accent. He had to be Wilhelm. "My father controls Uni Germany, back home."

"My parents head up the Bio-Chem Agricultural Quality Control Team on Titan," said the girl named Anastasia. She sounded so Russian I could barely understand her.

"And Jamal's own half of Europa," said the fiercely redheaded girl with the freckles.

Jamal threw back his dark head and laughed. "Only about a third."

I gulped. "And you?" I asked the redhead.

"Molly," she supplied, reminding me. She grinned through

her freckles. "Me, I'm just a scholarship student. My parents were some of the first colonists on Callisto, which makes me kind of royalty there, but that doesn't get me so much as a supper invite on Earth."

"Don't let her kid you," Bren said. "It got her a scholarship. Besides, she's got the most brilliant mind for fundamental economics. She'll change the entire economic structure of the planet the second she gets out of college. My granddad's already considering inviting her to board meetings."

I felt rather uncomfortable. "I'm nothing so interesting," I whispered.

Jamal and Wilhelm laughed as one. Tall as a mountain, Wilhelm had to bend down to peer into my eyes. "You own every one of us, *Liebchen*," he said fondly.

I knew I had turned red again, but I whispered, "No, I don't."

"Might as well," said Jamal. "Particularly—" But whatever he had been about to say was cut off by Nabiki, who elbowed him in the ribs. Jamal threw a surreptitious glance toward the only one of the party who hadn't spoken yet, and then he closed his mouth. I searched through the names Bren had rattled off. Otto, that was it.

I couldn't see Otto's face. He had long, shaggy black hair, which he did not keep pulled back as the other boys did. He hadn't looked up from his plate. "So who's Otto's family?" I asked.

There was an uncomfortable silence. I didn't understand it until Otto finally looked up at me. I froze. I had thought him either Asian or Caucasian, but he was neither. His eyes were yellow, and his skin, now that I looked at it more closely, was nearly blue. He was pleasant-enough looking, with a strong nose and a fine-featured face. But his coloring simply wasn't human.

"Otto doesn't talk," said Nabiki. She smiled at Otto, whose face remained entirely expressionless. She touched his shoulder in a way that told me their relationship wasn't entirely platonic. "He kind of doesn't need to."

"Wh-what is he?" I realized as I said it that I was being rude, but I couldn't help it. He unnerved me.

"Genetically modified from alien DNA found on Europa," said Anastasia. "Technically, you own him. And the technology as created him."

It took me a moment for the words to make sense. Her accent was so thick, and the words were impossible. "Me?"

Bren looked annoyed. "It was one of Guillory's pet projects. They banned most genetic modification just after the Dark Times, but Guillory's been lobbying for eases in the restrictions his whole life. Otto here is one of a hundred human embryos who were implanted with the Europa microbe DNA. Only thirty-four of them survived full gestation. Only a dozen survived past puberty, and of those, only four seem to function with adult minds. It was carnage. Otto is the biggest success, but he doesn't talk."

"Why not?"

Otto opened his mouth, with a hint of a smile edging the corners of his lips. A strange noise erupted from his mouth, as if someone were screaming by sucking in breath rather than exhaling. It was very quiet, and it sounded more dolphin than human.

I jumped, and everyone at the table laughed. "He loves teasing people," Nabiki said. She nudged him. "Otto, come on—be nice. She's almost as weird as you." Otto seemed to think for a long moment, then slowly held out one long-fingered bluish hand. I blinked at it. Nabiki looked annoyed. "Go on, take it!" she hissed.

I gingerly put my fingers on his palm, and with great gentleness, Otto's fingers wrapped around my own.

"Good afternoon, Princess," I thought in a voice that wasn't really my own. *"I am Otto Sextus."* The name came to me as 86 at first, and I knew, without explanation, that he and all the others had for some reason been named as numerals. Another thought came to me that wasn't as clear. It was almost, for lack of a better term, inaudible. *Treat us well, treat us well, treat us well.* It was a plea, accidental, a background drone of a thought. For a brief second, I saw Otto, and three other blue-skinned teenagers, with a background shadow of half a dozen half-formed figures.

I gasped. Those words and images had been my thoughts, but they hadn't come from me.

"Shh," was the word I thought, but the feeling connected to it was something along the lines of, *Don't worry, fear me not.*

My thoughts seemed to drift for a moment, until I wasn't sure what I was thinking about. *"Your heart is troubled. Your experience . . . interrupted. . . ."*

The first real expression I had seen flashed over Otto's peculiar face. I felt a blast of disconnected fear. *"I am sorry, dear Princess,"* he thought at me. *"Your troubles are greater even than my own."*

He pulled his hand away rather quickly and stared at me for a moment before he looked back to his tray.

Everyone was staring at me as if they'd just seen an alien. Which was ironic, considering the circumstances. Nabiki's eyes shot sparks. "What did you say to him?" she demanded.

I was trembling from the experience. I understood hardly any of what just happened. "I said nothing."

Nabiki frowned and then gently put her hand on the back of Otto's neck. He sighed, and the troubled look faded a bit from his eyes. Nabiki frowned again, but this time more chagrined. "Sorry," she said to me. "I thought you'd been rude to him."

I shook my head. "Never," I said earnestly. His circumstances horrified me, but he didn't.

I tried to find what I needed to say. "If what you say is true, and somehow I've inherited you and your family . . ." I hesitated a moment and took a breath. It was so horrific a thought, akin to human slavery. "I swear to you, the moment I come into my inheritance, I'll—I don't know—give you back to yourself or something. Sign the rights over. I don't know how it works. But I'm so sorry."

Nabiki smiled. "He says thank you. It isn't your fault." She hesitated, her brow furrowing. "He's sorry about this. But, ah, if you don't mind, he doesn't plan on touching you again." She turned to Otto, confused. "Really?" she asked. Otto slightly lifted one hand, either a shrug or a signal to go on.

Nabiki tossed her head. "Okay." She turned back to me. "He says there are too many . . . 'gaps' in your mind. Too much space. He nearly got lost." She shrugged. "Sorry—what he thinks doesn't always translate perfectly into language. What does he mean by gaps?"

I shrugged. "I don't know," I said, but I was afraid I did. Stass had been a series of breaks in my life. I stared at Nabiki. She seemed like a perfectly ordinary girl, Japanese descent, expensive earrings, fashionable haircut, but whatever relationship she had with this strange semi-alien-being spoke of a hidden depth to her. "Are you two . . . ?"

"Together?" Nabiki said, indulgently embarrassed. "Well, yeah."

Otto turned his head deliberately to her and flashed his hint of a smile.

"What are you . . . ?" I realized Otto wouldn't answer. "What is he doing when he . . . does that?"

Nabiki shrugged. "No one really knows all of it. Somehow he's able to manipulate the electronic impulses in your brain so you can think what he wants you to think. He can't control your actions or feelings or anything, though. It only touches surface thoughts. Apparently those little microbes on Europa have some kind of rudimentary communication via electro impulse, probably for breeding purposes. It came out in Otto like this."

"Can all your family do that?" I asked.

Otto shook his head slightly, then glanced at Nabiki, who took his hand again.

"Only one other of the . . ." She seemed to find the subject difficult, too. "The four," she finished. "And then three of the simple ones, but they don't think very clearly, so it's pretty useless." She glanced at Otto's expressionless face. "It breaks his heart."

"All right, that's enough drama," said Bren. "Speaking of which, Ani, you doing drama this year?"

I was too shaken by my encounter with Otto to concentrate. I tried for a few more bites of my meal before the tone sounded to send me back to class. As everyone stood up from the table, I caught Otto staring at me. I had the unnerving sensation that he was staring right through me, as if I were some magical creature made of glass. He blinked when he caught me looking back at him, and then he hurried to catch up to Nabiki.

What had he seen in my mind that scared him so?

—chapter 5—

My first afternoon at school went no better than the morning. Elementary astrophysics might as well have been graduate-school advanced theories, for all the sense it made to me. An hour later I trudged into my math class, and an hour after that I scurried out as fast as I could, unable to make head nor tails of it.

Then came history. My teacher began a brief overview of the first twenty years I had missed, and I was suddenly glad I'd been stassed through it.

The Dark Times came less than two years after I went into stass. I had assumed it was some kind of economic depression, which it was, to an extent. But the biggest problems had not been with the money.

I spent the class tying the facts that Ms. Holland was telling me—population statistics and weather patterns and economic fluctuations—to the events of my elongated childhood. It was quite gruesome, and I couldn't help but feel that I—or at least the structure of my parents' corporate society—had been deeply responsible for much of it. Likely, this class was intended as a warning to the children of the high echelons to avoid the mistakes of the past. But to me it still felt like the present—my time, my generation's mistakes. Revulsion and guilt stabbed through me the entire hour.

The first factor that led to the Dark Times was a steady population increase, which had been building for two hundred years. I'd seen that. There wasn't space for anyone when I was young. Even the wealthy had to abandon the concept of vast estates and settle into controlled gated communities, like ComUnity and Unicorn.

The next was an economic boom leading to widening gaps between the rich and the poor. I'd noticed that, too. The poor starved, while my family bought me designer mink coats when I was three and had a private state-of-the-art stass tube for me, worth the whole of Unicorn Estates together.

Some years before I was stassed, there had been a few seasons of difficult weather, due to a climate shift instigated by some volcanoes. This was no one's fault, exactly. There was a food shortage, which did result in a lot of deaths, I recalled, but mostly in marginalized countries. It hadn't touched our family.

The first sign that things were really going wrong was the resurgence of tuberculosis. It had begun in prisons, where inmates' health had not been carefully monitored. A resistant strain had developed in one prison in the South, and the habits of prisoner transfers and recidivism was such that before long, most of the prisons in half the countries in the world were riddled with TB. Countries with a high percentage of prisoners were particularly vulnerable. The disease wasn't caught before many prisoners had been released into the general population without adequate health care.

It spread. Newborns, the poor who suffered from malnutrition, all those with reduced immunity were susceptible. This included any HIV victims who hadn't received the vaccine in time, which meant half of Africa. It also included many of the affluent, among them millions who had been promised an extended life by having their organs regrown from stem cells and transplanted. TB spread unchecked for a few years before anyone noticed what was going on. Most people didn't realize when they had a cough that it was anything serious, and some of the carriers showed no symptoms at all.

They were instigating a series of mandatory TB status clinics all around the planet when I was put into stass. They seemed to have the tuberculosis under control when the next plague hit.

It really was the next plague, and not just a figure of speech. Bubonic plague resurfaced, in New York, two years after I was stassed. I was already cringing in horror from hearing of the TB deaths in Africa when Ms. Holland brought in the effects of this next plague on top of it, and I swear my heart stopped. When the tone sounded, Ms. Holland told us that the rest of the overview of the Dark Times would have to wait until next class.

I was not looking forward to it.

I dreaded hearing what had happened to everyone I loved. My mother and father, my beloved Xavier. Knowing they were dead was one thing. Knowing the details was harder to stomach.

Fortunately, the school day was over. I climbed into the limoskiff that Mr. Guillory had arranged for me. I rather wished I could have taken the public solarskimmer with Bren and a handful of others, but I didn't want to scorn Mr. Guillory's offerings. He was my executor, after all. He should know what was best for me.

It took me some minutes to realize that my limoskiff had settled beside my condo. The skiff's ride was so smooth that I hadn't even noticed it had stopped.

I really liked these new hover boats. I was told that the technology was barely thirty years old, but it had already replaced pretty much every land vehicle on the planet. They had been designed to skim over the water, to be used in swampy areas, such as the Everglades, but those who had them thought them so wonderful they continued to use them on land. It saved wear on the roads, and without friction and drag, it was cheap and easy to power them on solar energy.

Oddly, the hover boat companies were one business on which UniCorp had no monopoly. The corporation had tried buying out each of the manufacturers in turn, but the solar battery that ran the boats was public domain. It had been depatented during the Dark Times so that isolated areas could create their own renewable power. According to Guillory, it had proved dangerous to use NeoFusion to power the vehicles. NeoFusion reactors became very volatile when the protective casing was damaged. While it wasn't radioactive or inherently deadly—NeoFusion being the "safe, clean alternative" to almost all power needs—if involved in a crash, it almost invariably resulted in a fire, due to massive amounts of lost heat. Using solar power on the skimmers made them infinitely safer, and they were so convenient and elegant that UniCorp hadn't been able to bury them with competitors. Thus they were free from UniCorp's intrigues.

The boats did have one flaw—also their strength—in that they could travel over anything. The transportation commission had to create magnetic barriers that prevented the boats from passing over roads and onto pedestrian areas. All roads now had red-and-yellow magnetic curbs, and those UniCorp *did* have a monopoly on. Guillory had made a joke when he explained all this: "If you can't beat 'em, box 'em." UniCorp contained all their competition, one way or another.

I crawled my way out of the skiff, over the red-and-yellow curb. My limoskiff turned on its cushion of air and headed off to the garage. I dragged myself through the corridors to my condo. I pressed my hand to the antiquated fingerprint pad, and the door opened. I wondered if the old print pad still had a record of Xavier's fingerprints, as it had had before I was stassed. Apparently most doors opened to retinal scan now.

When I opened the door, I heard a noise. Patty and Barry weren't supposed to be home until after five: they both worked in the accounting department of the Uni Building. I swallowed. "Hello?" I called out. No response. My parents' training of hypervigilance and paranoia burbled in the back of my mind, and I poked my head around the corner, prepared to run in the opposite direction if the noise proved to be a threat.

It was not. A leash tied to the door handle of my studio was attached to a dog—a tall, silky-furred Afghan, his hair the same soft blond as my own. He stood up when he saw me, wagging his tail. I fell to my knees, wrapping my arms around his shoulders. With a dignified whine, the dog pushed his long nose to my cheeks and began to lick my face.

My stass-weakened eyes filled with tears, this time out of joy. It was the best feeling in the world to come home to something soft and friendly, something to love me unconditionally. And this wasn't just a dog. He was an Afghan, the prince of dogs, the four-legged human! My fingers laced in his silky fur, and I felt a piece of paper hanging by a string from his collar. I lifted it up, wiping the tears from my eyes to read it. FOR ROSE ON HER FIRST DAY OF SCHOOL.

I sniffed. It must have come from Mr. Guillory. Or maybe Patty and Barry had arranged to have him delivered. Mrs. Sabah? I didn't know. It didn't matter. "You're beautiful!" I told the dog. "The most beautiful dog in the world. So I'm giving you the most beautiful name: Zavier."

Zavier panted and licked my face again. Even school didn't seem like such an ordeal, not as long as I could have my Zavier waiting for me at home.

I'd always wanted a dog, ever since I was a kid. The closest I'd had wasn't even mine. It was Xavier's, and in truth, it wasn't even a dog.

I was fourteen, and Xavier was my best friend. He'd asked me over to his condo to look at his new toy.

It was a little black box. It looked a bit like a cell. It didn't strike me as being anything that would cause Xavier's green eyes to brighten with such enthusiasm, but he was showing it to me as proudly as if it were the doorway to enlightenment. "What is it?"

Xavier pressed a button on the side, and a Doberman suddenly appeared in the middle of the room. "Here, boy!" Xavier said, snapping his fingers, and the dog obediently strode up to him and panted, his head to one side. "Isn't it neat?" he said. "It's a holographic dog. They had them at the computer expo. Call him; he'll come to you. It has programmed reactions just like a real dog. It'll react to everything you say, and it knows a thousand tricks. Speak, boy!"

The dog sat down obediently and barked twice.

"Why didn't they program it to speak English?" I asked.

"Because then it wouldn't be a dog," Xavier said, as if it were obvious.

"It's still not a dog. What's the point of a dog if you can't pet it?"

Xavier shrugged. "I don't know. It's just cool. It has settings for more than a hundred different breeds, and the behavior modes for all of them." Xavier was poking at the controls on the box. The Doberman switched to a Dalmatian and then to a dachshund. "What breed should I set it to?"

"An Afghan," I said without hesitation. He poked at the controls until a regal, silky-furred Afghan stood in the middle of the room. It barked.

"There," Xavier said. "I think I can figure out how to hack

it into the touch pad for our door. I can get it to bark at anyone who enters."

"A real dog would do that, too."

"Yeah, but my mom's allergic. Come on! You have to admit it's a cool tech."

I perched on a stool and snapped my fingers. The holographic dog looked at me and then sauntered over, his ears pricked. "I will grant you that." I passed my hand through its head and waved it at Xavier. "Still would be better if you could pet it."

Xavier shook his head. "I don't get you. I thought you liked dogs."

"I love dogs. That's how I know this isn't one."

"If you love dogs so much, how come you won't get one of your own?"

It had been a bit of an issue in the past, when I'd picked up runaway dogs from other members of Unicorn and played with them for hours, keeping them from their owners. "I couldn't."

"Why not?"

I sighed. My parents were scheduled to oversee the coordination of the Luna colony, and they were going to be gone for months. "You remember that gazelle I had when I was eight?"

Xavier shook his head. "I was two. How could I remember?"

"Oh. Well, anyway, I had this gazelle. The stables took care of it for me, but it died while Mom and Daddy were on vacation, and I wasn't there. I felt awful about that. I'd hate to do that to a dog."

"I could take care of it while you were sleeping," Xavier said. "I'm sure my mom wouldn't mind, not if it was Mr. Fitzroy's."

I shook my head. "No. I'd hate it if I ever had to really be away from Mom and Daddy, and that's what I'd be doing. I wouldn't want to pop in and out of a dog's life like that. He wouldn't understand."

Xavier grunted. "Forget the dog—hell, I'm human. I barely understand, and you're my best friend."

I frowned at that. "Don't you have friends at your school?"

"Of course I do, but they're not you. Besides, they all tease me for having a name like Xavier, even the guys who say they're my friends. They call me 'X-man' and say things like, '*Ex*actly, Xavier!' and 'Are you doing *ex*tra credit, Xavier?' I don't even pronounce the damned *X,* but they all do."

"Well, *Zavier,*" I said, pronouncing it how he liked it. "Tell them to stop."

He shrugged. "They're guys. You can't stop 'em. It doesn't matter. You'd never do something like that. I can't wait until I'm old enough to go to the same schools you do. You and I have always been best friends."

It hadn't occurred to me before. I'd always thought of him like a little brother, but now that our ages were pretty close together, he was much more like a friend. "You are my best friend," I admitted. "Come to think of it, you're my *only* friend."

He scoffed. "Now, I know that's not true."

"It is, you know," I said. I didn't know why I didn't feel sad about that. I got off my stool and joined Xavier at the table. I reached up to ruffle his hair. As long as I knew he'd be there in the next condo, tearing some computer apart, it didn't matter that I didn't have anyone else.

"Come on," Xavier said, cringing away from my maternal tousle. "I'll bet you've got lots of friends."

"Not really. You know Mom doesn't approve of any of the kids at school, and she doesn't like me going out without her." I frowned. "I've never had any other friends. Not since the caretaker's daughter when I was little."

"How little?" Xavier asked.

"I think I was three or four. It was at our last house, in the city." I hadn't thought of Sarah for years. "She was bigger than me, all glamorous and adventurous. We'd spend the whole day together. We used to dress in matching outfits."

"At four?"

"Yeah. I guess it was her idea. But other than her, you're the only real friend I've ever had."

"Didn't you get invited to a sleepover the other day?"

"Polly only invited me because her mom was trying to get a promotion."

"What?"

"Her parents work for UniCorp."

"Oh," said Xavier. "Well, so do mine."

"True . . . but we've been friends forever. Almost as long as you've been alive," I reminded him.

Xavier turned back to his box. "Do you ever think how

it's weird?" he asked. "I mean, you haven't grown up the same way I do. I remember when you used to tower over me, and you told me stories because I couldn't read yet. Now we're like the same height. Almost the same age."

"I'm fourteen!" I said indignantly, and pulled myself up to my full height, which was still a few centimeters taller than him. "You're only eleven."

He looked at me rather pointedly. "My birthday was three months ago. I'm twelve."

I blinked. I'd been out of stasis for over a month. I hadn't realized my last stint had been so long. "I missed it? Really?"

"Really."

"I'm sorry. I'll get you something to make up for it. What do you want?"

Xavier's eyes searched my face. He hesitated for a long time before he said, "Nothing."

"No, really."

"No, really, nothing. I just wish you could have been there. That would have been the best present."

I smiled. "You're sweet."

"Don't tell anyone; I'll never live it down."

I touched his shoulder anyway. "I've got to go," I said. "Mom's taking me to the art supply store and then to the furniture designer. I'm out of burnt sienna."

"Oh." He looked disappointed. "I was kinda hoping you'd stay and help me wire this into the door key."

I looked mock horrified. "You want to start a fire? I couldn't figure out a circuit if my life depended on it!"

"But the threat of exploding wall sockets adds so much more excitement to the project!" He laughed.

I shook my head. "I'll just jinx you. Besides, I'd miss giving my opinion on color wheels. Mom's redecorating the front lobby, and she wants my help."

"Yeah, whatever," Xavier said. He turned back to his new holographic dog circuit.

Something bothered me. I wondered if Xavier knew I was going back into stasis soon. "Ahm . . . I wanted to tell you. Mom and Daddy are going on to Luna next week."

Xavier's head snapped toward me, his eyes wide. "For how long?"

"I don't know."

He stared at me openmouthed for a moment before he composed his face. "Well. Just don't miss my *next* birthday, okay?"

I reached forward to ruffle his blond hair. "Not for anything, Xavy."

He blushed. "I wish you wouldn't call me that. I'm not a kid anymore."

"No," I said. "You're not. But you are my best friend."

The holographic Afghan barked. "Girl's best friend," Xavier said, and then he barked, too.

Now I had a new best friend. He wasn't anything like as good as Xavier, but he was the best I could have had under the circumstances.

Zavier's real name, according to the information sheet I found in the kitchen, was Freefoot's Desert Roads, and he was a retired champion, having come an inch away from Best in Show three years before. He was well trained in general obedience and had a smattering of rudimentary guard training. He had a regularly scheduled grooming every two weeks. It was suggested that I give him a light once-over every day with a brush I found along with his papers. I asked him if he preferred Roads or Desert, or a dozen other combinations of his show name, but he didn't prick his ears at any of them. His call name must have been something entirely different, and I had no note of it, so Zavier was as good a name as any.

Patty and Barry were obviously expecting Zavier, as Barry came home with a bag of dog food. I couldn't bring myself to ask if they had arranged for me to have him or if it was Mr. Guillory. But it didn't matter. Zavier was mine now. That night, he curled up at the foot of my bed and kept my feet warm.

Unfortunately, he didn't quite keep the nightmares away.

—chapter 6—

The nightmares were relentless. They had been coming almost every night, ever since I came out of stass. In my dreams I walked through long, empty hallways. At first they were the corridors between the apartments at Unicorn, but the night I got Zavier, they were the halls at Uni Prep, complete with neo-Gothic windows and stone arches. Always there were mirrors around, confusing and frightening. I would catch movement and turn to see what caused it, to find it was only me, looking back at myself. I wasn't sure what I was looking for in these empty hallways, but I was afraid to find it.

Like always, I woke in a cold sweat, shouting for my mom. But the moment I fully awoke and realized she wasn't there, I was glad. She'd have been ashamed of me, calling out like an undisciplined child.

"Would she really have been ashamed?" asked Dr. Bija the next morning. We'd had a special session scheduled for the morning of my second day at school, so that I could talk over what the first day had been like. When Mina had asked how I'd slept, I'd slipped up and told her about the dreams.

"Probably," I said. "Mom always kept herself composed. It's best if you can refine yourself, so that people will only see perfection when they look at you. That's what she said."

Mina frowned. "Do you think anyone can really be perfect?"

I shrugged. "Like a statue, I think. If you can file off the parts that are rough, eventually you'll have a personality like Michelangelo's *David*."

She laughed. "Do you really think you have the power to file off your nightmares, like you would your fingernails?"

"I don't know." I sighed. I wished I could.

"So, how did school go yesterday?" Mina prompted.

"I don't understand anything."

"It's only your first day. But I wasn't talking about your academic performance. Do you have any friends?"

"Not really. Well, Bren, I guess."

"Bren?"

"Brendan Sabah? His grandfather's apparently Guillory's second or something."

"Ah, yes. I remember from the press conference. Do you like him?"

"He let me sit with him at lunch."

"That must be a comfort," she said. "It's good to have friends."

I shrugged. I wasn't sure that the relationship I had with Bren was exactly that of *friendship*. It wasn't anything like what I'd had with Xavier, even before we started dating, and I hadn't had any friends outside of Xavier, so I had no other point of comparison. All I knew was that I needed Bren badly, but I didn't feel as comfortable around him as I had with Xavier. That left me with a confused, unbalanced feeling that I wasn't sure I liked. Though I did like Bren. A lot.

I left the session trying to figure out exactly what it was with Bren. I wasn't sure I knew. But at the very least, Bren did treat me with friendly deference. I was glad. I badly needed a friendly face later that day, after my history class.

Bren caught me in the hallway as I fled, unexcused, from the horrors I had been learning. Yesterday, hearing about the preparations for the Dark Times had made me feel terrible enough. But today, as the Dark Times themselves loomed larger and larger on the wall screen, I shrank smaller and smaller, until I had to get out of there. I ran past Bren without seeing him, without seeing anything. "Rose!" His voice echoed in the otherwise empty hallway. "You all right?"

I whirled.

"Hey, what is it? You look like you've seen a ghost."

Ghosts. That's all that was left of my family, my friends, my Xavier. I choked on bile, looking desperately around the halls. There, a garbage incinerator! I stuck my head over the pan and vomited, losing the few precious morsels of food I'd managed to choke down over lunch.

For a few moments I retched alone, and then I felt a warm hand on my shoulder. "Hey," said Bren. "Should I get you to the nurse?"

I spat some of the vomit taste out of my mouth. "No," I said. I pulled back from the pan. "I'm not sick." I began digging through my pockets, hoping for a tissue.

Bren pulled one from the necessary dispenser on the wall. I blew my nose with the proffered square and then threw it onto the pan. I pressed the button on the side, and the pan disappeared into the lower confines of the incinerator, replaced by a fresh one. I could hear the quiet hum that meant the incinerator was destroying all evidence of my weakness.

Sickness past, all I felt was overwhelming grief. "You want to tell me what that was about?" Bren asked. "Was it lunch? You still suffering stass fatigue?"

"No. Well, yes, but that wasn't it." Another wave of nausea hit, but I suppressed it. "Why didn't anyone tell me how bad the Dark Times were?"

"We didn't?" Bren looked confused. "I thought Reggie told you."

"He told me some," I said. "But I don't think it registered." Between the stass residue and the shock, nothing had seemed to touch me at the time.

The tales this afternoon, of whole towns perishing in agony, of people waking up one morning perfectly healthy and being dead by the afternoon, the loss of infrastructure, which made everything worse . . .

Bren still looked confused. "What brought all this on?"

"History class," I said. "They're talking about how my parents died. How all my friends died. My boyfriend."

Understanding softened Bren's face. "Oh," he said. He looked a bit awkward for a moment and then said, "You want to talk about it?"

I sighed. "No. But I don't . . ."

"What?"

I was embarrassed, but I said it anyway. "I don't want to be alone."

Bren's brow furrowed. He put his hand on my shoulder, a heated weight to anchor me to the earth. "You're not alone," he said, his voice a velvet cushion. "Come on, let's get you some air."

"Don't you need to be in class?"

"Doesn't matter."

I wasn't about to argue with him. With his hand on my shoulder, he led me outside to the quad, where he sat me down on a bench under a weeping cherry tree, the flowers just blooming in the spring air. The gentle scent and the slight chill did wash away my nausea. Bren sat beside me, watching me with those eyes like new leaves. I wanted to bury myself in his chest and weep for a hundred years, but I didn't.

"Is there anything I can get you?" he asked. "You need some water or something?"

"No."

There was an awkward silence. "Anything I can do?"

I hesitated. I knew what he could do, but I wasn't sure he'd want to do it.

"Anything," he prompted, sensing my indecision.

"Tell me about the Dark Times," I said.

He frowned. "Arrre . . . you sure?"

"Yes," I whispered. "I'd rather hear it from a friend." Then I realized what I'd said. "You are a friend, aren't you?"

"Of course I am," he said brusquely. "Okay." He scratched his head. "Where should I start?"

"She was talking . . . talking about the plague hitting first in New York."

Bren nodded. "Apparently some American fashion guru decided that the next great thing in furs was marmot, so he headed off to China to collect as much as he could. His name was Marcus Alexios. He came back from China carrying a septicemic variant of plague. New York being New York, he hopped on the subway, went to the show, and then dropped dead.

"Apparently marmots carry plague. Who'd comm that? Usually plague is spread only through blood contact, but two little protein shifts had turned this into a particularly nasty strain, passed by human-to-human contact. Which meant that everyone Alexios worked with in China, everyone on the plane to America with him, everyone in that crowded subway station, and all the affluent fashion elite who had been at the show were all exposed. His autopsy wasn't performed until after all of those people were let loose on the public. One person got on a plane to L.A., one guy went to a homeless shelter in the East Village, one woman went on a train to Vermont, and you can guess how it all spread from there."

Bren was watching me, and I knew my face had gone white. "I'll skip the details," Bren told me, and I was grateful. "Now, they had medicine that could cure this plague, though it was resistant and stockpiles were low. But the transportation needed to ship them was out of commission. With a third of the population sick, nothing worked. By the time medicine got to any given community, most of the people were already dead." He gazed at me. "It was usually pretty quick, they say," he said, trying to reassure me. "Scary, apparently, but they didn't have time to suffer."

I covered my eyes, trying to compose myself. "Right."

He took a deep breath. This must have been ancient history to Bren, but telling me about it seemed awkward for him. "The plague swept through one summer, then it kept resurfacing. Later outbreaks were less widespread, but it could still be transmitted by human-to-human contact and by fleas. Meanwhile, tuberculosis was still spreading. You knew about the TB?"

"Yes," I said. "They had control clinics for it when . . . before."

Bren grimaced. "Yeah, those mandatory collections of people from all walks of life didn't help when it came to containing the plague. People would show up to get tested for TB, and come home half-exed from plague. It was strange. Everyone was so shocked that the problem hadn't come from some new disease but from the old diseases that everyone had neglected to prepare for." He sighed. "Then came the final blow."

I started, horrified. "There's more?" How could there be *more*?

"Yeah," Bren said. "Infertility. They tell you about the Global Food Initiative?"

"Yes, that was before I was stassed. Daddy was involved in that."

When the century-long ban on genetically modified foods was lifted so that high-yield seeds could be distributed to countries suffering from food shortages, my parents had taken me to a ceremonial banquet in their honor. UniCorp had developed many of those GM seeds. Mom and Daddy were thrilled to be included in the Global Food Initiative and lobbied extensively for it to be instated.

"Biggest lawsuit UniCorp ever had to deal with," said Bren. "Nearly sank the company, Granddad says. Apparently one of the seeds, a type of corn, was genetically modified as what is known as a 'terminator seed,' which means the crops won't produce viable seed next year."

"I know," I said. "It's good for business. It means the farmers have to keep coming back for fresh seed from the company. Daddy restructured the patents after they rescinded the ban of 2087."

"And everyone wishes he hadn't."

"Was it too hard to transport fresh seed after the population decreased?"

"Well . . . that didn't *help,* but no, the problem was in an unexpected mutation. That's the real reason they banned genetic modification, you know. In the end, the risk outweighed the rewards. It was just too dangerous. The terminator gene passed into the bloodstream and affected humans. Particularly males. It resulted in short-lived sperm, like, one or two hours' life span.

Which meant that unless a guy was getting it off pretty regularly, the sperm would die and he'd be shooting blanks. And even if he wasn't, if a woman's egg wasn't ready and waiting, panting at the edge of the cervix, the sperm didn't have a prayer of reaching it before it sang the final dirge and exed."

It was so gruesome and macabre that I was surprised I laughed, but I did. I'd been right: hearing about this from a friend did make it all easier to process.

Bren shrugged. "No one commed before the plague. People had been postponing pregnancy, and it wasn't that surprising that women from the age of thirty-eight to forty-five were somehow unable to conceive during the brief window they allowed themselves. But after so much death, everyone felt justified in having children, and it turned out that most people couldn't. We had lost so many, and we couldn't build the population back up. The killer corn had gone into the general food supply, and it mixed with everything, which meant it was everywhere. It was fed to livestock, which meant the livestock wouldn't reproduce either. That resulted in more food shortages." Bren shook his head. "Everything spiraled downhill. There were riots, resource wars, technology wars. TB was still raging, and the plague kept coming back. Nothing really started coming together for about twenty years."

"Is that all of it?"

"Yeah, pretty much. War, Famine, Pestilence, and Death showed up, got on their horses, played a little polo, and then headed back into the ether to wait for the next apocalypse." He held his arms wide. "And we're all still here."

"How?" I asked. "How could the human race survive all that?"

"Intervention, preparation, those handful of people in any population who are immune to some disease or other. Once the worst of it had calmed down, people were able to focus on how to repair the damage. My grandmother had to be externally fertilized to have my mom and her brother, and it was apparently, like, the fourth time my grandma tried before the embryos took. Glad they did, or I wouldn't be here. But with enough persistence, anything can start to grow again."

"I guess all you have to do is survive," I said quietly. My parents hadn't. Åsa hadn't. My Xavier hadn't. "I don't think I can go back into that class, though," I said. "Today was just the overview. She's going to go into each mistake and tragedy in depth, and I just can't take it."

"Well . . ." Bren thought for a moment. "What if I were to get you transferred into my history class? We just finished the Dark Times. We're starting now on the Reconstruction. It won't make much sense if you don't comm all the details of how bad it was, but it's less . . . depressing than the Dark Times themselves. Learning how we put the world back together again and all."

I looked up at him. His eyes were completely earnest. "Could you do that?"

"Sure I could. I'll ask my granddad. He can do anything in this school."

"You'd really do that for me?"

"Of course."

I couldn't help it. I flung my arms around him and buried my nose in his neck. He smelled of sandalwood soap. "Thank you!"

He held me briefly, then put me back. "Don't mench," he said. "It's no big deal."

"It is," I said.

He shook his head. "No, this obviously really bothers you. It's sky. I'll see to it tonight."

I hoped it really was sky. I couldn't bear another dose of *Apocalypse Then*.

Knowing I might soon be able to transfer out of my history class had no bearing on my nightmares. They were even worse that night. I was walking through corridors, but they were corridors of human corpses, bloated and red and sickly, images of the horrors my history teacher had told me about. This time, to my own horror, I knew what I was looking for. I was looking for something, or someone, *in* the walls, one of the thousands upon thousands of dead. And I wasn't sure, when I found the corpse, if it would truly be dead, or wake up and try to . . . I didn't know. It didn't matter. Whatever it tried to do would be horrifying.

I thought at first that every face would be the face of Mom, of Dad, of Xavier, but it wasn't the case. I made myself stare into the faces of the anguished, dripping corpses, and the smell was terrible, and I started to run through them, looking for somewhere to throw up, but there were only the halls of the dead. I knew Xavier was among them, and I knew I'd never find him.

This time when I woke up, I was crying. Zavier looked up

from the foot of the bed and whimpered, his eyes worried. "It's okay, Zavy," I told him, patting him on the head. "Good dog."

I took a deep breath and got up. Zavier whined but followed docilely at my heels. It was always pointless trying to sleep again once the nightmares started. They always came back. I missed my stass dreams. They never turned dark.

I slipped out the door and across the hall to my studio. The fish tank cast a quiet glow throughout the room. I turned on the lamp above the drafting table and uncovered the chalk drawing I had started that evening. It was a sketch of Bren. I stared at Bren's green chalk eyes and smiled. Xavier's eyes had been green. Maybe that was what really drew me to Bren. Bren and Xavier didn't otherwise look anything alike—from the shape of their eyes to the texture of their hair and the tint of their skin, everything was different. But those eyes of Bren's reminded me of my Xavier.

I was busy drawing Bren a green shirt that matched his eyes when I heard the noise behind me. I assumed it was Patty or Barry, though I was a little surprised they'd even bothered to come in. It was strange, going from my parents, who scheduled my every move, watched my every action, prevented my every mistake, to Patty and Barry, who barely spoke to me unless I went to them first.

The footsteps behind me were slow and precise. I was about to turn around when a harsh, creaking male voice said, "You are Rosalinda Samantha Fitzroy. Please turn around for retinal identification."

There was no way that voice was Barry's.

—chapter 7—

My hand slipped, marring Bren's portrait. I whirled, startled, and spilled half a dozen squares of chalk. They shattered on the wooden floor.

The black-haired man who stood behind me seemed unreal. His skin shone in the light of my lamp as if he were made of glass. He stood as straight as a rod. One hand held a strange circular device with little flashing lights on it. In the other he held a black stick with a red-and-yellow warning beacon on the tip.

He positively terrified me, but I managed to find my voice. "What do you want?"

The man's head twitched, which did not move his hair at all. "Voice match confirmed," he said. He looked Asian, but he spoke with a distinct German accent. He sounded monotone, as if he were uttering a prerecorded amalgamation of syllables rather than actual speech. "Please remain still for retinal identification."

Zavier began to growl behind me. The shiny man had no reaction. Instead he stared into my face and said, "Retinal match confirmed. Target confirmed."

At the sound of his voice, Zavier lunged, grabbing the man's leg with a fearsome snarl. I shrieked. I expected the man to kick Zavier away, but he completely ignored the snarling Afghan.

"Rosalinda Samantha Fitzroy. My orders are to retain and return you to the principal. If return proves impossible, my orders are to terminate. Remain still."

Terminate? I scrambled backward, painfully knocking my hip against the corner of my drafting table. He tried to come at me, but Zavier tore and snapped and snarled. I was surprised at the depth of Zavier's training; I'd heard that Afghans could be rather meek. Zavier's teeth had no effect on the man's skin, but his trouser leg was torn to ribbons.

The man looked down at Zavier. "You are impeding my retrieval. Cease and desist, or you will be eliminated."

"Zavier! Down!" I cried. But clearly my poor dog hadn't yet gotten used to his new call name. It had no effect.

"You have been warned," the man said, and touched Zavier with his stick.

Zavier yelped and stiffened, falling to the ground as lifeless as if he'd been stuffed. "You killed my dog!" I screamed, horrified. At the sound of my voice, Zavier began to whine faintly, much to my relief, though he still seemed incapable of movement.

My attacker came at me, stepping casually over Zavier. The circular thing in his hand opened, so that it seemed ready to snap shut like a clam. Two nasty-looking electrodes protruded from the back end of it. Suddenly I recognized it. That was a control collar. The collar disconnected the wearer's lower brain functions and made all movement subservient to an external force, usually a computer. They were invented for use in medicine, physical rehabilitation, and certain procedures for which the patient's compliance was imperative. If he got that thing around my neck, I would be forced to go with him, no question about it. So whatever I did, I had to avoid that collar.

My parents had been worried about kidnappers, so they had me drilled in self-defense. It had been a very real danger; they were powerful, highly visible people, and their daughter would have been a prime target. I had never been very good at it—no superhero rescues from me—but I'd picked up the basics. Run, they'd told me. Fight. Make as much noise as possible. Do everything you can to keep from being put into their power. Once they have you, they can do anything they want with you.

So I ran. Or tried to. My drafting table caught on my waist. I lost my balance and fell, dropping most of my weight on the back end of my table. The table tilted upward, like a seesaw, flinging my entire box of chalks against the wall and knocking down the clock. The clock fell into my fish tank, sending up a streaming flash of water. I went down, cracking my head against my easel, collapsing it under my weight.

Half-dazed from the blow, I reached behind me, scrambling in a drawer. I hoped to come up with an X-Acto blade or a paint knife, but what met my hand was a huge tube of oil paint. It was a start.

I squeezed it at the man's face, and a splurt of sticky green oil paint splatted into his eyes. He hesitated only a second, reorienting himself. To my horror, he seemed to have no reaction of pain, despite the fact that his open eyes were entirely covered. He didn't even move to wipe it off. Who was this guy? Or *what* was he? He seemed entirely inhuman, and I was utterly out of my depth.

And also incredibly lucky. The oil paint mixed with the water on the floor, creating slippery patches of oil over water. Unhurt but blind, my attacker skidded in the oil slick as he reached for me with his stick weapon. He flipped backward and landed with a clatter onto the wooden floor.

I didn't wait. I launched myself out the door and slammed it shut.

But now that I was out of the room, I didn't know where to go. Why hadn't Patty or Barry come running? What if he had killed them? I flung open the door to their bedroom.

Blackness. Their bed was empty. They must not have come home from the theater yet.

Leaving their bedroom door swinging, I fled down the hall, wishing Zavier was beside me. I didn't know where to go or what to do. Why was that man after me? Where had he come from?

I opened the door to the condo and ran down the corridors toward the lift, fighting my stass fatigue. I wouldn't be able to run much farther, but when I got to the lift, I balked. What if the shiny man wasn't alone?

I backed away from the elevator and opened the door to

the stairwell. Quietly. There was no one waiting for me in the harshly lit cement utility stairs. As softly as I could, I crept down them, hoping my bare feet would make no noise. In the end, I knew there was only one place I'd feel safe.

I crept to the subbasement and picked my way through the debris, the stored remnants of old tenants' lives. I stubbed my toe on a wooden crate and nearly screamed when a dusty coatrack lunged at me from the blackness and left a coat now forty years out of fashion grappling at my throat. I escaped these perils, found the old storeroom, and curled into my abandoned stass tube, shaking.

I had a brief thought of turning it on, letting the quiet waves of my colorful stass dreams take me from my nightmares, from the horror of my missing years, from whoever was hunting me. But fear of being captured while stassed kept me from pressing the activation switch. Instead, I curled quietly on the satin-of-silk cushions, wrapped in the dusty coat that I'd thought was attacking me.

The pervasive chill of underground seeped into my bones. I rubbed my cheek against the softness of the cushions and breathed in the perfume of stale stass chemicals. I think they affected me a bit. After the first few moments of shuddering terror, I drifted into semiconsciousness: not stasis itself but the beginning stages of it. What dragged me from my huddled stupor was my cell, beeping shrilly in the darkness. I pulled it from around my neck and pressed the receive button.

It was Patty. Her rigidly trimmed head appeared in a hologram before me, her mouth pursed in distaste. "Where are you?"

she demanded. "Do you know what your wretched animal has done? You keep that creature in the pet garden when you go out, or so help me I'll send it back to where it came from! I didn't want the stupid thing!"

"What's wrong with Zavier?"

"He's a menace! He's eaten half your green oil paint and completely trashed your studio. That's my one comfort; at least it wasn't *my* living room. You get over here and clean up before school, or contract or no I'll find some punishment for you."

"I'll be right there," I said, pressing the end button. I disentangled myself from the coat and headed to the lift. My fear had passed, thanks to the residual stass chemicals that were still affecting my fear receptors. If they hadn't been, I suspect I'd still be gibbering with terror in the basement.

When I got back, Patty was shouting at Zavier, who cowered under my drafting table. My studio was in ruins. Zavier actually must have been responsible for some of it. Dog prints and smudges circled the room, and the tube of paint I'd left on the ground had been chewed, leaving Zavier's blond fur streaked with green. Water on the floor had mixed with the oily paint, making wavery green archipelagoes on my wood floor. Punctuating this were brightly dissolving sticks of chalk, which were going to be useless after this. Patty kept her fashionable shoes carefully out of the detritus. "There you are!" she said. "Clean this up before school. And when you go out, take that wretched dog with you. Why on earth did you leave it shut in here?"

"Yes, Patty," I said obediently. I opened my mouth to tell

her about last night, but she was already gone. I wasn't sure how I would have broached the subject, anyway.

After she left, I tried to coax Zavier out from under the drafting table. At first he wouldn't come. When he saw that no one else was coming into the room, he gingerly heaved himself to his feet and crept over to me, whining. He was clearly in pain.

I pulled out my cell and pressed the button for the information drone. "I'm Hally, your information operator." The hologram of the beautiful composite woman asked very politely what she could do for me today. I asked her for the names of local vet clinics.

Of the names the drone rattled off, one had the same name as Zavier's grooming facility. I asked her to contact them, and within a few moments, the image of an exquisite receptionist appeared before me. "My dog is . . . hurt," I said.

"Would you like to make an appointment?" she asked.

"I don't know," I said, flustered. "I don't have a lot of time before school. I think he has a regular appointment with your groomers? His name is Freefoot's Desert Roads."

"Ah, yes." The receptionist smiled, her eyes glancing at a screen I couldn't see. "Desert Roads is down here as a prestige patient. If you will drop him off on your way to school, we'll do the rest."

"What's a prestige patient?" I asked.

"All of Desert Roads's care has been prepaid and pre-approved. You just drop him off, and we'll cell you when we know what's wrong with him."

"Thanks," I said, and disconnected.

I didn't have time to clean my studio and drop Zavier at the vet's before school. After fishing the wall clock out of the fish tank (which miraculously had not electrocuted any of my fish), I locked the door to the studio so that Patty couldn't see the mess, threw on a uniform, and led Zavier to my limoskiff. I ordered the skiff to the groomers and crept into the back with Zavier.

He got green paint all over the skiff and my uniform, and I didn't care. I hugged him around the neck. He groaned and whined, but he licked me tenderly.

When I dropped Zavier off at the vet's, I told them about the paint, but I omitted the story of the shiny man and his weird stick. They reassured me that they'd check his system for toxins as well as give him a thorough grooming. I headed for school feeling a little better about Zavier. I had buried the memory of the shiny man firmly beneath the stass residue, and I wasn't going to think about it for as long as I could manage.

Bren was waiting for me in the quad. "It's all sky," he said, grabbing my notescreen from my hand. I'd forgotten about my new schedule in the horror of last night and the troubles with Zavier. Bren touched my screen a few times and then handed it back to me, showing me my new schedule. "There you are: second period, history, Mr. Collier. We had to change your English class to the Romantics; hope you don't mind."

"No, that's great," I said. It actually solved two problems at once, as I'd been hard-pressed not to point out to my teacher that these so-called famous turn-of-the-century authors had been literary unknowns. I didn't want to offend her.

School was only marginally better now that I didn't have to dread my history class. But I was fortunate to be in class with Bren. He was a delight to watch, wildly animated in class, striking up debates with the other students, surprising the teacher with obscure facts he happened to have read someplace, drawing conclusions from seemingly disconnected details. He did everything I always wished I could do in school. Unfortunately I had never been intelligent enough to manage anything like it.

I really loved watching him. How his hands moved so deftly over his notescreen. True, he'd been using it since kindergarten, while I was new to the personal notescreen touchpads, but still, his long brown fingers seemed to perform a delightful ballet. I found myself wondering what it would feel like to have those fingers on me, touching my skin, holding me close.

I swallowed. No way. No way. That was not right. I didn't feel that way about Bren. I *couldn't* think that way about Bren. I loved Xavier. This weird thing I was feeling wasn't love, wasn't anything like what I felt for Xavier. But . . .

When Bren caught my eyes, I blushed and looked down at my screen. I couldn't meet his eyes. I couldn't think about him without strange fish swimming through my stomach. Oh, hell!

I left history class in a daze and actually got lost on my way to Chinese. The teacher didn't scold me when I ducked in five minutes late. I began to suspect that Mr. Guillory had given instructions on that as well.

I couldn't make heads or tails of the class. About twenty minutes in, my cell beeped, giving me an escape from the incomprehensible vocabulary review. I darted into the hall.

"Your dog seems to be all right, but he's exhausted himself," said the vet. "We checked for toxins, but the paint seems to be relatively benign. Did you take him for a long walk yesterday?"

I shook my head. "No."

"Well, our scans tell us that all of his muscles are fatigued. He's suffering from an overdose of lactic acid. Basically, your dog's muscles are overly stiff. He'll be all right in a day or two, but he should take it easy. Are you sure no one overworked him?"

"Not that I know of," I said. I wasn't sure how to tell him that my dog had been hit with a weird baton by a shiny, mechanical-sounding man who told me he wanted to terminate me.

I headed back to class. I didn't want to think about the shiny man, I couldn't understand anything in most of my classes, and now that I knew Zavier was going to be all right, he didn't weigh on my mind. Which left me thinking of Bren.

I didn't know exactly what I was feeling. The only boy I'd ever loved had been Xavier, and that had come so gradually, over so many years, with so many changes, that I didn't know how to handle this kind of rushing fondness. It hurt my heart. It hurt more so because I had no idea how he felt.

I'd always known how Xavier felt. I'd known him for so long, through so many moods, that there was no way to misinterpret his actions. He would never hide anything from me, anyway. He was my best friend, my brother, my love. And now he was dead, and I grieved for him. I wondered if it was that grief that was reaching out for Bren now, or if it was something more than that.

I considered how he had saved me, how Bren of all the people in the world had been the one to stumble over my stass tube, how he had been the one to wake me . . . wake me with a kiss, just like Sleeping Beauty. I hadn't thought of it as a kiss at the time. I wondered if he ever did.

I caught sight of Bren as I exited my last class, now Romantic poets. My heart quickened, and I found myself running up to him. "Thanks so much for everything," I told him. "The Romantics are so much better than turn-of-the-century lit. I was . . . a little put off by that."

He smiled. "Yeah, my granddad said you'd probably like that better. He remembered reading turn-of-the-century lit when it was new, and he hadn't been impressed by it then. What did you think of history? You prefer the Reconstruction?"

"It's fascinating. How did they manage to maintain the out-planet colonies?"

"We haven't gotten to all of that yet," Bren said. "But I do know we abandoned the outposts on Ganymede and Ceres, and we had to abort a planned colony on Enceladus." He looked over his shoulder. Nabiki and Otto were standing there, clearly waiting for him. "Ahm, I gotta go. I'll miss the skimmer."

I sighed. The stass chemicals had faded entirely, leaving me scared and jumpy, and I was afraid to be alone. Even though I couldn't bring myself to tell anyone about my encounter the night before, I was shaken. I also wanted to be with Bren. "I could take you home in the limoskiff," I offered, trying not to sound as desperate as I felt. "I mean, we're both going to Unicorn."

Bren hesitated, then shrugged. "Okay." He jerked his head at Nabiki and Otto. Nabiki shrugged and headed off to the skimmerport. Otto stood and stared at me for a moment, his yellow eyes glinting in the sun.

It made me uneasy.

"Have I offended Otto somehow?" I asked.

Bren turned to look at his alienesque friend and grinned. Otto gave his forced smile back, waved, and followed Nabiki. "Nah," Bren said. "He finds you interesting. But, technically, you own his patent, which means . . . well, he's human enough that he has human rights, but it's complicated. He's always afraid they'll try another experiment. Once you come of age, that would be your decision."

I balked. "I wouldn't do something like that! Didn't you say most of them died?"

"Horribly," Bren said. "Don't worry about it. I think he just wishes that he dared to talk to you, but you scare him."

I gulped. "Do I scare you?"

Bren turned his regard on me, his brow furrowed. It was like having a strong light shone on me. I was suddenly aware of all my flaws. I hadn't had my hair done professionally since the press conference. My clothes were rumpled and paint stained from bringing Zavier to the vet. I'd been chewing on my nails in my classes, either out of nervousness or boredom. Under Bren's gaze I turned into a pimply, skeletal orphan, lost in time. "You do have to comm you're odd," he said finally, and the light turned off. "Half your turns of phrase are off—it's like talking to my grandmother. But then you'll do something or say something that seems . . . don't take this the wrong way, but very childlike. No offense."

"None taken," I said.

"So, you're different. Almost like someone from another country, but not. I don't know." He looked nervous. I suddenly wanted to reach out and ruffle his hair. "That answer your question?"

"I guess." I swallowed. "The limoskiff meets me down here," I said awkwardly. He followed me to the skiff and climbed in after me. "I have to make a stop on the way home. Do you mind dogs?"

"Nope. Had one up until last year. Finally succumbed to old age. Poor Jack."

"What kind?" I asked.

"Retriever," he said. "He was a great fielder. He'd fetch any tennis balls that escaped the court."

When I brought Zavier into the skiff, he tilted his head at Bren and then sniffed his legs. "Hey there, boy," Bren said. He ruffled Zavier's ears.

"Be gentle with him," I said. "He had a rough night. He ate some paint."

"Did you eat paint?" Bren asked Zavier in a low, confiding voice. He looked up at me. "Where'd he get paint?"

"My studio," I said.

Bren stared at me with new respect. "Your studio?"

"Yeah, I . . . putter," I said shyly.

"The Piphers gave you a studio?"

"Guillory did, I think," I said. "It must have been in my records somewhere that I liked art."

Bren shrugged, turning his attention back to Zavier. "Not that I saw," he said. "And I tried looking you up."

"You did?"

"Couldn't find you anywhere. Actually, I couldn't find any records of your parents even having a child. I guess they guarded their privacy. I found a picture of you at about age ten or so with your parents, buried in one of the UniCorp archives, but you aren't even labeled in it. You're pretty much a ghost. No digital trail. Couldn't even find your birthday."

"Like I never existed in the first place," I said. "I feel like that sometimes. Everyone I ever knew is dead."

Bren let Zavier go and sat back awkwardly. "I'm sorry."

I shrugged. "I'm getting used to the idea."

"I'm still sorry."

The limoskiff moved too quickly. We were already at the condo, and I was still scared to be alone. "Would you like to see my studio?" I asked. "It's a bit of a mess. Zavier kind of knocked stuff around, but . . . Well, I have to get it cleared up before Patty and Barry get home."

"You're alone until then?" Bren asked.

"Yeah. 'Cept for Zavy."

Bren seemed to hesitate and then said, "Yeah. Sure, I'll come up."

When I opened the door to my studio, I expected to see it in the ruin I'd left it in this morning. However, the maid had a key and apparently hadn't heard Patty's admonitions. She had cleaned the room for me, leaving it considerably more tidy than I ever could have.

"Wow!" said Bren as he stepped inside. He looked around at the paintings. I was a little glad now that my chalk drawing of him had been destroyed. I could see the crumpled, dampened remains of it peeking out of the incinerator tray. If he'd seen my drawing yesterday, it wouldn't have bothered me. I'd have told him the truth, that I always drew the people around me. I even had a couple of sketches of Patty and Barry around, and one of Mr. Guillory in pencil. But as of today, with this awful fluttery feeling he gave me begging for a name I wasn't sure I wanted to give it . . . well, I would have felt awkward.

I longed to paint him, though. I would place him on a stool in the corner, with the bookshelf as a background. Or maybe against the window, particularly if I could persuade him to open his shirt just a little. Maybe even more than a little. Maybe take it off entirely, let the sun glow on his skin, bring out the contours of his well-muscled chest. I'd bring the color of his eyes into the foliage in the background, and . . .

I realized he had just asked me a question. I shook my head to clear it of visions of Bren half-naked in my studio. "What was that?"

"Why aren't you in any art classes in school?"

"I don't know. Guess Mr. Guillory didn't think I needed one." I gestured around the room. "I don't mind. I've got all this."

Bren went up to the wall where my biggest painting to date was still drying. It was one of my stass landscapes, an oil painting of brightly colored undulating hills and lightning-flecked clouds, which came off cheerful rather than foreboding. I was calling it *Blue Dunes.*

"You painted all these?"

"It's just a hobby."

Bren glanced at me. "They're good," he said. "Don't put yourself down." He tilted his head as he stared at my painting. "Noid, that's so sky," he said, bemused. "There's something very . . . visceral about these landscapes."

I looked at him. "Did you really just use the word *visceral?*" I asked. I hadn't heard such a word since I'd left stass.

Bren shrugged. "My grandparents always dragged us all to these galleries. I've learned how to describe art."

"Landscapes have always been my strength," I told him. "I won an award for one once."

"Really?" He raised an eyebrow, looking more closely at the canvas. After another moment he nodded. "I can see that." He turned to look at some of my other pieces. "That would be, what, sixty years ago?"

"Sixty-two," I said. "It was just before I was stassed."

"What was it called?"

"*Undersky.*"

"No, sped, the award," he said, chuckling.

"Oh. The Young Masters Award. I was supposed to win a month-long art tour through Europe." And a scholarship, but I probably wouldn't have been able to accept it.

"You didn't go?" Bren asked.

"Well, I was . . . indisposed when the trip came up," I said.

I had been stassed right before the tour. Not that I would have gone, anyway.

"Oh, right. Sorry."

"That's okay," I said. "I know it's weird."

"Only a little." He flipped through some finished drawings on the counter. "Is this my mom?" He pulled out a sketch done in pencil on copy paper.

"Yeah," I said, looking over his shoulder. "I did it in the hospital." Mrs. Sabah had been an easy study. Her features had clean lines and a natural flow. I just hadn't been able to bring out the startling green of her eyes.

"Could I make a copy of this? She'd love to see it."

"Give it to her," I said.

"Are you serious?"

I shrugged. "It's just a sketch."

He looked at me, almost excited. "Would you sign it?"

I frowned but dug a pencil out of a drawer. "Why?"

Bren laughed. "Because with this skill, you'll be a famous artist any minute, and it'll probably be worth Mom's weight in gold."

I wrinkled my nose. "No, I won't," I said. "Mr. Guillory needs me at UniCorp."

Bren scowled. "*Ev*eryone says that." He turned back to my sheaf of sketches. "It drives me nuts. You should do what you want."

"I don't know what I want," I said. But I signed *Rose Fitzroy* below Bren's mother's portrait and titled the portrait *Annie*.

"You got everyone in here. Noid, look at that!" He pulled

out the sketch of Mr. Guillory. "You drew him like a troll in this picture!"

I tilted my head sheepishly. "Who, me?" I said innocently.

Bren laughed. He pulled up another sketch. "Who's this? I think I recognize him. Kid at school?"

I frowned. "No," I said. I turned away.

Only then did Bren notice the five other drawings of Xavier already on the walls. There were lots more, of course, but I doubted he'd connect the baby pictures with the portraits of Xavier as a young man. His tone turned more serious, and he asked, "Who is he?"

I didn't want to tell Bren this. And yet I did. I wanted Bren to catch me up and tell me that he was sorry for me, tenderly kiss my forehead, my eyelids, assure me he would make it all okay. I turned to my drafting table and watched the fish behind it. "Just my old boyfriend."

"Oh," he said. Then, only half of what I wanted, he added, "I'm sorry."

I shrugged.

There was an awkward silence. I could feel the heat of him behind me, drawing me toward him. "Well, ahm . . . thanks for the sketch. Mom's gonna love it."

"Anytime," I said.

"Guess I'll see you at school."

By the time I turned away from the fish, Bren had already skittered out the door.

—chapter 8—

I didn't sleep at all that night. I huddled in my bedroom, my hand firmly on Zavier's collar, my cell within easy reach. At every little click of sound, every time Zavier shifted his weight, at every light flickering over the walls from a passing skimmer, I was convinced I was about to be attacked again. At dinner I'd considered telling Patty and Barry about my attacker, but I really couldn't bring myself to. They had such indifference toward me, and it seemed so impossible. I wasn't an idiot; I'd checked the security logs—there had been no break-in. As far as official records went, it had never happened. It didn't make any sense.

As daylight began to glow through my window, I picked up my cell. "Dr. Bija's office," said the holoimage of her secretary.

"I'd like to make an appointment," I said. "For this morning, if that's possible."

The secretary was brusque and dismissive. "This is urgent?"

I considered this question. My usual impulse when someone asked such a thing was to say *no*. "Yes," I said, feeling ashamed.

"Do you attend the school?"

I nodded.

"Name?"

"Rose Fitzroy."

"Oh!" The secretary's demeanor suddenly changed, and her eyes began to dart away from mine, looking toward her screen. "Well, I can't get you in before school starts, but I can arrange for an appointment at ten, at the start of third period. Dr. Bija can file an excuse for you over the net."

"Thank you," I breathed.

"Of course, Miss Fitzroy." She disappeared, looking relieved to be off the phone with me.

I slept through social psych. I stayed awake in history to watch Bren, but by third period I was glad of the excuse to miss Chinese.

Dr. Bija seemed concerned when I showed up in her office. "Is there a problem, Rose?" she asked. "My secretary told me you'd scheduled an extra session."

"I know I'm not supposed to meet with you until Monday, but I can't sleep."

"Have the nightmares gotten worse?"

"Not exactly," I said, but I'd been wondering that since I'd gotten home the day before. There was really no evidence of the shiny man's existence other than Zavier's exhaustion, which might have come about from him going wild in my studio while I slept. "Sort of. Maybe." I sat down on the couch, feeling confused and exhausted.

"What seems to be the trouble?" Mina asked.

"I . . . I thought I was attacked the night before last," I said. "By this shiny, dead-eyed man who wanted to put a control collar on me . . ." I told her the whole thing, including how I'd run down to the subbasement and fallen asleep in my stass tube. "And when I came upstairs, my studio was trashed," I finished.

"Did you tell Patty and Barry about this . . . experience?" Mina asked.

"No," I said. "Patty was so angry when she got up and the room was a mess, and then I had to go to school. And by the time they got home last night, it seemed too weird."

Dr. Bija nodded. "You realize that your building is a high-security zone, don't you? No unauthorized persons can even set foot in the grounds, let alone walk through the corridors and into your condo, without a hundred alarms going off."

"I know," I said. "I checked the security logs. He wasn't there. And most of my dreams involve being hunted by something, but this one felt so much more real. And my studio . . ."

"Could your dog have done it?" Mina asked.

"Maybe. But how could I have a dream that my studio was trashed, then wake up and have it true?"

"That happens very often," Mina told me. "We hear things while we're unconscious and incorporate them into our dreams. I'm more worried about the possibility of you sleepwalking. Have you had any experience with that before?"

I shook my head. "No. I didn't really have nightmares before now. But last night I was so scared, I just sat up all night."

Dr. Bija nodded. "I'm going to arrange for you to get a prescription sleep aid. Something mild," she reassured me, "non-habit-forming. Take it only if you have real trouble getting to sleep, like last night. Do you know the name of your doctor? I'll have to have him prescribe it."

"No," I said.

"I'll contact Mr. Guillory. He should be able to tell me the name."

"Do you have to go through Guillory?" He still made me uncomfortable.

"I won't tell him anything about this," Mina said. "But I can't prescribe the medication myself."

I sighed. "Okay. Rose the freak gets freakier."

Mina laughed. "Do you really think you're a freak?"

"What else do you call a teenager who's a hundred years old?"

"I think it's only seventy-eight," Mina said, and I knew I'd said a bit much. I'd realized a few days ago that when Bren woke me up it had been a century since the day of my birth. A century and going on seven weeks. There were some things it was better that Dr. Bija didn't know.

I didn't have any more dreams of the shiny man, nor did I sleep-walk, as far as I knew. The pills Dr. Bija had sent over did help with my nightmares a bit. Or rather they helped me get back to sleep once I had them.

I continued going to school, which remained steadily dreadful. I continued my physical therapy, which was finally starting to take. It got to the point where I could actually take Zavier for a nice long walk after school without my muscles shutting down, though I still couldn't run easily. I continued my art, which was surprisingly more polished than ever before—sixty-two years of stass dreaming hadn't gone entirely to waste. I continued to see Dr. Bija once a week. And I continued, almost against my will, to watch Bren.

"Did you bring in any of your artwork for me today?" Dr. Bjia asked as I walked into her office.

I shook my head. It had been almost four weeks since my sleepwalking incident, and for all of our sessions, I'd never remembered to grab one of my landscapes before I left home. "Sorry."

Mina raised an eyebrow. "I see you've brought a sketchbook. Is there anything there you'd be willing to let me see?"

"But these are just sketches," I said, surprised.

"So? I don't need to see the *Mona Lisa*."

I shrugged. "Okay." I passed her the sketchbook.

The first few pages were landscapes. "Tell me about these," Mina said.

"Just landscapes," I said.

"Where did you draw them?"

"Ahm . . . during class, mostly," I admitted. Over the last month I'd filled considerably more pages in my sketchbook than I had done schoolwork on my notescreen. Very few of my sketches were in color, but she seemed to appreciate even the charcoal-gray landscapes. Lots of them featured lightning storms — my stass dreams often did. She turned a few more pages. "And who's this? Bren?"

I licked my lips nervously. "No," I said. "That's Xavier." I'd forgotten I had sketches of him in there. I had been trying so hard to avoid mentioning anything about my old life, and here I'd just handed her a lead to it.

"Who's Xavier?"

"Someone I used to know . . . before."

I could suddenly feel her burning with questions, all of the questions that she had avoided asking about my old life. I did not volunteer any more information, and to her credit, she respected that. She simply turned another page.

"That's Nabiki and Otto," I said.

"Yes, I know."

"You know Otto?"

"Otto's a little like you. I think everyone knows him," Mina said.

I caught something in the words that I probably shouldn't have. "Is he a client of yours?"

"I can't answer that," Mina said. "You should ask him if you're curious."

I sighed. "I can't. He won't talk to me."

"You'd be surprised how much Otto can say, if you'd let him."

"I know all about that," I said. "But he won't touch me. My mind scares him for some reason."

"Ah," Mina said thoughtfully. "Did he tell you why?"

I shook my head. "Nabiki couldn't translate it very well."

"Have you tried asking him personally?"

"I told you: he won't talk to me."

Mina pursed her lips. "Have you tried contacting him over the net?"

I stared at her as if she'd gone insane. "If he can't talk, he can't use a cell, either."

"Through your notescreen," Mina clarified. "He writes very well."

I simply hadn't thought of that. I rarely even opened my notescreen, and it hadn't occurred to me to use it to contact anyone. I'd never had anyone to contact before. "I'll think about it," I said, turning another page of my sketchbook. "*That*'s Bren."

Mina smiled. "He's a handsome one. Look at those eyes!"

I stared at them. "I know," I said quietly. I'd highlighted his eyes in the sketch. They seemed to shine out from shadow space. Bren's eyes always drew me, until I found myself drawing them.

I'd drawn the entire lunch table crew on different pages of the book, so Mina was able to put faces to all the names I'd mentioned. Then she turned the page and landed on another portrait of Xavier. "Now, this is the same boy as before," Mina said, "but he looks younger. Is it his brother?"

"No," I said. "That's Xavier, too. I knew him for a long time."

"How long?"

Pain stabbed me. "All his life," I said.

Then she asked me the first solid question she'd really asked about my situation. "You miss him?"

I considered brushing it off or changing the subject, but I didn't. "Every day," I said. "I try not to think about him."

"Yet you draw him."

I sighed. "I can't think about him, but I can't forget him, either. It's not right to forget someone you love."

There was a long, long silence. "You think?" Mina finally asked.

This line of questioning had gone seriously awry. "Anyway, that's my sketchbook," I said, taking it back. "Just a bunch of doodles."

"They're very skilled," Mina said, returning to her chair. "Do you think you'll continue with your art?"

"Of course I will."

"I mean, do you think you'd like to do that for a living?"

"I have UniCorp to tend to," I reminded her.

"Ah, right," Mina said. "That is a tricky one. Do you think you have the skills to run a multitiered interplanetary corporation like UniCorp?"

No one had ever put it quite like that before. My shoulders sagged. "No," I admitted. "But maybe I could hire someone to run it. Maybe after college . . ."

She laughed. "Fortunately, you don't have to worry about that right now."

"No, you're right," I said. "I should study harder."

. . .

I should study harder. That became both my litany and my shame, because as much as I said it, I couldn't bring myself to do it. I knew I was too stupid to understand, so how could my school subjects interest me?

But Bren interested me. And Otto interested me even more.

I was very interested in Otto, but I found it difficult to find out more about him. I felt awkward offering him my net-number, particularly with Nabiki around (and she was always around). Nabiki liked to talk about him, though, and I managed to find out some. He was always there when I gleaned my little knowledge, and it felt very odd not to be getting the information directly from him—though at least we weren't talking about him behind his back.

From what I could find out, Otto had won the Uni Prep scholarship without telling anyone exactly who he was. The scholarship had been awarded on the basis of an essay. Otto couldn't speak, but he had a brilliant mind, and that came out in his writing.

Despite the scholarship, Otto almost didn't get into Uni Prep. It took him six months and a civil rights lawsuit before he earned the right to an outside education. Before he'd come to the school, he and his family had been educated in a UniCorp laboratory, every nuance of their brain activity monitored and recorded.

Otto worked very hard at Uni Prep. His siblings—the other three Europa Project children who weren't simple—were still being monitored by UniCorp, and he visited them on weekends. Though they weren't being mistreated, all of them looked forward to the moment when they would come of age and be officially under their own guardianship.

Bren was a thing of pure energy in my head, a fluttering bird of feeling that consistently distracted my thoughts. Conversely, Otto was a weight. He lurked, a heavy burden standing in the corner of my mind, until I was dragging it everywhere. It ate at me that all of his hardships stemmed from the company I was supposed to own.

It didn't help that I often caught him watching me—staring at me, really—but his face was virtually expressionless. I couldn't read him. Other than the forced smile he'd obviously cultivated as a social lubricant, there was no way to tell what he was thinking. He was either interested in me or violently angry with me; I really couldn't tell.

My opportunity came through pure accident. At lunch a few days after I showed my sketchbook to Dr. Bija, Nabiki and Otto left the table very quickly and both forgot their screens. I surreptitiously reached across the table and turned Otto's on. There it was. I threw his number onto my own screen, so that I could contact him later.

And just in time. Nabiki came running back, and I picked up both screens to cover my prying. "You forgot these," I told her, holding them out to her.

Nabiki looked a little annoyed. "Thanks," she said.

She was always polite, Nabiki, but I could tell she didn't really like me.

I felt strange as I linked up with Otto's screen later that evening. It was an antiquated technology, on its way out even when I was a kid. The technology had been replaced by the cells, which responded to voice cues and used their little holo-recorders to make it seem as if you were really there with the person. It felt as outdated to me as a quill pen would have felt to someone in the Gates era.

I pulled up the keypad on the touch screen, took a deep breath, and began writing. Otto, sorry to bother you. This is Rose.

I waited.

When the reply chimed on my screen, I was almost too nervous to read it. No bother. Wow. Hey. Nice to talk to you.

Yeah, hi. Now that I'd started, I didn't know how to continue. I thought I'd just say hi. I was glad he couldn't see the face I made as I realized what an ass I sounded. Sorry. It's just awkward talking through Nabiki all the time.

It is. I'm glad you thought to write me. This is really . . . wow. This is so sky! Hi! I really wasn't expecting this.

I hadn't been expecting this, either. Otto sounded so friendly compared to his cold stare and Nabiki's quiet coolness. Sorry.

What for?

Interrupting you, whatever you're doing.

You aren't interrupting anything. I really wanted to talk to you, too. It's just . . . this would have been the only way, and I couldn't figure out how to ask. It's kind of a weird thing to send through someone else. That and most people find this kind of thing too antiquated.

Actually, I do, too.

Really? I'd have thought you of all people had done it before.

Well, I have. But only when I was a kid.

I thought so.

There was a long pause. I didn't really know what to say next.

Was there a specific reason you wanted to talk to me?

Sort of, I wrote. Dr. Bija was the one who suggested I write to you.

Mina? Isn't she nice?

I like her. Do you go to see her?

Weekly.

Me too.

I know.

She wouldn't tell me if you went.

She didn't tell me. You did. She was in your mind.

Oh. I'm not sure how I feel about that.

Don't worry. I show no one what I see in other people's minds. I have a code of ethics about it. As strong as Mina's. As any doctor's.

Really?

You have my word. In writing.

I wasn't sure why I could hear humor in that little written sentence, but I could.

Thanks, I wrote. I wanted to ask you something a little personal, and I didn't want to go through Nabiki.

Hm. Why not?

I tried to think of something that wouldn't sound offensive, since I really had no reason to dislike Nabiki. In fact, I thought she was probably very—what was that word they were using now?—very *sky*, considering her taste in friends. She doesn't seem to like me very much.

Ah. I'll have to tell her. She's not hiding her hostility very well.

Is she trying to?

Desperately.

So she really doesn't like me?

There was a bit of a pause before he replied. **She doesn't blame you for it. She knows full well it isn't your fault.**

What isn't my fault?

There was another long pause. **She's jealous,** he wrote finally.

I was indignant. Jealous? What on earth for?

Just who you are, I think.

Oi! Tell her for me, she can have it. My whole life. She can have the whole bloody company, the blasted reporters, the stass fatigue, another two years of physical therapy — not to mention all the nightmares! I'd change places with her in a heartbeat.

The moment I sent that message, I regretted it. Sorry, I wrote immediately.

She knows all that. It isn't that.

Now I was confused. Then what is she jealous of?

I find you interesting, and she finds that unnerving.

I swallowed. Oh.

Yes. It doesn't happen very often, you see. Most people bore me. Most minds are very simple.

I'm not very smart, I wrote.

It has little to do with intelligence, though I did not see stupidity in your thoughts. No, it's being willing to think and consider that I find interesting. Everyone has the ability to broaden their mind, but few people use it.

I didn't know what to say to that, so I asked another question. Is Nabiki interesting?

Very. She has many layers of thought. Which is why she can feel hostility and sympathy for you at the same time.

How did you two get together? If that isn't too personal a question.

It's not. When I first got to Uni, I was in a bad space. I was about as alone as you are, and even more strange. There was a lot of harassment. Nabiki has always been fiercely protective of me, ever since we first knew each other. Something about that reminded me of a mother lioness. She was so flattered by the thought that she fell in love almost instantly.

Wait, after one compliment?

Well. It's sort of hard to explain. First, a compliment from me is usually pretty, well, intense. God, that sounds arrogant. But it's true. I'm weird, and that's one of the weirdest things about me. And second, Nabiki's just like that. Everything she feels, she feels wholeheartedly, nothing held back. It was very strange absorbing the thoughts of someone falling in love with me. It was as if a colored rainbow of light came through her mind.

I liked that description of love.

I hadn't planned on a girlfriend, but it was such a beautiful thought that I found myself warming to it. We've been together more than a year now.

That's a nice story.

Nicer than most of yours, I suspect.

I shrugged, even though he couldn't see it. True.

Don't worry. I have plenty more nasty stories than nice ones.

I'm sorry.

I'm not. I can live no one's life but my own. What was that personal question you wanted to ask me?

Oh. Just the one. What so scared you about my mind?

You don't want the answer to that question.

I do.

If I could answer it properly, you wouldn't have to ask it in the first place. I'm not used to having to find words for that sort of thing.

I sagged in disappointment. I'm still asking. Answer any way you can.

It's your mind, Otto wrote. What do you think I saw?

When you touched me, I just felt confused.

And lonely. And frightened. And lost. And a little resentful.

I'm not resentful toward you.

Not toward me. To some golden statue.

Oh. That's how I think of Reginald Guillory.

Oh, that's funny!

A thought struck me. Do you laugh?

Not very well. I sound . . . odd. I tend not to in public.

Why don't you talk?

I can't. I've tried. There's a resonance chamber in adult humans that enables speech. Mine is still the same shape as an infant child's. I can whisper sometimes, if I'm desperate, but it still sounds odd, and people have a hard time understanding it. I know sign language, but it's useless if others don't know it, too. It can be really frustrating.

And your expressions? Your skin?

I think, as the heir to UniCorp, you have access to my medical records, if you'd like.

No, that's okay, I wrote as quickly as I could. Sorry.

I don't mean to sound rude, Otto wrote. I don't think much of UniCorp.

I don't blame you.

I don't blame you, either.

That was nice to hear. I'm glad. I still want to understand. I wish I knew why I scared you, so this wouldn't be the only way we could talk.

Fine. Let me think. There was a long pause before the words began again. **This is annoying,** he finally wrote. **It would be so much easier to SHOW you, but if I could show it to you, I wouldn't have to in the first place, because I'd be in your mind, and the problem wouldn't have arisen.**

That's ironic, I wrote.

Quite. All right. There is an . . . emptiness in your mind. It's not lack of intellect, and it isn't blocks or gaps in memory. Your memory seems solid. Stronger, in some places, than most people's. So strong it feels a little like running into speed bumps. I didn't see much, so bear with me if I say something that offends you.

I doubt there's anything you could say that would offend me, I told him truthfully.

There's something about the areas around those speed bumps of strong memory. Either before or after them are vast holes, and I'm afraid to look into them. I feel that what is inside them is dangerous. Some kind of terrible briar might drag me inside, and I'd be trapped forever. But I don't know why I feel that.

I swallowed. Otto? I wrote. Have you ever gone into stasis?

No, but I plan to, one day. My sisters and brother and I would like to go to Europa after we reach the age of ascension and have the right to do anything we coiting well please.

I smiled at that.

Why do you ask?

Just wondering if that's what you were seeing.

I doubt it. There's more than just the one gap.

Well, there was more than just the one stass.

Really? Why more than one stass?

I had to change the subject. You think you'll get to Europa?

They won't be able to stop us once we're twenty-one.

I'm glad you're human enough that UniCorp can't own you completely.

They can still make more of us, Otto wrote. We do not even own our own blood. Prick us, do we not bleed? Not without written permission. UniCorp owns our reproductive rights, too. If we could ever have children, they'd own them as well.

That's awful!

Yes. But you're almost as bad off as I am, at the moment. UniCorp owns everything about you as well.

Until I supposedly come to own UniCorp.

If your golden statue will let you.

A terrible sense of foreboding engulfed me. You think he wouldn't?

I know he likes power. He was extremely affronted when I won the scholarship to Uni. He's made us all nervous ever since.

When I read that, I felt ill. I tried not to think of my long-lost Young Masters Award.

Of course, I am not truly free, Otto continued. Uni is still run by UniCorp. That was the only reason why I won the lawsuit. The judge decided that any school run by my guardians was the same as any other run by the same, and that if I had the ability to earn the tuition, I should therefore have a choice. Direct legalese quote. There was a pause in his steady stream of letters and then they started again. I have to go. They turn lights out at eleven for the boarders, and Jamal's my roommate. He complains if I leave my screen running.

Good night, Otto.

Good night, Briar Rose. Write to me again. I still find you interesting.

—chapter 9—

It was nice talking to Otto. For one thing, writing to him just before I went to bed helped me feel less alone at night. That was the first night in weeks I didn't have a nightmare. I was perfectly willing to repeat any performance that might keep the horrors at bay.

So I was glad the next day at lunch when Otto threw his deliberate smile at me while Nabiki wasn't looking. He tapped his notescreen twice and then held up both hands. Ten. I nodded silently.

At ten o'clock that evening, with Zavier keeping my feet warm, I sat down and turned on my notescreen. I hadn't even had time to open a file before a page linked through. **Hello again.**

Hello, I wrote. And to what do I owe the pleasure?

I just wanted to talk to you.

What about?

Anything. Everything. I want to ask all the banal questions you never answered for the reporters.

What are you talking about? I did nothing but talk to reporters for days!

Telling them exactly what they wanted to hear. Am I right?

I hesitated. Um, I finally wrote, almost as a joke.

You're funny. Tell me the truth. What did it feel like to wake up sixty years after you went to sleep?

Stass isn't exactly sleep, I wrote, avoiding the question. Though it does leave you rested. And there are . . . dreams, for lack of a better term.

They aren't really dreams?

No, I wrote. It's more like seeing inside my own head. I frowned. I think it's a little like what you did when you touched me, only it's just in my own head. And most of it takes the form of images — storms, and seas, and lots of colors.

Oh! There was a long pause. Must be pretty spooky, then.

No. Stass chemicals eliminate the fear centers of your nervous system. You can't feel any fear in stasis. Worry and sadness are partially eliminated, too, since they're mostly based on fear.

That's odd.

It was necessary. Before the fear suppressors, people would instinctively panic as their bodies stopped working. It's a weird process. I mean, your cells stop aging or dividing, and you feel yourself — well — dying. You aren't, really, but that's the only comparison your body has. You can only feel it for a second, but before the suppressors, it made getting out of stass extremely unpleasant. People were frozen in a state of terror for . . . however long they were stassed for. There's also the claustrophobics, who'd panic even before the stass started, and . . . My knowledge failed me. There's other reasons. Before they introduced the second load of chemicals, stass was much too unpleasant to use.

You know a lot about this.

I've done a lot of stass.

You make it sound like a drug.

I blinked when I read that. I didn't reply for so long that Otto wrote, **Rose? Still there?**

Still here, I wrote. You took me by surprise is all. You're right. In some ways, I guess it is a little like a drug.

I'm sorry. I just realized that was a bit insensitive of me. I didn't mean to say I thought you'd been high for sixty years.

Sixty-two, so they tell me, I said. No, it wasn't a sixty-two-year high. More like meditating on my artwork for a really long time.

Did it help your art?

Seems to have. Not that I would have chosen that way of studying. Kind of hard on my relationships. And stass fatigue isn't much fun.

I can imagine it's not. How long were you in the hospital?

It should have been three weeks, but they shoved me out after one. The reporters were coming. It was four weeks before they put me in school. I still can't run the mile.

Now, *that* I can do. All of us are fine runners. They chose very fit embryos for us. Tristan's the fastest, though.

I realized he was changing the subject for me, and I took it gratefully. Tristan?

Tristan Twice. My sister.

That's an unusual name.

32. We all figured out names based on our embryonic numbers.

How did you end up with Otto, then?

It's technically Octavius on my court records. It kind of degenerated. Octavius Sextus. Better than 86, I think.

Court records?

Yeah. We fought for real names.

When did you do that?

There was a longer pause than I would have thought he needed for such an innocuous question. When we were thirteen, Otto wrote.

Why not before?

That was — then he didn't write anything for a long time — when we started to die, he finished.

I'm so sorry. You don't have to go on.

There was another pause. No, it's fine, Otto wrote. I thought it would be hard for me, but actually this form of communication seems to be coming in handy. I forget how intense thinking everything at people is. I can't tell people about it the way I normally talk to people. I choke up. Even with Nabiki. But this isn't bothering me much. Oddly.

Well, that's good. I guess.

Yeah. Weird. Okay. There were thirty-four of us at first. We lost half a dozen from unexpected complications during childhood, mostly early, before five. But when we reached puberty, we started dropping like flies. Sixteen of us died within eight months, seven who weren't simple. Including my best friend. She was called 42.

So what happened? What made you choose names?

It was Una. Una Prime. 11. She was pretty sure she was going to die. Of course, I was pretty sure I was, too. It was the ones who can do what I do who died the fastest.

You mean with the mind reading?

Yeah. There were more of us who could than not, when we were all kids. Then things started to fall apart inside. Some of them went mad before they died. Some got massive brain hemorrhages, bled out. That's what happened to 42. We were all scared. Particularly Una. She did die, as it turned out. There's only me and Tristan now. We're the only ones who aren't simple and who can share thoughts who made it. There was a pause. Well, made it so far. No one's really sure of our life span.

Oh, God. You're scaring me.

Me too. I'm used to it by now. But Una Prime was afraid to die and have only Eleven on her tomb. So those of us who were left chose names. Apart from me, only Tristan, Penny, and Quin made it this far. The simple ones still go by numbers.

Who are Penny and Quin?

Pen Ultima is my other sister. She was 99. And Quint Essential is my brother. He was 50. Quin can talk. You should meet him. He's funny.

I'd like to meet your family. Did you always think of yourselves as family?

Yes. But we weren't officially brothers and sisters until we took names. Una wanted family to preside at her funeral, so we actually sent it through a judge and adopted one another. Now we're siblings with inheritance rights and everything, so if we die (presuming we're free by then), UniCorp won't get our property. Anything we own will go to one another. It always bothered me that 42 died before we did that. Feels like she died alone.

Aren't you, like, really related?

Not really. We all have different mothers and different DNA inserted from different microbes. Well, the same microbe, as in genus, but different individual ones. I think they were hoping we'd try to breed among ourselves. Too weird, though. We just don't see one another that way. We've always been together. Well, until I went to school.

Something about that struck a chord in me. The memory of the Young Masters Scholarship still haunted me. It would have been hard to accept it and leave Mom and Daddy. I wasn't sure I could have accepted. Rather than open that can of worms, I asked Otto, Does your family resent you for going to Uni?

No. All four of us tried. We knew only one of us had a chance at getting in. Quin found out about the scholarship program from his tutor. He had a different tutor from us because he can talk. Tristan and I used to share one. We needed someone trained in psychology, because our communication is so—here he paused for a moment before continuing to write—different. Penny's tutor is deaf, because Penny can only communicate through sign. And writing, like this. Unless I'm with her, of course. Then I can translate.

That must be weird.

You should see it when Guillory comes to check on our progress! Tristan and I refuse to touch him, and he won't learn sign, so Quin does all the talking. And as I said, Quin has a sense of humor. You should see the look on Guillory's face! Quin has been known to strut up and down making *beep, beep* noises, just to freak him out.

You've got me laughing, I wrote. Thanks. I don't laugh much.

I've noticed that about you, Otto wrote.

I'm glad I'm not the only one you refuse to touch, I wrote. Though I'm a little chagrined that my companion is Guillory.

There are thousands I refuse to touch, Otto told me. You are far from alone.

Does everyone else scare you?

Most people bore me, or disturb me. Most people's minds aren't pleasant places to be in.

I sighed. Not surprised you don't want to touch me, then.

I do, actually, he wrote. Only I fear it. It's annoying. I've never been faced with this problem before. After living most of my life on a biological death row, there isn't much that scares me. There was a bit of a pause before he said, So I'm glad you keep linking me. This is nice.

It is, I wrote. It was. Did you tell Dr. Bija you wanted to talk with me?

Of course. I can't lie very well, and if I'm feeling open, I don't hide things very well, either.

What does Dr. Bija think about me?

Here we go again. She doesn't think about you or any of her other clients when I'm with her, and if she does accidentally, I avoid the thought and don't read it. It takes a lot of trust on her part, but she's sincere. It's kind of like being in a room with classified documents, and you've sworn you won't read any of the ones that aren't thrust under your nose. Keep your eyes straight ahead, and don't pay attention to the rest of the room.

Oh. I didn't mean to try to breach your code of ethics. I was only kind of hoping I could see how other people see me.

I can say how I see you, Otto wrote.

I was a little afraid to hear it, but I wrote, Okay.

You're very quiet. You talk more with me than I ever see you do in school. He was right. I think I wrote more with him than I even spoke to Bren or Dr. Bija. You seem sad to me, he went on. Your eyes are dark, and I'm not just talking about the deep tea of their tone. Hm. Otto had an eye for color. You're diligent in your art; you're always drawing. It seems to be very important to you. A kind of outlet. More than a hobby, I think.

You're right, I wrote, volunteering information, since he'd said so much about himself. I use it to understand things.

You have trouble understanding things?

Yes. I've always felt like a bit of an outsider, even before all this. Drawing helps.

That's good. Let me think. What else? Well, personally, I worry about you. You don't complain, even though I can tell you hate just about everything about school. It makes me wonder if something's happened to you. Of course, everyone agrees skipping some sixty years is bound to mess you up a bit.

So everyone sees me as messed up? Great.

Of course they do. Most of them are wrong about how, though, I think. According to gossip (which I do not hold as sacred as I do people's thoughts), most people think you wanted to be stassed and that you just wanted to be the center of attention and the dowager to UniCorp. Most people think you have an eating disorder because you're keen on staying beautiful.

I look like a skeleton.

I think so, too, and I keep watching you *try* to eat.

It's stass fatigue.

Ooh. I'm sorry.

Lots of things don't work in me right. All my organs are protesting being dormant so long. They tell me they put little nanobots inside me, to keep my kidneys functioning and my heart happy.

Quin's got some of those, Otto said. They hope to take them out when he's old enough. Probably around our emancipation.

When will that be?

Twenty-one.

Why does he need maintenance nanos?

We were dying. They did *try* to keep us alive. Half the simple ones needed maintenance, too. Especially since they can't really tell anyone when they're hurting.

Is their life very hard?

They try to keep them happy. We visit for an hour or so on the weekends. They like us, particularly me and Tristan, because we can show them pretty mind pictures and stuff. A pause. Lights out. Jamal's being a sped.

Okay. Good night.

Good night, Briar Rose.

I smiled. I was starting to like being called Briar Rose.

—chapter 10—

Despite my resolve to study harder, school continued to be a drain on me, mentally and physically. I wasn't really trying. I spent my days disappearing into my sketchbooks and into my studio. The only time I woke up at school was in history, when I could watch Bren and his glinting green eyes.

Even seeing him down the hall brightened the day, as if a ray of sunshine had pierced the clouds. I didn't know what I was feeling. It hadn't been this giddy, confusing rush of conflicting emotion with Xavier. With Xavier my affection had been concrete, immovable, my touchstone. Xavier had been the only real constant in my life, and now that he was gone, I felt rootless. If Bren were gone, I knew my world would not completely crumble, but there was something almost addictive in watching him. What I felt for him had similarities to what I felt for Xavier, but it wasn't an exact match, and that was confusing.

I frequently invited Bren to ride home in my limoskiff. He accepted more often than not, which I took as a good sign.

He'd tell me about upcoming tennis matches or the work-
ings of UniCorp, which he heard a lot about. He told me the
gossip about his friends—how people took it when Otto and
Nabiki had originally hooked up, how Anastasia had a huge
crush on Wilhelm, who was obsessed with a senior from his
advanced astrophysics class. It was fun talking with him.

I'd have said Bren and his friends were my saviors, but it
was fairly clear to me that apart from Otto, who didn't talk,
his friends put up with me only because Bren seemed to like
me. It wasn't that they *dis*liked me, but there was no obvious
warmth toward me, either. It wasn't surprising. Apparently the
entire group of them had been friends since middle school.
They seemed very diverse, coming from all over the planet
and the colonies, but something about their parents' standing
in UniCorp had drawn them together, almost as if they were
UniCorp nobility, with Bren as the crown prince. The only
additions had come three years ago, at the start of high school,
when Anastasia's parents had sent her over from New Russia,
on Io, and Molly and Otto had won their scholarships. For all
that Otto had called me "Princess" when he'd first spoken to
me, I did not seem to fit their idea of UniCorp royalty. Technically, I should have had higher status than Bren, but they'd
never heard of me before a few weeks ago. They didn't know
what to make of me.

Bren, on the other hand, seemed completely oblivious to his
friends' coolness. He genuinely tried to bring me into the group
discussions when we sat down together at lunch, and for that I
was very grateful.

And a little obsessed. When I wasn't suffering nightmares, I tried to fill my dreams with Bren. Xavier was too painful a memory, and nothing else was powerful enough to engage my attention. I did portrait after portrait of him, using different angles and different expressions, trying to understand what went on behind those eyes. I feared him seeing my sketch-book and knowing how often I thought about him.

Until I realized that such stealth was silly. I *wanted* him to know how I felt.

Otto?

It was less than ten seconds before my screen chimed back. We linked up almost every night at ten now. **Here! Hello again!**

Hi. Can I ask you a question?

You always ask me questions. My turn.

Damn, I wrote. Just trust me: there's nothing very interesting about me.

Humor me. You avoided my question when I asked it before. What was it like coming out of stass?

It hurt, I wrote. Really, Otto, it doesn't make much sense. Between the shock and the stass, everything was a blur for the first week. Then things just crumbled from there. I didn't know how to work the stove; all the computers were incomprehensible; I could barely understand half of what people were saying to me. I couldn't go out to buy underwear without half the reporters in the world following my every move. Before school started, I felt like a stranded jellyfish, sort of formless and electric. As if the water I was meant to swim in had been taken away. Patty and Barry might just as well not be here. Everyone I knew was dead. Couple that with stass fatigue and worldwide infamy all in one fell swoop and I'm probably about as miserable as you.

I'm not miserable. Not anymore.

Not since Nabiki? I asked, thinking of Xavier. And Bren.

Not since the scholarship.

That sounded hollow to me. I felt bereft without Xavier. All the scholarships in the world wouldn't have helped that. Nabiki has nothing to do with it?

All my friends have something to do with it. Jamal brought me into the group. He was my roommate from the beginning. Bren and Wil were his friends.

I sighed. Did they warm up to you right away?

Of course not. I take some getting used to. There was a moment before he continued writing. **It surprises me that you warmed up to me as quickly as you did.**

You're nice.

You figured that out from talking with me exactly once? Upon which I immediately rejected you?

Well . . .

I'm used to people avoiding my gaze, acting awkward, even with outright loathing. You did none of that.

I'd be pretty hypocritical if I did, I wrote back. Besides, you did freak me out at first.

You freaked me out, too, he wrote.

Pair of odd ducks.

True enough. So what was it you wanted to ask me?

Oh. It was just about Bren.

What did you want to know?

122 –

Well, how well do you know him?

Known him for nearly three years.

Can you tell if he actually likes me or if he's just being polite?

I will not tell anyone what I see in someone else's mind.

And I wouldn't ask you, I wrote, a little offended.

Oh. Sorry.

No, just from observing him. Or what he's said. Or what other people have said. I'm asking for gossip, really.

There was a long, long moment before Otto wrote, **I'm really not the one to ask.**

Well, who, then? I wrote, feeling exasperated. Apart from you and Bren, I don't talk to anyone else.

You don't?

No!

I'm sorry. Why not?

I don't know anyone.

If you'd talk to people, that would change.

I don't know how to get to know anyone. I've never done it before. I've only ever had the one friend, really. And with him it was kind of like what you can do; I could all but read his mind.

How did that happen?

I'd known him since I was seven.

Was he your boyfriend?

Yes.

You lost a boyfriend you'd known forever?

Yes.

He let that sink in before the word printed itself on the screen. **Owtch.**

I laughed in spite of myself. Yeah. Big owtch.

I'm so sorry.

I'm getting used to it.

Is he that boy you're always drawing in your sketchbook?

How do you know that?

I watch over your shoulder. I recognized all the faces except one. I take it you have a crush on Bren?

Okay, I thought you couldn't read my mind unless you were touching me.

Well, all right. I quietly borrowed your sketchbook at lunch last week when you weren't looking. That boy and Bren are all over that thing.

You little blue thief!

That's me, he wrote, without apparent chagrin. **And how did you get my screen number, may I ask?**

Touché, I wrote.

I'm sorry if it was private.

It isn't, really. Particularly not to you, who knows everyone's secrets. I can trust you not to blab anything around, right?

Doubly so.

I almost laughed at that. I just wish you could have asked.

Sorry about that. I was curious. I wanted to know what you thought you needed to understand better.

I chuckled. Everything. I'm out of my element in this time.

What are you trying to understand with the landscapes?

I thought about that for a long time. Me, I think, I wrote. Life. Stasis. Landscapes are more . . . I guess you could say they're more meditative than the portraits. Though my portraits are meditative, too, in that I'm understanding a person.

Nice sketch of me and Nabiki, by the way. I didn't think you'd have captured her so . . . sweet-looking, since she's always so cool with you.

She was looking at you.

Ah, Otto wrote. **That would do it. So, do you have a crush on Bren or not?**

I don't know what I have. Except too much free time and not enough sense.

I don't know if he likes you or not. He doesn't have a girlfriend, if that's what you're asking.

Anyone he does like?

Not that I've noticed.

Okay. Good to know.

Now I have a question, Otto wrote.

Fire away.

What do you see in him?

Apart from the obvious?

What's the obvious? I'm afraid I'm not a teenage girl.

I tried to figure out a way to say it that didn't, in fact, sound like a gushing teenage girl. He's very aesthetically pleasing.

That's it?

Well, he's nice to me. He talks to me. He's nicer than everyone else.

Even me?

Nothing personal, Otto, but you don't talk to me.

Yeah. I know.

I don't really know what it is. There's just something that draws me. I *am* fascinated by him. I keep wanting to draw him. That has to mean something, right?

Of course you want to draw him, with his athlete's muscles and the wood-tone skin and the eyes like a beam of light.

I blinked at the screen. Well, yes. Where did that come from?

Molly, about a year ago. But she got over him.

I went over Molly in my mind, assessing my competition. I wasn't worried. Since she was born on Callisto, her skeletal structure was more compact than would be considered attractive. She'd obviously spent plenty of time doing gravimetric exercises, but her parents weren't rich enough to afford the full corrective exo-surgery kit, and it still showed in her figure. Then I caught a glimpse of my own toothpick wrist and wondered what I was doing feeling confident.

Still there?

Yeah. I was just musing over my own aesthetic configuration. Or lack thereof.

I think you're very pretty.

You said I looked like a skeleton.

I said you'd look better if you filled out more. Not that you weren't pretty.

Oh. I suddenly wanted a mirror. I glanced at myself in the window instead. I was only a shadow. Thanks.

Of course, I don't think *pretty* is the best compliment I can give you.

Stop with pretty. Go any further and I won't know how to handle it.

I believe that.

Besides, there's not much else going for me.

Oh, I could try talented, accepting, enchanting, or demure, but I'll stop with pretty. Don't want to overwhelm you.

Stop it. You've got me blushing.

Burn it. I'm missing it. There was a bit of a pause. If you really want him, I think you should go for it.

You really think I've got a shot?

I don't know. All I know is that you should be happy. Can I ask another question?

I guess. I was afraid it would be more about Bren, and I was starting to feel embarrassed. I needn't have worried.

You weren't offended when I said I wouldn't touch you?

Not at all.

Why not?

I shrugged, then remembered he couldn't see it. I don't know, I wrote. It just seemed . . . I don't know. I think if I had to encapsulate what I was thinking, it was something along the lines of "of course."

Are you that used to rejection?

I don't think so, I wrote at first. Then I thought about all the schools I'd gone to, and all the maids our family went through, and all the times Daddy told me not to get in his hair. Yes, I wrote.

There was a bit of a pause before Otto wrote, Me too.

I didn't really know what to write. After a minute Otto added, I wish I could talk to you. I really wasn't trying to reject you. I'm so glad you wrote me.

I'm sorry I scared you.

I'm sorry you have to have things in your mind that do scare me. Do you have any idea what they are?

No, I wrote. Those moments of bright memory I can answer, though. Stasis holds thoughts in your head until they stay more clearly than they would have.

There were an awful lot of those, he wrote.

I swallowed. Yes. I suppose there were.

Then what are the shadowy, briary, tangled places? Because they aren't the same thing as the bright spots.

I don't know, I wrote. I wasn't sure what about my stass visits would have caused tangled bits in my mind. I don't think I have any memory gaps.

I don't think so, either. They felt more like emotion.

I frowned. Maybe I'm just messed up about losing everyone.

That might be it, he wrote, but I don't think either one of us believed it.

You lost people, too, I wrote. I wished I could whisper it; it was such a terrible thing. Do you recognize it?

I do, Otto wrote, but that's something else, too. I think it was more immediately brutal to me than it is to you. There's something of a dreamlike horror to your situation. I think there's probably a part of you that still thinks you're going to wake up and find everything back the way it was. Am I right?

How can you know me so well?

Observation, Watson! Besides, it doesn't take a genius to realize that there's something less concrete about waking up and finding everyone gone, compared to holding your best friend as her brain hemorrhages.

I blinked at that coldly written phrase. Oh, God, Otto. You were touching her?

He waited a long time before writing. I died with her. Or my mind did. God, I can't believe I'm telling you this. They had to drag me away, and I knocked four of them unconscious before they realized they couldn't touch me. They just don't think.

I'm surprised you don't hate them.

It's not their fault. They're just employees.

The way he called everyone who cared for his family "them" made me wonder. Didn't any of them love you?

You're astute, aren't you.

I miss my parents, I told him honestly, as an explanation. It was an explanation that made sense to him, apparently, because he didn't ask for clarification.

No one's ever asked me that before. We love one another. We have no biological parents. Some of our surrogates—the implantation mothers—got together after we were born and made sure we were given human rights. But only Penny's surrogate was part of that group. The other few were all carriers for the simple ones. They visit on the weekends, too, sometimes.

And Penny's surrogate?

Got married and had another child. Still sends Penny Christmas presents.

That's it?

Yup. Doesn't matter. We're glad to be designated human.

I can imagine so! But they didn't give you foster parents, or anything? Who cared for you as babies?

Registered nurses. They were tender, but it was a job. We've had tutors, supervisors. Lots of them are nice enough, but no. They're all hired by UniCorp. We don't belong to them. Or with them.

I swallowed. For a long time, I considered whether or not I was going to write it down, and then I decided, what the hell. I had nothing to lose. You could belong to me, I wrote. I had to write it quickly, or I knew I'd never get it out. I'd love you. I'm as much of an anomaly as you, and I don't seem to belong with anyone. You're the only thing that seems to really fit. We can be family.

The moment I pressed send, I wished I could erase it. There was a pause at least as long as the one I'd left before I'd written. I sat there feeling like an idiot. Even reading it over I sounded desperate and hopeless. I'd said too much. No doubt I'd scared him and he was about to run screaming.

Thank you. The words appeared on the screen. **That means a lot.**

I hoped he meant it.

There was a long pause before he wrote, **Are you going to ask Bren out?** as a way of changing the subject.

By comparison, this was actually an easy subject. I don't know yet.

Well, maybe Mina can help. She helped me sort out Nabiki and me a dozen times.

I can imagine it's hard for you to have a relationship.

Easier in some ways. Harder in others, I suspect. It's hardest on Nabiki. She gets a lot of grief over it. And her parents don't approve.

Why not?

Would you approve of your daughter dating a blue-skinned alien?

If the alien was as adorable as you, absolutely.

There was a bit of a pause before Otto wrote, **Did you know I blush purple? Jamal's teasing me about it.**

Is he reading this? I asked, horrified.

No.

Sorry I made you blush.

I'm not. Good night, Briar Rose.

Good night, blue-skinned alien.

"Okay," I told Dr. Bija. "I genuinely have something you can help me with."

"What's that?" Mina asked, her face brightening.

"How do you know if you like someone?"

The question seemed to confuse her. "Pardon me?"

"How can you tell if you like someone? I mean, dating like."

"I'm not sure what you're asking me. Generally people just know."

I frowned. That didn't help me.

"Why are you asking this? Is this about Bren?"

"You could tell?" I asked sheepishly.

Mina shrugged. "Process of elimination. You don't talk about anyone else."

"I really don't talk *to* anyone else."

"You don't?"

I shook my head. "Except Otto. But we don't really *talk*."

"No one else?"

"No."

"Why is that?"

Sometimes it was really aggravating how she just kept asking questions. "I'm a freak," I said. Wasn't it obvious? "I'm out-of-date, out of touch, out of time."

"Do you think you're making any progress assimilating?"

I sighed. I tried my hardest to talk about only the most trivial aspects of my life with her. We talked about my art a lot. And Patty and Barry, about whom I was hard-pressed to find something to say. I knew basically nothing about them. They were still complete strangers, with whom I shared the evening meal. "I don't know."

"What's going on that you had to ask?" Mina said.

"'Cause I think I like Bren. But it . . . it isn't the same." I wasn't sure what I was trying to say, but Mina was.

"Not the same as with Xavier?"

I nodded.

"How did you and Xavier meet?"

"I was seven," I said, but I didn't finish the story. It would mean explaining that I'd come out of a long stint in stasis suffering from a mild bout of stass fatigue, so I couldn't do much for a week besides sit in the garden. And Mrs. Zellwegger, the next-door neighbor, had had an infant son. He was less than a year old, just learning to crawl, and she would take him out into the garden to get some fresh air. Since my eyes hurt if I read too long, and I was only seven, I hadn't had a lot to do. So I'd taken up with little Xavy. I had had endless fun putting toys in the grass and crawling with him. We'd laugh and laugh. I'd sit him on my lap and tell him stories, and as he grew a bit, we'd draw pictures in the sandbox.

The garden was still there at the condo, but that sandbox was long gone now. Just like Xavier.

"So you'd known each other for a long time."

"Yeah," I said. "I really don't want to talk about Xavier."

"That's okay. Do you think you're going to tell Bren how you feel?"

"You think I should?" I asked.

"I can't answer that for you," Mina said. "Do *you* think you should tell him how you feel?"

I sighed. "The trouble is, I'm not sure *how* I feel."

"Well, I can tell you this. Every love, every relationship, is different. It's never going to be the same, not with anybody."

I sighed. I was more than a little disappointed by that thought. To never have a touchstone again, to always be a floating seed, rootless, was a horrifying thought.

"It might be just as good," Mina said. "But it'll always be a little different."

I took a deep breath. If that was the case, maybe this giddy, unyielding confusion and awe was a new, different type of love. Or at least the beginnings of such. And if that was the case, I really *did* want Bren to know how I was feeling.

So I'd tell him.

—chapter 11—

The next day, startled birds beat against my chest with my resolve. I wasn't really sure how to go about this kind of thing. With Xavier it had been so easy. We'd known each other for so long that our relationship was natural. Still, I had a general idea of how to manage it. I'd seen enough holomovies.

I told myself to wait until we were alone together in my limoskiff. I was terrified I might fail to catch him. If he took the Uni solarskimmer, I wasn't sure I could stand another day of anticipation. I literally ran out of my last class, catching Bren in the quad just as he was about to go up to Otto and Nabiki. "Youwannaridetoday?" I babbled.

Bren seemed taken aback at first, until he deciphered my accelerated question. "Oh. Um." He glanced at Nabiki and Otto. Nabiki rolled her eyes and walked away, but Otto just stared at us. At me, actually, as had become his custom. "Yeah, I guess."

I felt a peculiar mixture of relief and horror at his acceptance. The first hurdle was over with. I knew what I had planned to say; I had plotted it out a hundred times since the night before. But the moment I had Bren alone in the limoskiff, all my careful preparations fled into the quad, leaving me with my mouth dry and my hands sweaty.

Bren tried to tell me about his next tennis game, but I barely heard one word out of twelve. The miles fled beneath my hovering skiff, and all my precious time alone with him was left behind. The skiff turned into the condo lot. Time was up.

All that wasted time!

"I want to go out with you," I blurted.

Bren had been casually leaning back, telling me about the angle of the court and how to adapt to the nearness of the audience. He stopped midsentence and stared at me, his back rigid. "What was that?" he asked.

"I . . . I like you, and . . ." I swallowed.

His response was the worst I could have anticipated. I didn't expect him to fall at my feet with protestations of adoration. But I really didn't expect him to scramble for the door of the limoskiff, desperate to get away from me, his face twisted with a trapped panic that tore my heart. He dropped his notescreen in his confusion and picked it up awkwardly from the ground. "Sorry, Rose. No," he said once he was safely out of the skiff.

I don't know what perverse imp caused me to continue talking. But I couldn't keep my mouth shut. "I know," I said. "I didn't expect you to say yes. I mean, it's not . . . not that important. I just . . ." My cheeks were hot, and my ears were hot. I felt on fire with embarrassment, and I heard my own voice finish. "I thought you liked me."

"Coit!" Bren swore. "Look. Rose. Oh, burn it." He glanced up at the sky as if looking for strength. "I'm sorry if I gave you the wrong impression, okay? I wasn't trying to lead you on. I—I think this is probably my fault, and there's probably some kind of . . . culture . . . thing . . . going on. It's just that my granddad told me to look after you. I mean, he and Guillory are worried about the company, okay? They just told me to make sure you weren't . . . I don't know. 'Led astray' was, I think, the phrase Guillory used. Actually I think Granddad was just worried about you—he's not as mercenary-minded as Reggie. So I've been here for you, but I really didn't mean to give you the wrong idea, and I don't know how this kind of thing worked sixty years ago, and I've probably put my foot in it or something. I'm sorry. I'm so sorry."

He didn't sound sorry. He sounded panicked.

"So . . . you don't like me," I whispered.

"Not . . . like that. I mean, you're nice enough, but you give me the creeps! You're like a ghost or something!" He bit off his next words, realizing he'd already said too much. "Sorry," he added. "That's not your fault. You're really sweet, but it's just . . . I can't, okay?"

A fierce hand gripped my chest, squeezing my lungs. No, it wasn't my lungs. It was my heart. It was breaking.

Wasn't I stronger than this?

"I'm sorry," I whispered.

Bren stared at me, and the panic left his face. Behind it I

saw remorse, and . . . oh, no. I didn't want that look. That was pity. "So am I." He pulled his notescreen to his chest and stared at me awkwardly. "I'll . . . I'll still see you at lunch tomorrow. It's not like . . ." He trailed off.

"Right," I whispered.

"Okay," Bren said. "Bye."

I sat in the skiff for a long time after he had gone. My stass-fatigued eyes were often burning and blurry, so I didn't realize I was crying until I saw the raw wet patch on the skirt of my uniform. I dashed the wetness from my face and headed up the lift, hoping that neither Barry nor Patty had come home early from work. I was in luck. They were out. As usual.

Zavier met me at the door, his tail wagging, waiting to be taken out. I couldn't bring myself to walk him today, so I dragged myself out to the garden and sank to the grass.

Zavier ran around and chased butterflies. I wished I could be so carefree. The tears started falling again when I looked at my surroundings. In sixty years, many of the plants had changed, some of the paths had been altered, but many of the ornamental trees were still there, arching over the courtyard with their blossoms and their red leaves. But now they were four times as thick around, and now when I walked beneath them, I would never again find my Xavier.

It had been so perfect with Xavier. Friendship had melted into love so quickly that we could hardly tell the difference between the two.

．　．　．

Mom and Dad had let me out of stass, and we had a fabulous champagne breakfast to welcome me back. It had been late autumn when I'd gone into stass, but it was early summer now. I'd just missed the end of school, and I was glad.

After our breakfast, Mom took me down to Jacquard's to go shopping, and we had a spree. She got me a whole new wardrobe, the latest summer fashions. Indian cotton was in this year, replacing the light silks that had been popular in my last wardrobe. By the time we were done it was midafternoon, so Mom had gone home and settled in for her afternoon nap. Daddy was somewhere doing something for UniCorp, and I didn't feel like napping. I could have gone down to the pool or the tennis courts, but I didn't feel up to it. I'd been in stass long enough to feel a stiffness in my muscles, the first hints of stass fatigue. Rather than settle into my room, I dug around until I found a sketchbook and headed to the garden to draw.

I didn't recognize him. Not at first. I thought the tall, rangy youth who was walking the paths was a new tenant, so I avoided him, taking a different path. There was a pause in the crunch of the footsteps behind me, and then he began to run after me.

"Rose?"

I froze. I'd know that voice anywhere. Ever since he'd lost his lovely soprano at thirteen, Xavier's voice had been a soft leather couch, warm and brown. I turned. "Xavier? Is that really you?"

Xavier had changed. A lot. His ash–blond hair had darkened

to a brownish gold in the last nine months, and he had shot up like a weed. He towered over me now. Ten centimeters wasn't so much, but I'd always been taller than him. I'd also always been older than him. This Xavier was no longer a child. The downy fuzz he'd been cultivating when I went into stass had transformed overnight into a well-manicured goatee. When I said his name, the smile he flashed me was no longer wholly innocent. But most of all, his eyes watched me with an appetite I had never seen before.

My hands reached out to him, grabbing at the lapels of his open shirt, beneath which he wore a shirt with the UniCorp logo of a charging white unicorn. "Look at you!" I laughed, looking up and up at his new face. "You're so *tall!*"

He laughed. "You always say that."

"It's always true." I was stunned by his appearance. I reached up to touch his face and was surprised by the rough stubble left behind by a razor. "What's *happened* to you! You're . . . *different.*"

He was smiling at me, his green eyes shining in his freckled face. "Good," he said. "I like being different for you." His hand reached up and touched my hair, wrapping a lock around his finger. "You're just the same, though."

I shrugged. I didn't want to talk about me. "What'd I miss?" I asked. I patted his newly muscled chest. "I mean, apart from the obvious."

His fingers kept playing with my hair. Little trills passed down my scalp. That was . . . different. He'd played with my hair before now. Just yesterday, in fact . . . or what I thought of as yesterday. So why did this feel different? Well, he was different, I guessed, but something else had changed.

"Not a lot," Xavier said. He gazed into me, and his eyes were soft. "How long has it been?"

I couldn't keep the laughter out of my voice. "You'd know better than I would."

He smiled. He pulled me against him and squeezed me tightly. "I *missed* you!"

"Me too," I said. I'd never meant it so much. I'd missed so much of him. He squeezed me even tighter and lifted me off my feet. I gasped. He'd never been strong enough to do that before. I laughed and he looked up at me, delighted. With a mischievous grin he spun me around in a circle, and I squealed. "Stop it! Put me down, you colossus!"

He did, setting me lightly on my feet. "What do you think?" he asked. "Think I've filled out well enough?"

"I always said you'd make a handsome rogue!" I said, teasing him. But I wasn't really teasing. I was amazed. I looked him up and down, his newly developed chest, his beautiful crop of hair, the strong arms that still held my shoulders. I shook my head. "Look at you!" I whispered.

"You like me, then?"

I tried to think of exactly what to say and found myself at a loss for words. "Ahm, yeah," I said. "Ah . . ." I trailed off, finally stating my approval in an expressive whistle.

"Mmm." It was a very low sound. He closed his eyes and his breathing quickened. He looked away from me for a moment, as if wrestling with himself. Then his hands tightened on my shoulders. "Rose?" he asked, his tone deadly earnest. "We've always been friends, right?"

"Yes," I said. "I suppose we have been."

"You know . . . that won't ever change. No matter . . . what else might change."

I was afraid of this. I'd always known that one day I'd come out of stass and he would have outgrown me. A boy won't follow his big sister around forever. "Yeah, I know that." I sighed. "I just . . . brought out my sketchbook; you can go do . . . whatever. I'll see you later."

"I wasn't planning on going anywhere," he murmured.

Now I was confused. "Then what was with the . . . ?" I trailed off, distracted by his gaze. It was very, very deep. "Xavier . . ." I whispered.

"Ah," Xavier groaned, closing his eyes. "You look just the same. I meant to wait on this, at least a few days, but I don't think I can."

"Wait on what?"

He stayed silent for a moment, his brow furrowed, looking deep into whatever blackness was inside his closed lids. "Rose," he said at last. "If you don't want this, just say so. It won't make any difference."

"What?"

"Shh." He put a finger over my mouth and stared at me. His eyes burned with an amber flame deep amid the hazel green. "It's just I've been thinking about this since last autumn. Well, every impossible day for the last four years, really. And if

I don't do something about this now that I . . . *can,* I think I'm going to go crazy."

He pulled his finger away, and I opened my mouth. "About what?" I whispered, but I thought I knew.

"This," Xavier murmured, and he moved in closer to me.

Time went very slowly. I had time to think about all the repercussions if I were to let him kiss me. Nine years of friendship, changed in an instant. Sixteen years, if we went by his time. I'd helped change his diapers when I was seven. Now here we were, and he was taller than I was, handsome and charming and confident. So confident. This was not the move of a boy who had never before kissed a girl.

That thought alone was enough to drive me to him, to make me loosen my hold on my sketchbook, so that it fell abandoned into the grass. As the heat from his breath touched my lips, my hands went up to his neck, to his newly darkened hair, and I clutched him to me. Xavier was *mine*! He had always been mine! What right had some other girl to take his first kiss from me? And here I stood, giving *my* first kiss to him.

The moment our lips met, there was a riot of color that I could feel, not see. An explosion of light, with all the intensity of a stass dream, only it was real and tangible, a solid, impenetrable connection to my Xavier, my constant. My hands were wild, trying to pull different pieces of him into me, his hair, his shoulder, his neck, the back of his head. I laced my fingers into his hair. His arms were steady, firm, and as solid as stone, pulling me as close to him as it was possible to be. His teeth lightly gripped my lower lip, his tongue explored my mouth, and I was angered anew by his confidence, his evident experience.

My jealousy pulled me even closer to him, and the bright colors of my body began to go gray, along with everything else. My leg snuck around him, trying to hold him to me so he couldn't get away. And even as I kissed him, I was crying.

After a moment Xavier pulled away. I blinked at him, gasping. His face was gray and the sky was gray and the world was gray. I had no breath left.

"Easy," he whispered, his voice hoarse. He held me tightly enough that I didn't fall in a heap at his feet. Sensing my shakiness, he slowly brought us both to our knees on the bright grass. Xavier kissed the tears from my cheeks, from my eyes, then he ducked his head and whispered into my ear, "I know."

Did he know what I was feeling? Did he know why I was crying? I wasn't sure I knew myself. I was breathing hard, and as the oxygen returned to my system, so did the colors around me. We held each other. Xavier had his lips against the hair behind my ear. I buried my nose in his neck, smelling the familiar scent of him mixed with the new heady smell of man sweat, which had not been his the last time I had seen him.

As our breathing slowed, Xavier squeezed me around the shoulders. "Wow." He breathed a sigh into my ear, and I shuddered at the sensation. "I wasn't quite expecting *that*."

"Who was she?"

Xavier pulled away a little to look at me. "Who?"

How could he ask *who*? "The girl who took you from me. The girl who stole your first kiss, who taught you all that."

Xavier smiled, but it was a little trepidatious. "Does it matter?"

"Yesss!" The word came out a poisonous hiss. I hadn't realized I felt so possessive of him.

"Her name was Claire," Xavier said, "and I met her in school. But Rose, she wasn't important." He gently touched my face, leaving trails of warm color through my skin. "She was a . . . means to an end. She knew that. I surely wasn't her first. She's been through four more since. It was you. Always you." He pressed his lips to my hair with a sigh. "The only reason I even let her touch me was so that I'd know what to do when I finally saw you again." His lips traveled with painful sweetness over my forehead, along the side of my hairline, along my jaw. "Oh, I've been waiting for you," he whispered with a heavy sigh that left me no doubt as to his sincerity. "She didn't love me, and I certainly didn't love her." His nose caressed my cheek. "It was *nothing* like this."

Distracted as I was by what his lips were doing to my skin, I managed to hear him. "Are you . . . saying you love me?"

Xavier pulled away and stared at me with frank shock. "Rose!" he whispered. Then his eyes softened. "I've *always* loved you." He moved to kiss me again, and this time it was hesitant, almost teasing, or it would have been if his eyes hadn't been so desperate. When our lips met again, it wasn't frenzied or furious, and the passion was less a raging fire than a warm, diffuse, powerful glow. It felt better than the first few minutes of stasis, better than the drifting safety of the first chemical infusion. When Xavier and I kissed this second time, I knew, without a doubt, that I was home.

The nose that touched me now belonged to my dog, who had begun to get worried by the constant stream of tears falling from my eyes. He licked them from my cheeks, and I laughed hollowly. My Zavier kissing my tears away. It just wasn't the same.

I dragged myself to my feet and led Zavier inside. He expected me to begin working in my studio, as I did every afternoon, but I couldn't bear to go in there. The faces of Xavier and Bren would stare at me, grind my heart into chalk dust. I curled up on my rosebud-print bedspread instead, still in my school uniform. I didn't move even when Patty told me it was time for dinner. I still couldn't eat much, and the idea of trying to choke something down while I felt like this was abhorrent.

Sometime in the night, I dragged myself to the bathroom and drank a huge glass of water to replenish the moisture I'd lost from my tears. Five minutes later, I ran back and threw it all up into the toilet. This time when I went back to my bed, I took the glass with me and drank slowly, making sure my stomach could absorb each mouthful before I took another.

Around ten my notescreen dinged, but I didn't feel up to explaining what had happened, not even to Otto. I ignored it, and it didn't ding again.

It was a terrible night. My pills made me just drowsy enough to throw me into nightmares but not enough to keep me asleep, so I oscillated back and forth between nightmares and tears. The nightmares were particularly terrible, as they now involved being attacked by shiny, dead-eyed versions of Bren or Xavier, being beaten again and again with the stick that my attacker had been carrying during my adventures in sleepwalking.

I welcomed the alarm that signaled a reprieve from my nightmares. I fed Zavier and climbed into my limoskiff, scorning breakfast.

When I got to school, I opened the door. Only then did I realize I was still in the creased and tear-stained uniform I'd worn through the night. I winced as the cacophony of the school invaded my skiff. Kids shouted at one another across the quad, and the Uni volleyball team was singing some rhythmic sports chant that seemed to be in Arabic. Cells beeped; footsteps clattered. My head ached before I'd even set my feet on the ground. And then I saw *him*.

Bren was with his friends in the middle of the quad. I knew I looked a mess. I felt as if I'd been pulled through a hedge backward. Had I even remembered to brush my hair this morning? Bren looked his usual radiant self. He glanced in my direction, and he must have seen my limoskiff, because he quickly turned his back, laughing with Anastasia. My heart twisted.

Otto pulled a little away from the group and looked at me. His expressionless face tilted on his neck, and he regarded me silently. I would have given anything in that moment for an expressionless face like his. Mine crumpled, and the tears started welling again. Otto took a step toward me, his hand reaching out as if he could touch me across the quad. How much did he know? I couldn't bear it. I climbed back into the limoskiff. "Home!" I told it. "Home, home, home, home, home!"

The skiff obediently closed its doors and glided off.

When I got to the condo, I pushed a bag of Zavier's dog food under my bed and left it on its side, open, so he could get to it when he needed to. I knew he could get water from the toilet. I stole a brief moment of comfort by hugging him, but this was too big even for my beautiful fluffy dog. I wiped my tears off on his fur and left the condo, heading purposefully for the lift.

It moved very slowly down into the subbasement. I felt calmer just thinking about my coming oblivion.

I climbed hungrily into my stass tube and stabbed the preset button. We'd rarely had to use it before. My parents had always known when it was best to take me from stass. I set the timer for two weeks and lay back as the music began to swirl around my head.

The perfumed chemicals quickly wiped the horror and grief from my mind. I breathed them in deeply and thought of Xavier. I half hoped that when I woke up, this whole terrible incident would never have happened. It would be just a few weeks or months since my parents had closed the stass tube, and Mom would be looking down at me, offering me a champagne breakfast. Xavier would still be my next-door neighbor, and I could throw myself into his arms and apologize for every missed moment.

Anything seemed possible in those first few moments of stass.

—chapter 12—

With only three percent vision, he had made his way back to his station. His target had fled from the known location. He was not programmed to believe that the target would return there. As he was unable to locate his target, his directives were suspended. He sat himself back down, flipped into standby mode, and waited.

"The famous Rosalinda Fitzroy was reported missing this morning, sparking rumors of a possible abduction. Fitzroy's last known location was her family's condominium in the UniCorp town of ComUnity. Police are standing by."

NAME ALERT: TARGET REFERENCED. ROSALINDA SAMANTHA FITZROY.

The new location was known. It didn't occur to him that it was the same as the last known location. Patterns of behavior were not something his programming took into account.

He implemented his primary directive. RETURN TARGET TO PRINCIPAL.

He scanned through the net. Since he was running on 98.7 percent capacity, the scan took only an hour.

PRINCIPAL UNAVAILABLE.

Electrons firing, he reinstated his secondary directive.

TERMINATE TARGET.

ON STANDBY, PENDING REDUNDANT SCAN.

His status check automatically pointed out that his vision was still at only three percent. It took his nanos about four hours to remove every speck of the dried oil paint from his eyes before he rose from his station to implement his directive.

When I opened my eyes this time, the face looming over me was not in shadow. I hadn't been in long enough to suffer further stass fatigue. Brendan glared at me, eyes flashing as if there were goldfish swimming in the green pools. "You realize threatening suicide is abusive behavior, right?"

I shook my head, regretting the loss of the stass dream. This one had featured Xavier, only Xavier and Bren had somehow gotten mixed up, and I was never sure which one I was with. I told Bren that I missed him, but it was really Xavier I was missing. The boy, whoever he was, held me, and we were swimming in the brightness that pervaded my stass dreams. It bothered me in a vague way that the boy in my arms kept changing. But it had been much better than the angry face of the boy who really stood above me now. "I wasn't threatening suicide," I said. My voice was still languid from the stass chemicals.

Bren glared. "Right. What else do you call climbing back into your glass coffin?"

I blinked. I'd never thought of it like that. I looked down at my comforting stass tube. The smooth satin-of-silk that cushioned me, the gentle music that filled the final moments before the stass began, the first sweet scent of the gases that created a final dream state before deep stass took hold. A coffin?

Bren snorted at me and flung himself away. "Get back to your family. They're worried."

I knew that was a lie. Barry and Patty barely noticed me when I *was* there—how long had it taken them to notice that I wasn't? I swallowed. "How long?" I asked.

"Two days," Bren snapped. "When they told me you disappeared, I guessed you might be down here."

"No one else did?"

Bren glared at me. "No one else has any reason to think you were trying to make someone feel guilty."

I gripped the edges of the opened tube and climbed onto the floor. "I wasn't trying to make you feel guilty."

"Oh, weren't you," Bren said, incredulous. "It never once went through your self-centered little mind that you'd crawl back into stass, and *then* I'd be sorry."

That was unfair. "No," I said. "I actually kind of thought you'd be glad."

Bren raised an eyebrow. "Glad? Burn you! You think I'm a total creep, just because I won't go out with you?"

That confused me. "No."

"So why do you think I'd be glad? Just because I don't

want you doesn't mean I want you hurt or dead or . . . disappeared into coiting stass."

I shook my head. "It wasn't like that! I just didn't know what else to do."

Bren scoffed. "Yeah, given a choice between life and death, of course this was the proper option." He shook his head.

"But . . . this is what I always do."

"What do you mean 'always'?" he asked. Then he froze. "Coit. You've . . . done this before?"

"Yeah. All the time."

He stared at me in disbelief. *"Why?"* he asked, drawing out the word.

I shrugged. "Mom called it our coping mechanism. When we'd have a fight, or they were too tired, or things got really hard for me at school, or they needed to go on a trip, they'd put me in stasis."

Bren seemed to lose his footing. He sat down hard on a dusty trunk. "You mean, your parents put you in stasis all the time?"

"Yeah," I said. "How did you think I got there in the first place?"

"I . . . didn't know. You weren't put into stass for protection from the Dark Times?"

I shook my head. "They hadn't started yet when I was put in. Not really. There was some circulation of TB, but it wasn't that bad."

"Your parents really put you into stass . . . over and over again? Just because they were going on vacation or something?"

I shrugged. "Yeah. They said that no one could raise me as well as they could. It was the best thing for me, really."

Bren was staring at me in disbelief.

"What?" I asked.

"You . . . you know that's illegal?"

"What is?"

"To stass an individual for one's own convenience is considered a class-one felony. It falls under the same category as assault."

I didn't know what to say. Stass was welcoming and comforting, a calming release from the pressures of life. How could anyone compare it to assault?

"Your parents did that to you?" he asked, his voice soft. "All the time? Just stole great chunks of your childhood away?"

"No," I said defensively. "No, it wasn't like that at all. They were keeping me from having great chunks of my life wasted. The longest they ever kept me in was four years, and that was only because they had to oversee the formation of the mining colony on Titan." As I said that, I frowned, trying to remember if that were true. I wasn't sure. I often lost track of time while I was stassed. "They had a party for me when they came back," I said, trying to get back on track. "It was my seventh birthday."

Bren gave me an odd look. "Seven . . . like, you're now sixteen going on seventy-eight?"

"Oh," I said. "Yeah, I guess so."

"Rose . . ." he said. "How many years did it take for you to reach the age of sixteen?"

"Well . . . I'm not sure. I realized a few weeks ago that I'm actually a hundred, technically. The last stass was sixty-two years ago, so . . . thirty-eight years? I think." I shrugged.

Bren rose slowly to his feet and did something that really surprised me. He put his arms around my shoulders and wrapped me in a warm, strong hug. "I'm so sorry," he whispered in my ear.

Now, this just wasn't fair. It was as if he were trying to tear out my heart, just so he could grind it into the dust. His breath was heavy in my ear, and his body was as comforting against mine as sleep. I couldn't hold back a gasp of relieved shock, but I was angry. He didn't mean it. He was just torturing me. I pulled away. "What for? I'm fine." I was surprised my voice sounded as strong as it did.

He stared at me, his face as soft and open as I'd ever seen it. He shook his head slowly. "Rose, you are *not* 'fine.'"

"Yes, I am," I said, glaring at him. "Who are you to judge my coping mechanism? You go hit a tennis ball; I go into stass. No difference."

Bren stared at me in disbelief, and then he slowly closed his eyes. He shook his head a few times. "Fine," he said, opening his eyes. "Believe that if it gives you comfort." He grabbed my hand. "We gotta get you back home."

I balked. "No."

Bren turned to look at me. "No?"

"I'm not ready to go back yet."

Bren stared at me for what seemed like a full minute. "Too bad," he finally said. "You've got half the police of ComUnity on the alert. Your foster parents are in hysterics. Guillory and Granddad are so riled up that they're about to come to blows. So grow up, get a grip, and get upstairs."

I winced. "Just leave me alone," I groaned. "Tell them I'm fine. Tell them where I am. I just can't go up there yet." I pulled away from him and sat down on a crate.

"Why not?"

"It's too . . . soon," I said. "Everything's supposed to have gone away. It's supposed to have been long enough that it doesn't matter anymore." I stole a glance at him—wretched beauty—and my heart twisted. Nope, not long enough. "It hasn't been."

Bren still stared at me. He crept forward, as if I were a feral cat, and crouched at my feet so that I would meet his eyes. "Rose," he said. "I really am sorry. I shouldn't have said what I said to you. It was . . . cruel, but you took me by surprise. I misinterpreted you." He sighed. "I'm not very good at getting to know new people; our little group is pretty . . ."

"Insular," I supplied.

"Yeah. That'll do." He smiled ruefully. "And you're so quiet. That's what I meant when I said you were like a ghost; it wasn't anything to do with the stass stuff. It's hard to get to know you when you don't talk. I really didn't see it coming. Not in the least." He struggled for the right words. "You're unreadable. To me, anyway. Otto saw you that morning, when you left school. He was worried about you. I told him you just had a crush on me and were overreacting, but he thinks . . ." He hesitated.

"Otto thinks there's something wrong with you. Not with *you*, I mean, he doesn't think it's inherent or anything. But you have these *gaps* in your mind. I didn't know what he meant, but now I think . . ."

"It's not the stass," I said firmly. "You wake up one morning and find your entire world gone, everyone you've ever known and loved dead in one fell swoop, every place you've ever been to changed so radically that you don't recognize it—even the expressions on people's faces are different—and see how whole your mind is!" By the end of that little speech, tears had welled again in my weakened eyes. "Coit!" I muttered, trying to force them back. I was right. I hadn't been stassed long enough.

"That's the longest speech I've ever heard you make." He touched my face. "You can cry," Bren said quietly. "I'd cry, too."

"No, I can't. I can't let anyone see this. I'm too high-strung. I need to control myself."

"There's no one here to see you but me."

"It doesn't matter," I said. "It isn't proper. I need lots of time to wind down. That's why the stass, okay? I'm too emotional. Besides, I spent all of last night crying. I shouldn't need to cry anymore."

Bren tilted his head, amused. "Last night you were in stass," he pointed out.

"Oh," I said. Bren's mouth quirked to the side, and then he came and sat down beside me on the crate. He put one arm around me and rubbed my shoulder. It seemed entirely platonic, but actually heartfelt. I sighed. This was the first touch I'd felt since I came out of stass that hadn't felt forced. Unless you counted Zavier. My head tilted until I leaned against Bren's shoulder. "I'm sorry if I made you uncomfortable yesterday," I said.

"Three days ago," Bren reminded me.

"Right," I said. Organizing time when you'd been stassed was always a conundrum. "I've never really dated anyone. I don't know any signals."

Bren snorted lightly. "No one really does," he said. "It's always hit or miss. I thought you said you had a boyfriend."

I nodded. "Xavier," I said. "But he and I didn't need to know any signals. We knew each other so well it was like water joining water. I knew him all his life."

"You wanna tell me about him?" Bren asked gently.

I took in a deep breath. "He was the son of our next-door neighbor. I met him as a baby when I was seven. We used to play in the garden. We grew up together. He was like my little brother, and then . . . somehow he became my best friend. My only real friend. He was the only one who understood, the only one who listened. When we were both fifteen—or, I think he was sixteen by then—we . . ." The tears started again, and this time I just let them go.

Bren squeezed my shoulder and pressed his cheek to the top of my head. "I'm so sorry, Rose. It must be so hard to have had someone like that and never have had a chance to say good-bye."

But that was what made it even worse. "I said good-bye," I said, and my tears distorted my voice. "I just never had a chance to say sorry."

Bren didn't understand that, but he didn't need to. All I needed from him just then was to let me cry myself out.

I didn't get the chance. A harsh voice pierced the silent gloom of the subbasement, startling me from my grief. "You are Rosalinda Samantha Fitzroy. Please remain still for retinal identification."

—chapter 13—

I pulled away from Bren. "Did you hear that?" I whispered, praying he'd say no. I'd rather be hallucinating than have that thing really be after me.

"Yeah. Hello?" he called into the darkness. "Who's there?"

There was no immediate answer, except from me. "Coit!"

"What's wrong?"

"He's *real*!"

Bren looked confused. "What's real?"

I looked at him, panicked. "I thought he was a dream, but—"

"Voice match confirmed. Please remain still for retinal identification."

I closed my eyes and dodged out of the way, pulling Bren with me. I huddled behind the crate and looked left and right for a way out. There was nothing. Just corridor upon corridor of dusty crates and boxes. Maybe there was a weapon or something. . . .

"What's going on here?" Bren asked.

"No time!" I said. "Run! He's after me, not you!"

"Run? What are you—?"

But I was already running.

He had lost sight of his target. It had hidden behind the crate, and then run down one of the corridors of shelves. He activated the warning signal. "Remain still. My orders are to retain and return. Should return prove impossible, my orders are to terminate."

Meanwhile, he was walking up and down the corridors. He could not hear his target or the noncombatant, as his hearing mechanisms were not up to optimal performance after so much time in standby mode. He connected to the net and searched for a diagram of the subbasement.

STATISTICAL ANALYSIS, CONCEALMENT POSSIBILITIES BY SIZE. He began a strategy program, ready to systematically search each corner of the basement while blocking access to the exit.

BEGIN STRATEGY PROGRAM.

The maze of storerooms and shelves in the subbasement proved too much for my stass-fatigued body. I lost track of Bren, and I couldn't get to the hallway with the lift. Panting, my chest burning, I crouched in a corner behind a broken chair and tried to remember which direction the lift was in. A hand grabbed my shoulder. I shrieked and then bit my arm, hating myself for the noise. It was only Bren. "Why didn't you run?" I hissed. "He'll be here in a minute. Don't wait for me."

"Who will? What are you talking about?"

"Didn't your parents ever teach you how to evade a kidnapper?" I asked.

"No," Bren said. "Why would they?"

My mouth hung open at this oversight.

"Rose, will you tell me what is going on?" Bren sounded more exasperated than worried.

"This shiny, crazy plastic-looking man attacked me in my studio the other night. I thought he was a dream, but I guess he's not. He was going to put a control collar on me and return me to some principal."

"Oh." Bren stood up and looked down the corridor. "You mean him?" I looked. My attacker was advancing, slowly but steadily. He was halfway down the corridor, but he was going to get to me eventually.

"Oh, God!" I breathed. "Come on!" I tugged at his arm. "He'll get you, too!"

Bren took hold of my shirt, keeping me from running away. "It's not a he," Bren said, rather arrogantly, I thought. "It's a machine. Quit trying to run; it'll keep itself between you and the lift, and you'll get tired long before it will."

"He said he was going to terminate me!" I said. "What am I supposed to do, offer him tea and crumpets? Last time he nearly killed my dog!"

"What did Barry and Patty say last time?"

"Nothing."

"You got people trying to ex you and they said nothing?"

"I didn't tell them," I hissed.

"Why not?"

I opened my mouth, but I didn't really have a reason. I'd convinced myself it was a dream, but why didn't I say anything that first morning? "I don't know."

Bren stared at me for a moment, and then he shook his head. "Ae, Rose. Learn to *talk*!" He stood up and pointed at the man. "Abort mission!" he said in a loud voice. "Abort, abort, abort!"

"Bren!"

"Abort! Abort! Target at specified return location! Abort! Abort!"

"Voice match invalid," said the flat, mechanical German accent. "Secondary target impeding mission. Terminate secondary target."

Bren froze. "Coit," he whispered. He grabbed my shoulder. "You were right the first time. *Run!*" He pushed me away from my broken chair and down one of the corridors. He ran the other way.

Of course, the thing came after me. I ran as fast as I could, but now that the thing had me in its sights, it was going much faster. My heart pulsed with an arrhythmia as my overworked nanos protested the exertion. With a terrifying screech, a wall of shelves collapsed behind me, shedding boxes of out-of-date clothes and plastic toys before landing with a terrible crunch.

With inexorable determination, the shiny man plodded through the rubble, crushing the aluminum shelving beneath his feet. Bren was right—this thing was definitely not human.

It was just like my nightmares. I wanted to run, but my stass-fatigued body was already past capacity. My lungs were burning, my heart was racing, and my feet seemed stuck in treacle. I couldn't possibly go fast enough.

The thing jogged behind me, and I could feel him, nearer and nearer. Until something struck me in the back.

He hadn't hit me; he'd only touched me with his cylindrical baton. But even through my uniform jacket, the stick could clearly do its job.

My body stopped working. It was as if I were the machine, and I'd been turned off. I wanted to scream, but couldn't. I collapsed like a rag doll, every muscle tensed and powerless, as if I were a puppet cut from its strings. It was worse than if I'd merely been electrocuted. Shooting pain radiated out from the point where the stick had touched me. I was sure he'd shorted out my nanobots. How long could I survive with my organs functioning purely on their own?

I felt a burning touch as my attacker turned me over. I couldn't move. A strange sound was coming from my throat— the sound of the raw, agonizing pain I was suffering.

I could still move my eyes, and they focused on the control collar my attacker was pushing toward my neck. I knew that once he had that thing on me, my body would no longer be my own. There was nothing I could do now. At least he hadn't gotten Bren.

Then my eyes widened as I saw, over my attacker's shiny head, what he could not. Another one of the tall shelves began to tip. Everything was moving very slowly. I watched a box fall off the shelf, then a crate, then two boxes, and then the entire storage unit came right down on my attacker's back, and onto my legs.

My attacker seemed jolted rather than truly disabled. I whimpered as fresh pain shot up half my body. Bren stood triumphant behind the shelves, but he started when he saw me. "Rose!" He picked his way over the rubble and began pulling me out from under my attacker. "Come on," he said. "We have to get you out of here."

"I really hurt," I complained. I couldn't think clearly enough for anything more coherent.

"I know," Bren said. He slid his arm around my shoulders and hoisted me to my feet. I could barely find them to put weight on them. I actually whimpered, just like Zavier had. "You've been hit with a stumble stick." He reached through the rubble and plucked the stick from the unresisting hand of the shiny man. "We have to cell the police. You have yours with you?"

"I think it's by my bed," I muttered. I hadn't really been together when I went down into stass.

"Let's get you upstairs and away from this thing before it resets."

"Thing? Resets?"

"Yeah, thing," Bren said. He dragged me through the storeroom to the door of the subbasement. He pushed me through and then pulled an old-fashioned biometric key card from his pocket. A wave of nostalgia hit. I hadn't seen one of those since before coming out of stass. He passed it through a slot beside the door. "Override, Sabah," he said. "Lock."

A small whine came from the slot, and a click sounded from the door.

"There," Bren said. He took me around my shoulders again and pressed the button for the lift.

"What did you do?"

"I have a master key card," he said. "Only my parents and I can open that door now." The lift doors opened and he pulled me inside. I panted as the lift slowly climbed. Every part of my body hurt. As the lift stopped, my legs buckled, and I fell to the floor. "Burn it. Hold this." Bren pushed the stumble stick into my hands and scooped me up like a child.

"Don't," I said, as it became clear that he meant to carry me to my door. "I'm too heavy."

"How do you think I got you out of the basement the first time?" he asked, wrapping one arm around my shoulders and the other under my legs. "You're only barely heavier now."

I blinked as Bren picked me up like a new bride. "You *carried* me?"

"I couldn't just leave you there," Bren said brusquely.

The idea of him carrying my unconscious body up out of the cellar was both embarrassing and compelling. A real Prince Charming. Apparently tennis built some strength, or at least encouraged stubbornness. I closed my eyes as he cradled me, telling myself that even this, right now, meant nothing. My body wasn't listening. I laid my head against his shirt, breathing in the smell of his sandalwood soap and of him. He smelled like heat itself. His arms felt so strong around me, damn him. He kicked on my door. No one answered. I heard raised voices coming from inside. Were Barry and Patty having a fight? "Open the burned door!" Bren shouted.

To my surprise it was Mrs. Sabah who opened my door, and her almond eyes opened wide at seeing me in her son's arms. "Good God, get her inside!" she cried.

"She's fine," Bren said, though the strain of carrying me was beginning to show in his voice. He pushed past his mother and into the living room.

Mr. Guillory was shouting at an older, white-haired man I assumed was Bren's grandfather. I hadn't seen the old man since the day I came out of stass, when he was just a white blur. The argument continued as Bren lugged me into the room.

"No, I do think the feds could do the job; I just don't think we need any more forces than the ComUnity police!" Guillory said, his voice sounding very loud in the subdued apartment.

"What if she's no longer *in* ComUnity. Did that ever occur to you? We'd never find her! Ach, why am I arguing this with you? You'd just as soon we'd never found her in the first place!"

"I wish none of this had happened, true!" Guillory shouted. "It's a logistical and public relations nightmare! It's not going to get easier, you know. You think you'll be able to keep all your little pet projects once she gets her hands on the board?"

"Hey!" Bren snapped, drawing their attention. "Get out of the way."

The two men started, identical looks of surprise on their faces. Then they hurriedly stepped away from each other, clearing a path to the couch. Bren pushed between them and tenderly laid me down. "Ro—Is she okay?" asked Bren's grandfather.

"Cell the cops," Bren said, ignoring the question. "She just got hit with a stumble stick."

"Those are illegal," said Guillory.

Bren pulled the stick from my hands and passed it to his grandfather. "Tell that to the Plastine downstairs."

"A Plastine?"

"Yeah, someone's trying to assassinate her."

"Where was she?" asked Bren's grandfather.

Bren hesitated, then said, "Down in the subbasement. She was, ah, opening boxes. Trying to see if anything of her parents' was left in storage."

I briefly wondered why he didn't just tell the truth, but I was too sore to say anything.

Bren's grandfather stared at the stumble stick with his eyes narrowed. He glanced at me, then backed away toward the door. "I'll cell the police, and an EMT," he said. "Where's the Plastine?"

"Resetting itself in the subbasement," Bren said. "I aborted its plan. It'll take it a minute to formulate a new one." As his grandfather turned his back to leave, Bren called after, "Take Mom, you'll need her key card to open the door!"

Things were swimmy and incoherent for a while after that. There were a lot of people coming and going. Someone sat me up and checked my vitals, then reassured interested onlookers that the stumble stick hadn't done any of the tricks to my system that they are wont to do. My nanobots did need to be reactivated, but one of the EMTs had a remote that could manage it. My heart felt better after that. Someone tried to question me, but the same EMT had given me an injection of something that was supposed to ease the muscle tension. Unfortunately, it seemed to work in conjunction with the rest of the stass chemicals in my system, and I was basically down for the count. Through my stupor, I could hear Bren's confident voice telling everyone about what had happened to me.

One moment stood out, when the sound of shouts half roused me. "What do you mean there's nothing there!" That was Bren's grandfather, and an angrier, more terrifying voice I had never heard. "You get down to that subbasement and you *find* that blasted thing!"

Keeping my eyes closed, I cringed away from the shouts.

"Dad, hush!" Mrs. Sabah said. "You're waking her up."

A soft hand touched my hair, so gently that I felt my heart ache when it left me. If I'd been more awake, I'd have sighed. I wished *my* mom was still around to caress my hair, to care whether or not I was unhappy.

"I'm sorry," the old man said. He took whatever he was shouting at, his cell or the police, out of the room, and the irate conversation faded to a distant murmur. I lost track of time again.

—chapter 14—

When I woke up properly, my foster parents, Mrs. Sabah, Mr. Guillory, and one of the police officers were sitting around the room talking quietly. "I understand," Patty was saying. "But how long are we talking, here? We gave up a lot to be here for her, and now you're going to take her and leave us?"

"Don't sound so concerned," Mrs. Sabah snapped with palpable sarcasm.

Before Patty and Barry could defend themselves, Mr. Guillory reassured them. "We'd still need you to maintain this apartment until we bring her back, and isn't there a dog? Wouldn't want that to starve."

Barry groaned. "Why a dog?" he demanded of Guillory. "Why on earth did you send her a dog?"

"You don't like it?" Mr. Guillory said absently. "Doesn't matter. Don't worry, officer. I can keep her perfectly safe."

"If you can give us some assurances of that, Mr. Guillory," said the policeman.

The unfamiliar voice made me open my eyes. The cop was standing by the fireplace, notescreen in hand, while everyone else sat quietly on various chairs. Bren had squeezed in at the end of the green couch, and my feet had ended up on his lap somehow. I blinked at them a few times. Someone had taken off my shoes, and my socks were filthy. I hated to think what the rest of me looked like, after rolling around on the subbasement floor. Bren looked as fresh and pressed as a Uni Prep brochure. There was something too intimate about having my feet on his lap. I experimented with sitting up. It didn't hurt too badly.

"It lives," said Bren with half a smile. "Drugs out of your system yet?"

I groaned. "Unfortunately."

Mrs. Sabah laughed. "How are you, dear?"

Bren smirked at her. "That's a silly question. How does she look?"

Mrs. Sabah twitched her eyebrows in acknowledgment, but it was Mr. Guillory who spoke. "Do you have any idea who did this to you?"

"If you don't mind, Mr. Guillory," said the policeman. "I think I'd better be the one to ask the questions."

"I think Rose would probably like to use the restroom first—wash her face," Bren said. Without waiting for my agreement, he seized my hand and pulled me to my feet. I was shaky and sore, but he was right. I definitely wanted to freshen up before I had to undergo an interrogation.

"All right, make it quick," said the cop.

Bren led me out to the hall, where another cop was talking on her cell. Bren took one look at her, then came right inside the bathroom with me.

The bathrooms in the condo were spacious, but there still didn't seem to be enough room inside. He was too close. I could feel his heat not an inch from my skin, that wretched seductive scent of him. Between the stass and the drugs, my emotions weren't working at their most optimal. I wanted to throw my arms around him, and I wanted to hate him. Mostly I just wished he would go away, so I'd stop feeling like this. "What are you doing?" I asked as he closed the door.

"Don't tell them you stassed yourself," he said.

I didn't know what I was expecting him to say, but that wasn't it. "Why not?"

"Because they'll label you class-A maladjusted, and you'll have half a dozen doctors shrinking your head," Bren said. "That might not be a bad idea, except then Guillory would use every dirty trick in the book to see you declared unfit to manage your parents' assets, and he'd be in control for life. You'd have everything you needed, and you'd technically own the company, but Guillory would own *you*."

I swallowed. "Oh," I said. "Thanks. But what'll we say about where I've been the last two days?"

"Patty and Barry didn't even notice you were missing until this morning," Bren said. "*I* noticed before they did. And just because you skipped school for two days running doesn't mean you went anywhere. Just say you were feeling nostalgic and skipped school to look through those old crates."

"What was I looking for?"

"Doesn't matter. Say that—say it didn't matter, just anything."

I nodded. "Okay." I glanced at myself in the mirror. I was filthy from head to toe. There were deep hollows under my eyes, and there was a crease on my cheek from the couch cushion. I looked like one of the beggars who used to mob me when I went into the cities. And Bren had to see me like *this*? "I really would like to use the bathroom now."

He took the hint. "Sure. I'll meet you back in the living room." He slipped awkwardly out the door.

Five minutes later, I came back looking a little less like a street urchin. I considered changing out of my creased uniform but decided that in the end it didn't matter. Someone seemed to be keeping the reporters outside. When I peeked out the window, I saw the white head of Bren's grandfather, placating them by the front entrance.

The first thing the police made me do when I got back was tell them everything I remembered about the first attack. Patty and Barry demanded to know why I didn't tell them before. "I don't know," I said. "Partly, I wasn't sure it had happened at all. I've been having nightmares, and they all seem pretty awful. By the time I got home, the maid had been and gone, and I wasn't sure I hadn't just dreamed the whole thing up."

This was the truth, but it wasn't the whole truth. The truth was that I hadn't felt it within my rights to bother Patty and Barry with my problems.

I followed Bren's advice and told them that I was just poking through crates in the basement. I hadn't run away. I hadn't meant to frighten anyone. I had no idea that anyone would notice me gone and cell the police. Everyone reassured me that I hadn't done anything wrong. I wondered what they would have said if I'd admitted I'd gone to stass myself. Bren seemed to think their reactions would be pretty bad.

"Well," said Guillory. "You shouldn't go poking around alone for a while. Not with a Plastine on the hunt for you."

"What exactly *is* a Plastine?" I asked.

Three answers hit me at once. "A robot," Guillory said.

"A weapon," said the policeman.

"A corpse," Bren said.

I shuddered. "What?"

"A Plastine is a human cadaver that has been plasticized, which makes it virtually indestructible," Guillory told me. "They were in the experimental stage around the time you were put into stass. They have all the functions and abilities of a human warrior, but they're about twenty times stronger and entirely insensitive to pain. Amazing constructs. No emotion, of course, but they were able to integrate programming through existing neural pathways, which makes them almost as intelligent as a human. And humans are smarter than you'd think, if you consider all the calculations of trajectory and wind variance and a thousand other things it takes to, say, catch a baseball.

Plastines aren't as quick to adapt as a human, though, as Bren proved this afternoon."

"They're deadly," Bren said. "They'll follow any order given to them, from taking out the garbage to committing genocide. The robots we make have an inability to harm humans hard-wired into their programming. Plastines have no such program. With human neural processors, there's no way of even implementing such a thing. In that way, they're all too human. They were developed as soldiers and assassins. They've been banned by international agreement for the last thirty years, though they're still in use in some of the outer colonies, where it's hard to find living humans for out-dome tasks. Bloody risky if you ask me. Not to mention a morbid exploitation of human remains."

"You're just like Ronny," Guillory said to Bren. "I don't see you complaining about organ donations. You and your grandfather don't see the potential for humankind if the ban were lifted."

"I see the potential for abuse in the whole system! Let's murder people so we can ex more people." Bren turned to me. "Plastines were mostly made out of executed prisoners who sold their bodies to get money for their families. They had to start healthy, you see, so they had to be *killed*—they couldn't die naturally. China was one of the worst; the body probably came from there. The largest Plastine laboratory was in Germany, though. Ask Wil. His granddad used to run the place. It was a slaughterhouse. Literally."

"But they volunteered—" Guillory began.

"Perforce!" Bren shouted back.

"Neither here nor there," said Mrs. Sabah, interrupting an obviously old and multibranched argument. "The ban *hasn't* been lifted, which means that whoever sent that thing is breaking international law."

The policeman cleared his throat. "Kidnap and assassination, no matter what tool you use, is a breach of international law."

I was shaking. That Plastine had scared me when I didn't know what it was. Now that I did, it was ten times worse. "Can it be stopped?" My voice came out in a panicked whimper.

"They're difficult to stop," the policeman said, with no attempt at reassurance. "It would take a tank, a flamethrower, and probably twenty men. Besides, there might be more of them ready to replace this one. It would be better to find who sent it and force them to rescind the order."

"Well, who's after me? Do we know that?"

"Unfortunately, no," said Guillory. "You're a public figure, and not everything UniCorp has done has been considered for the greater good. We all have our enemies. If someone fixated on something your parents did in the early days of the company, they might have decided to take their revenge out on you. It also might just be some nut who fears or envies your newfound fame. There's no way of knowing."

"Couldn't you ask it or something? Wouldn't there be some way of reading its orders?"

There was an uncomfortable silence. "We could," Guillory said, "but unfortunately the Plastine is nowhere to be found."

An icy grip of horror assaulted me. "It's gone?"

"I'm afraid so," said a new voice, and Bren's father poked his head around the door. I hadn't seen Mr. Sabah since my stint in the hospital, when he'd visited once or twice with Bren. I found him interesting; his facial expressions and movement patterns seemed African, and there was still the slightest hint of an accent to his deep voice as well. "We've been over that subbasement a dozen times with every sonar tool and olfactory sensor the police could find. Sorry, honey," he said, looking at me. "The thing has disappeared like a ghost."

Mr. Sabah looked so much like Bren, it was distracting. I wanted to smile at him, but I was too worried. "How is that possible? The door was locked."

"Yes, it was," Mrs. Sabah said. "No one can understand it."

"Since we could not apprehend the Plastine," the policeman said, "and you tell us it has attacked before in this very apartment, we're going to have to take you someplace safe for a few days."

"Reggie's got a lot of options," said Mr. Sabah, sliding into the love seat beside his wife. "Sky's the limit for him, isn't that right, Reg?"

"Absolutely," said Mr. Guillory.

"For tonight, how about you stay with Roseanna and me? You'll have to share a room with Hilary, but if you don't mind . . ."

"I'd love it!" I said too quickly. Then I looked over at Bren, and I half wished I hadn't agreed. But what were the alternatives? And I *liked* Mr. and Mrs. Sabah, and despite everything, I still liked Bren.

Half looking for a reason to back out, I said, "But . . . what about Patty and Barry? If that thing comes looking for me and finds them . . ."

"Plastines don't think that fluidly," said Mr. Guillory. "If its orders are for you, it will look for nothing but you. Patty and Barry could walk right past and hit it with a baseball bat and it wouldn't bother hurting them. As long as they didn't impede its progress toward you, it would just let them go."

"Okay," I said. I didn't want to spend the night alone. "Can I bring Zavier?"

"Just for tonight," said Guillory. "We can't bring a dog where I'm planning on taking you."

"Is that all right?" I asked Bren's parents.

They nodded. I went into my room to collect an overnight bag. I grabbed enough clothes for a long weekend and then slipped into my studio for a fresh sketchbook. I looked longingly at my oil paints. I hoped they'd find this robot corpse soon, so that I could have my studio back.

Mrs. Sabah was waiting in the hall with Zavier on a leash. "You ready to go?"

"Yeah," I said. "I can't thank you enough, Mrs. Sabah."

"Please call me Annie." She took the bag from my hand despite my protests. "You're still suffering from the stumble stick," she said. "I'll bet every muscle is screaming. The first thing I'm going to do is put you in a nice hot bath, with sea salt and bubbles."

"You don't have to do that."

"Why shouldn't I?" she asked.

"Thank you so much for inviting me, Mrs. Sabah . . . Annie."

She laughed. "Actually, it was Bren who suggested it to Mamadou. You should thank him."

I wasn't sure how I felt about that.

Bren's apartment was a mirror image of mine. But while mine was quiet, and still echoed from a sense of emptiness, Bren's suite was constantly filled with noise and movement and usually trouble. Bren was the oldest of three.

Hilary was golden brown and kept her hair in tightly managed cornrows. She had just turned fourteen and was going to start at Uni Prep next fall. Kayin was ten, black as ebony, jumpy as a cricket, and going through a horse phase. I'd apparently met them both in the hospital after I'd first gotten out of stass, but I didn't remember them at all. Half the country, it seemed, had passed through my hospital room in those days. Remembering everyone was impossible.

While Zavier was commandeered into the garden by Kayin, Mrs. Sabah followed through on her threat to stick me in a bathtub. But not just any bathtub. All the tubs at Unicorn Estates were huge sunken whirlpools, but Mrs. Sabah poured in enough bath salts and perfumed oils and designer bubbles that sinking into the water was almost like going into stass. I nearly found myself falling asleep, but Hilary came in with a plate full of delicacies, and I realized I was ravenous. I hadn't eaten since lunch on the day of my doomed attempt at romance with Bren, and then I'd been too nervous to do more than nibble. That would have made it more than twenty-four hours, even if the time in stass didn't count. Which to an extent, it did, because after you digested what you had in your system, stass just kept you from needing any more. I made sure to eat slowly so that the nausea wouldn't hit.

When I crawled out of the bath, I looked at myself in the mirror. I usually didn't spend much time looking at myself. Before that final stass, Mom used to spend much of her time dressing me up, sometimes several times a day, so I never had to worry about what I looked like. And lately, I'd been so blitzed from stass fatigue and culture shock, I hadn't developed a habit of looking in a mirror. I saw myself enough to brush my teeth and hair, and that was about it. Standing alone in my silken pajamas, I really looked at myself now.

No wonder Brendan thought me a ghost. I was all but emaciated. Nearly two months out of stass hadn't been enough to fill out my muscles. My cheeks were hollow. Shampoo and vitamins had almost restored my hair to the lustrous blond mane I remembered, but my skin still looked very pale. My eyes frightened me. The calm brown pools I remembered from my childhood were now shadowy places hiding devils. I gulped, then scrabbled in my bag. I pulled out a charcoal pencil and set about sketching this horrific face that stared back at me. I always understood things better when I sketched them.

This was my first self-portrait since Bren had rescued me. I didn't like what I saw on the page. Otto was right. There were gaps behind my eyes.

—chapter 15—

Dinner was quiet and friendly. There was a rule that everyone had to say something about their day. Mr. Sabah complained good-naturedly about having to create a new lock for the subbasement door. Hilary had reached a new level on some hologame. Kayin had started reading *Misty of Chincoteague* for the third time. Bren grinned, saying he'd battled against a merciless, unconquerable foe, bent on my destruction. Kayin laughed until Hilary said, "No, Kayin, he's telling the truth."

Then it was my turn. "Who, me?" I asked.

"You're at the table. Those're the rules," said Kayin.

I didn't know what to say. Today I was struck by a stumble stick. Today I broke down and told someone about Xavier. Today I'm still suffering from residual affection for a boy who doesn't want me. "Today I drew a self-portrait," I said finally.

Bren looked at me thoughtfully.

Mrs. Sabah spoke up. "Today, I prevented your grandfather from giving himself an aneurysm yelling at police officers. Who's up for dessert?"

After dinner we watched an old movie on the holoview. Old for them; I'd never seen the thing. There were sixty years of holovisions I'd never even heard of. I actually thought that might be the first entirely good news I'd had about my sixty-year jump.

Bren showed me and Zavier to Hilary's room once the movie was over. I felt awkward, but my parents had taught me to be a gracious guest. "I've had a really great time tonight. Thanks."

"Good," said Bren.

I wanted to get something out of the way. "Your mom says it was your idea to invite me," I said. "You didn't have to do that."

"Yes, I did." Bren looked uncomfortable, but he squared his shoulders. "You know, the reason I was so mad at you this afternoon, when I thought you were trying to make me feel guilty, was because it had worked. I was unconscionably rude to you, and what I said wasn't even true. Well, no, it was true that Granddad asked me to keep an eye on you, but as soon as he said it, I realized he was right. I mean, you don't know anyone. I probably would have tried to be nice to you anyway. Besides, Otto wanted to meet you."

"He did? From the beginning?"

"Yeah. Why do you think he wouldn't look at you at first?"

"I thought he was shy."

"No, he's just noticed that he makes people uncomfortable, so he wanted to be sure you were firmly seated before he surprised you. He's actually quite bold. Tends to delight in freaking people out. Doesn't have a lot of friends, but, no, he's not shy in the least."

"Oh." Otto didn't have a lot of friends? If that was the case, I was rather flattered that he wanted to spend time writing to me. "Um . . . can I borrow your notescreen? I should probably tell him I'm okay. I'll bet he's worried."

"Yeah, he probably is. Hil's got a wallscreen; you can reach him through that. Otto's number is on our household linkup."

"Thanks," I said, really grateful.

"Good night. If Hilary gives you any grief, tell her I'll tell Mom and Dad about the website I found on her screen." He grinned evilly.

I laughed.

Hilary put me up on a daybed that otherwise held a vast collection of well-worn stuffed animals, too beloved to consign yet to a trunk in the subbasement. She didn't complain about Zavier curled up at the foot of her bed. She was friendly and helpful, giving me a few pointers on the makeup that had resurged to popularity in my absence. When I was first in high school, makeup was considered out-of-date. I tried out the new tone scanner, which presented me with a list of the perfect cosmetics for my skin tone. The list was half a meter long.

"You know something?" I said suddenly. I set the tone scanner down on Hilary's vanity with a click. "I don't think I care what the fashions are anymore."

Hilary looked at me with frank confusion.

"I spent every waking hour of my old life listening to what

people told me I should be wearing, thinking, and doing. And it always changed within a year, or less." Always less for me, as I never spent an entire year unstassed. I was always having to start over again. I shook my head as the sheer futility of it all overwhelmed me. "What a waste of time!"

Hilary looked at her honey-brown face, altered with makeup, in the mirror. Her dark eyes darkened further. Only Bren had picked up his mother's green eyes. "Maybe you're right," she said. She frowned, but it was thoughtful.

I asked if I could use her wallscreen, and she pulled a chair up for me. "All yours," she said.

I hooked through to Otto's screen number and dropped him a line. Hello?

It took a long time before a message came back to me. I glanced at the time—after eleven. Oops. I debated giving up, but I thought Otto should know I was okay.

Do I know you? was the message when it finally came.

Sorry, it's Rose, I wrote. I'm using Bren's sister's screen. Sorry I'm an hour late. Is Jamal going to bug you?

Rose! You okay?

I'm fine, I guess.

You were in stasis, weren't you.

I licked my lips. Did Bren tell you?

I guessed when you disappeared. You do use it like a drug.

Does that make me weird?

You'd be weird anyway. Just like me.

Well, do you think it means I'm messed up. Or crazy?

There was a bit of a pause before Otto wrote, **I think you're** facing problems no one else understands. But no. As scary as your mind is, I'm pretty sure you're not crazy. You are a little messed up, but I imagine your life would mess up anyone. I'm sorry about Bren.

Sigh, I wrote. C'est la vie.

Laugh, he wrote back. **Que será, será.**

Look, I wrote. It might be hard to contact you for a few days. I'm not sure where I'm going.

You're going somewhere?

I have to. Apparently, someone's trying to kill me.

There was a bit of hesitation. **All right, I'm hoping that's some kind of analogy.**

It's not an analogy. It would seem I've got this Plastine after me.

A PLASTINE?

Yes. And I am under the impression that that's bad.

You're burning right it's bad! Have you heard some of the horror stories that have come out of Wilhelm's mouth? No, better that you haven't. For once I'm glad you don't talk to anyone; that kind of thought is the last thing you need right now.

You aren't helping.

I just found out someone I care about is under the gun of an undead killing machine! I thought I was used to my friends being under death sentences. Guess I'm not; I'm feeling actively sick.

I'm sorry. God, I can't do anything right.

Will you worry about yourself for once?

I'm not sure I know how, I wrote truthfully. I'm not worth much.

Say that one more time and I'll show you you are, gaps or no. Are you all right? Did it hurt you? Or did you only hear about it?

No, I definitely saw the thing. It hit me with a stumble stick.

I was about to write more, but Otto jumped in with, **Did they reactivate your nanos? Someone has to.**

They did.

Good. Coit, those sticks HURT!

How do you know?

You don't want to know. Part of it's that ethics thing again.

Oh, right.

Not that I can pretend I'm such a saint any longer. Are you safe?

Yeah, I'm safe right now. I'm at Bren's, remember?

Oh, *that's* got to be interesting. Did he change his mind?

No.

Otto didn't write anything, so I added, And I don't want him to. There was a bit more hesitation. **Yes, you do.**

I don't.

He's the only thing you've expressed a wish for since I've known you. It didn't go away that fast.

No, it didn't, I wrote. But I'm pretending.

That's good.

What did you just mean by you can't pretend you're such a saint? Did something happen?

No. But something should have. There was a long pause before he wrote, **You nearly broke my code of ethics three days ago.**

What? How?

I was hoping you were still too nervous to ask Bren out. When I tried to reach you that evening, I was hoping you'd still be debating or building courage. And I could have told you not to. When you didn't answer, I knew I was too late. Saved me my most deep-seated sense

of ethics, and I felt awful that I'd upheld them. I wished I'd just grabbed you and told you in the quad.

Told me?

That Bren wouldn't say yes. I broke my ethics twice, once by probing his mind to see if there were any latent thoughts that might lead to a yes, and again by wanting to tell you that there weren't. You're a corrupting influence.

I wouldn't have asked you to do that.

I know. But it would have saved you heartache.

Maybe not. I would have felt just as rejected had the rejection come from you.

Yeah. But I would have been gentler about it. Sped.

Why do you say that?

I basically saw the whole thing through his mind. He got angry at me when I exuded disapproval. I think we might be at odds.

Oh, God. I'm ruining your friendship. Don't worry about it; it wasn't his fault. I deserved it.

You probably think you deserve this assassin, too. You really hate yourself, don't you.

I didn't know what to write. Otto was very good at cutting to the core of things. Don't blame Bren, I wrote, mostly to change the subject. He didn't understand. And apparently, he feels guilty.

He should! Coit, I have to go. A night monitor saw I've got my screen open.

I'll try to reach you when I can, I wrote, but he didn't respond. I guessed the monitor had cut him off.

I turned off Hilary's wallscreen.

"What were you writing?" Hilary asked me.

"Just writing to a friend from school."

"That screen has a cell feed."

"He doesn't talk on cells," I said.

"Oh." Realization struck. "Oh, you were talking to Otto."

"Yes."

She frowned. "Is he nice? I know he's Bren's friend, but he kind of gives me the willies."

I stared at her, and my face burned. By contrast, my voice was ice. "Otto is the nicest person I've met since I came out of stass."

"Oh. Sorry."

I swallowed it back. Otto *was* odd, and she hadn't meant anything by it, really; she was only asking. "It's okay."

We turned out the light to sleep. After a few moments, I heard Hilary's voice through the darkness. "What's high school like?"

I frowned into the dark. "I'm really not the one to ask."

"But you're in high school."

"I never really stayed in any one school long enough to know what it was like," I said. "I only ever knew what it was to be the new girl in class. And that wasn't any fun."

"Oh," said Hilary. "I didn't know that."

"No," I said. "You'll probably like it. All you need to do is have a few friends."

"I hope I will," she said.

I considered this. "Do you have any now?"

"Yeah, but not all of them are going to Uni next year."

"That's okay," I said. "If you can make friends now, you'll be able to make friends later."

"Did you make friends?" she asked.

"Like I said. I'm not really the one to ask."

—chapter 16—

I didn't sleep well. In my dream, the Plastine chased me and Bren down the corridors of the subbasement. Bren ran on ahead of me. I couldn't catch him. I ran and ran and ran, but his dark form kept getting farther away from me. And then when he turned the corner, he looked at me, and he was Xavier. "Come on, catch up!" he shouted, but I couldn't. The Plastine's robotic footsteps plodded inexorably after me, and I woke up nearly shouting for Xavier to wait for me.

I opened my eyes to strange surroundings, and I panicked until I felt Zavier's comforting weight at my feet and remembered I was in Hilary's room. I slept only fitfully after that, waking myself at the first hint of a dream. I hadn't brought my sleeping pills, but I don't know if I would have used them anyway, considering the Plastine wasn't a madly intense nightmare after all. Otto's comments on using drugs had gotten under my skin.

Hilary's alarm clock freed me from bed early the next morning. I wasn't expecting Guillory until ten, but I got up for breakfast with the family. Bren used his tennis racquet to serve me an amaranth honey bar the moment I poked my head into the kitchen. "Catch!" he called out, lobbing it with expert accuracy into my hand.

I was startled, but managed to catch it before it hit the ground.

"Woo!" said Hilary, pouring two glasses of juice. "I still can't catch anything he serves at me."

"Painting gives you precision hands," I said. "And I think the physical therapy is starting to pay off."

Bren kept using his racquet to toss little bits of his own amaranth bar into the air and catch them in his mouth. "Oh, quit showing off!" said Kayin, trudging into the room. She grabbed one of Hilary's glasses of juice and disappeared again.

"Hey!" Hilary called after her sister. Kayin made no reaction. Hilary shrugged. "Well, that one was supposed to be for you," she said, pushing her remaining glass at me. She pulled another from a cupboard and filled it for herself.

Mr. Sabah sat sipping coffee as he perused a news scanner. It was kind of like my notescreen, only noninteractive, preprogrammed to make news searches easier. "Kayin, ask first!" he called out the open kitchen door.

"Sorry," came a muffled, disingenuous reply from the other room.

The more time I spent with Bren's family, the more I liked them. Unlike Patty and Barry, the family seemed genuinely interested in one another's welfare, interests, accomplishments. But unlike my parents, no one was hovering, telling everyone everything they had to do, what to wear, how to eat, what to think. It was . . . comfortable.

Bren touched my shoulder as he left for tennis practice. "Hey, hang in there. See you when we sort this out."

"See you," I said, a little forlornly.

"Cell me if you need to talk," Bren said.

The condo seemed very quiet once all the kids had gone. I wandered into the living room. My little travel bag was already packed and waiting. I considered pulling out my sketchbook, but I just didn't feel like it. Instead I went to the shelf above the holoview and pulled down the book I had seen there the night before.

It was a photo album. I curled up on the couch, and Zavier climbed up beside me, laying his head on my ankle. A quick glance at the album and I realized it was a selection of "best pictures," carefully selected and organized by date. I wished I was completely over Bren, but I wasn't. I started at the back, the most recent photos of Bren with his family.

I smiled. There was Kayin on what must have been her last birthday, opening a present of a huge ceramic horse, half as tall as she was. Bren was helping her rip the paper.

There he was again, holding a tennis trophy. His arms were still pumped from the match, making the sleeves of his shirt bulge. His hair was a little sweaty.

I don't know how many photos I got through before I

noticed Mrs. Sabah watching me. "Oh, sorry," I said. "I was just . . . looking . . ." I really didn't have any excuse to be thumbing through her things.

"There's a great picture of him on our last skiing trip, in the hot tub in the snow," she said, sitting down beside me. She flipped the page over. Sure enough, there he was, athletic chest revealed, surrounded in steam, just as stunning as I'd imagined it in my studio.

I was a little embarrassed. "Am I that obvious?"

"No. All the girls he brings home want to see that one," she said seriously. She looked back to the photo album and absently turned over another leaf. "He'd have quite a collection of groupies from his matches, if he wanted them. But he doesn't seem to think about girls much. He's always on about his tennis. Says he'd like to be a professional. His dad doesn't approve." She touched a photo of her husband, ski poles in hand. "Wants him to join UniCorp once he gets out of college."

"Do you think he will?" I asked.

She shrugged. "I don't know." She turned another leaf and there was a family portrait, Mr. and Mrs. Sabah, Bren, Hilary, and Kayin in the front, and Mrs. Sabah's parents at the back, her white-haired father and a friendly-looking—the best word I could think to describe her was *cute*—older Asian woman with a warm smile. Beside her was a man I assumed was Roseanna's brother, with the same green eyes, and two kids—Bren's cousins, I guessed—though their mother didn't seem to be in the picture. "My brother and I were both UniCorp brats. We had good entry-level positions in UniCorp through Dad, though he never really cared what we did. We just took the path of least resistance, which in this town almost always leads to UniCorp."

She touched the picture of the green-eyed man. "Ted always regretted it," she said. "After his wife left him, he took the kids on a colony tour to Europa. They won't be coming back for another four years, if at all." She sighed. "I always wonder if it's a good thing, to have something so huge and pervasive dictating our lives. I'm not sure it wouldn't smother Bren."

"But your husband thinks it'll be good for him?"

"Yes. But Mamadou fought to make his way into UniCorp's good graces. He's dedicated and works very hard for the good of all, the general welfare as well as the company. Still, it's a losing battle. He was never a part of what Dad laughingly calls the Royal Families."

"Royal Families?"

"His, Guillory's, and the Nikios. And of course you, now."

"Nikios?"

"They're in charge of most off-planet accounts—you haven't met them. But all three of these families have been involved almost from the beginning. The children of people hired by your parents. Once UniCorp has hold of you, it doesn't seem to let you go. It grabs you by the bloodline." She touched her brother's face.

I stared at the man. He had a kind face, but seemed a little lost. I wanted to draw it. It seemed familiar. Then I realized they all did. When I looked more closely, I saw Bren in every face in that photograph. I turned away as if the paper had bitten me, and I focused my attention on Mrs. Sabah. "You don't need to stay with me."

"I'll wait with you until Reggie gets here," she said. The proximity chime on the door dinged. "Speak of the devil."

She left me on the couch staring at Bren's family portrait. Envy suddenly stabbed me. I wanted *his* family! My heart hurt. I slammed the album shut and picked up my bag, dashing tears from my eyes.

—chapter 17—

I dropped off Zavier in my apartment, fervently hoping that Patty and Barry were serious when they said they'd take care of him. Knowing them, they'd probably hire a dog sitter, but I didn't care. Just as long as he was all right until I got back. I felt a little guilty for wanting to go off into stass and leave him behind for two weeks. Somehow being stassed didn't feel as real to me as leaving did.

Mr. Guillory led me down to his own private limoskiff, which made mine look like a canoe. It was a huge hover yacht, with seats made of soft indigo-dyed kidskin. I could see at least one reason Guillory didn't want me to bring Zavier; he'd have chewed on the cushions.

Once we'd settled into the wide seats and the yacht took off, Guillory opened a little bar set in the wall and offered me a wine cooler. I didn't know how to tell him my stomach was still uneasy, so I accepted. If I nursed it slowly, it probably wouldn't be too bad. "Would you like to hear some music, or start a holoprogram? We've got quite a ways to drive yet."

"Music would be fine," I said. I realized that Guillory found this just as awkward as I did. He rattled off a few names, but the only one I recognized was a band I'd heard the kids at school talking about. At the end of the unfathomable list, he added, "Or I have some cello suites from Bach."

"That would be great," I said, seizing on the familiar.

As the thick, sweet toffee strains of music flooded the cabin, I curled back in my seat, wishing I had Zavier's comforting head to scratch. Or Xavier to snuggle, as long as I was wishing. I watched out the window as ComUnity was left behind, and we entered a grayer urban landscape.

I'd expected to be horrified. I always was when I went into the city proper. But it didn't take me long before I realized the city, as I had known it, was dead.

Gone were the pushing throngs of harried people. Gone were the poisonous fumes and the sounds of gang wars. Gone were the starving children who would come up to my windows at traffic stops, tapping with little pebbles to make a noise. Gone were the uniformed private security firms, with their electroguns and lethal antipersonnel shields, who would seize the beggars and pull them into dark alleyways.

I couldn't believe it. "Are we skirting the city?" I asked, convinced we were avoiding the most unpleasant neighborhoods.

Guillory looked out the window. "No," he said. "This is it."

I suspected some kind of ghetto scheme, a concentration camp. "Where do they keep the poor?"

Guillory studied the streets for me. "I think that's one," he said. He pointed to a young mother who had her small child in a secondhand stroller. She was busking, playing a rather battered guitar for passersby.

I frowned at her through the tinted windows of the hover yacht. She was not starving. Her clothing was old, but neither ragged nor filthy. Whatever her circumstances, she had had enough free time when she wasn't scrounging for money or food that she had learned a luxury skill, such as music. Her child had a toddler's cup of juice in one hand and seemed to be laughing with the music. "You're kidding," I said.

"Nope." He smiled at me. "Looks different, doesn't it? After the Dark Times, there weren't enough people left to waste."

"But where are the security guards?"

"If no one's desperate, there isn't as much need to riot. Most security firms went out of business toward the tail end of the Reconstruction." He frowned. "UniCorp lost a lot of good stock in those," he mused. "Good thing we were diversified."

I stared at him. How could Guillory only be concerned with how much profit UniCorp had lost when the security firms were no longer needed? He was younger than I was, if you took my birthday into account. I was already in stass when Guillory had been born. Yet he was not young—mid to late fifties, I supposed—which meant that he was born in the midst of the Dark Times. In his childhood he would have seen much of the same squalor and inequality that I had seen. The Reconstruction had mended all the horrific gaps in society that I had taken as a matter of course during my lifetime. They'd told me this in history, but the words hadn't been real to me until I'd seen it. If it hadn't been the product of total and utter collapse, I would have considered it a miracle.

Guillory happened to be wearing a deep-blue suit today, which made him look a little less like a golden statue, but he still unnerved me. I didn't want to try to make conversation. I pulled out my sketchbook and started another drawing of my Xavier.

It amazed me that I never forgot his face, but I knew that was probably because of the stass. The memories of days just before going into stass always seemed more concrete than other memories. Stass held them fresh in your brain until long after you would ordinarily have let them drift into your subconscious, until they were indelibly imprinted. I still remembered the look on Xavier's face when I said good-bye . . . as much as I wished I didn't. Instead I tried to think of all the times he'd caught me in his arms, how nice it was to wake from stass and find him and Åsa waiting for me.

The year I spent with Xavier when I was fifteen was the best year of my life, though it had started a bit rocky. For the first time, I had feared going into stasis.

It was one thing to wake up and find that my dear friend had grown from five to six, and I'd missed it. It was another to be away from my boyfriend for four, six, nine months. Time had never seemed so precious to me.

And for once, I was fortunate. Usually whenever I came out of stass we had a new maid. This time was no different.

Two weeks after Xavier and I shared our first kiss, my mom hired Åsa.

Åsa was from Sweden. She had hair the color of honey, with lines of silver white in it. She was a sergeant major of a servant. She'd force me into cleaning up my own bedroom, something no other maid had ever done. She taught me how to do my own laundry, how to cook simple meals, how to fill out college applications. I thought it was a little early to do such things, but she insisted that I learn. I thought my parents would choose my college for me . . . whenever that happened. But she thought I should know things, "Just in case." "Just in case" was a big phrase with Åsa.

I never told my parents how strict she was with me. I figured they'd fire her if they knew, and I rather liked her. She seemed very real to me.

A week or so after Åsa came, Mom caught me by surprise just before dinner.

"I have something for you," she said.

"Really?" I popped over and stood with my hands clasped politely. Mom laughed and kissed me, and then she held out both fists. "Pick one."

I frowned and picked the left one. It had a caramel in it. I was a bit disappointed, but I took it anyway. "Thanks."

Mom laughed and opened her other hand. "Oh, wow!" I said, and gently took the BitCamera that she held out to me. It was the size of my pointer finger, small enough to keep around my neck, and it automatically adjusted to take the clearest digital photos of any device on the market.

"It's so you can take pictures and reference them later. For your paintings."

"Oh, Mom, thanks so much!" I hugged her tightly and she smoothed my hair.

"Go dig out a chain for it from your jewelry box. I think the silver square link would look best with it. And while you're at it, you should change for dinner. Royal blue tonight. I think you have two dresses that color this season, but you can choose between them."

"Thanks."

"By the way, you should know," she said as I headed toward my room. "We're going to a business retreat at the end of the month."

I stopped. "Oh," I said. I turned back to her, gripping the BitCamera in my hand. "Do you have to?"

"Yes, dear. Do you want to go to your tube tonight, or wait until the day we leave?"

"I'd like to wait, Mom," I said.

Mom frowned. "Are you sure? We'll be busy these next few days, packing and such."

"How long will you be gone?"

"Only a month or two. No need to worry."

I gulped. "Right," I said.

Later, I could only nibble at my meal.

I found Xavier in the communal garden after dinner. I fell into his arms and he wrapped himself around me without comment. After a few moments, he kissed my forehead. "What's wrong, Rose?"

"Mom and Daddy are going on a business retreat," I said. "Already."

Xavier pulled back, appalled. "But it's only been a few weeks!"

"I know," I said. It wasn't fair. "Will you wait for me?"

Xavier's eyes were full of pain. "I always wait for you. . . . But . . ."

"I know," I said, and my voice reflected the pain in his eyes. "How long?"

"They say only a month or two."

"That's what they said last time, and it was more than seven."

I sniffed. "I'll be back," I said. "I will be. I promise you."

"I know you will. I know you will." He covered my face with kisses until my knees buckled and I melted in his arms. "I'll miss you!" he hissed. "Oh, hell!" And he gripped me tight enough to bruise. "It's not fair!"

"It's for the best," I said, more to reassure myself than him.

"That's what you always say." He ran his fingers through my hair. "Can't you see that it's different now?"

"Of course I see that!" I pulled away from him. "Do you think I want you to leave me behind?"

"You're the one leaving me," Xavier pointed out. "Can't you tell them to leave you out? You're nearly sixteen; isn't it right to give you some freedom?"

"No," I said. "I'm not old enough to be alone. They know that."

Xavier's shoulders sagged. "I could ask Mom and Dad if you could stay with us."

"They'd never permit it," I said. "They'd never go against Daddy."

This was true. They worked for UniCorp just like everyone else in ComUnity. Daddy was king here.

Xavier tossed his head as if trying to force a solution out of it. "Could you ask them to take you *with* them? We could talk over the net. That would be better than . . . than . . ."

"I know," I said. "But there's nothing we can do. We still have a few days before they go. Can't we just enjoy them?"

Xavier clenched his fists. "Ask them. Please, just *ask* them!"

I didn't want to ask them. It felt wrong to question them. But for Xavier . . . "I'll try," I said.

"Of course you can't come with us, honey," Mom said when I tried the next evening. "We'll be working all day. You'd just be underfoot."

"I know," I said. "But I could, you know, learn about the company, for when I grow up. And . . ."

Daddy laughed. "You won't have to worry about that, little one. You just keep playing with your little paint set."

"But I . . ." I knew it wouldn't work. But for Xavier, I'd try anything. "I think I could be getting old enough to look out for myself. With a little help, I could stay here. You could hire a tutor or . . ."

Mom started as if she'd been whipped. "You want to stay

here by yourself? What are you thinking! You're a child! Mark, talk some sense into your daughter."

"Listen to your mother," Daddy said without looking at me.

"But Daddy—"

He turned to glare. "Did you just say *but* to me?"

"No, sir," I said, looking down at the ground.

But by now Daddy was angry. "You do not contradict me in my own house, do you hear me? I get enough of that at work. When I get home, I expect to be obeyed."

"Yes, sir."

There was a weighty pause while Daddy regarded my bowed head. "That's better," he said, petting my hair gently. "Now, apologize to your mother."

I turned my gaze back to her. "I'm sorry, Mom."

"That's all right, honey," Mom told me, wrapping me in a warm hug. "I think you're a little overexcited. You go into your room and get things in order. I think we should put you in stass tonight."

"Tonight?" I tried to keep the shock out of my voice when I looked up at her.

"Don't *you* think you're overexcited?" she asked, looking earnestly into my eyes. Her own blue eyes shone with concern.

I thought about this. I did feel flustered and unhappy. She was probably right. "Yes, Mama."

"That's a good girl," Mom said, kissing me on the cheek. "I knew you'd make the right decision. I'll order us a nice dinner before you turn in. Lobster or quail?"

"Quail, please," I said, forcing a smile.

"Of course, honey. Anything you want."

What I wanted was to stay with Xavier, but I didn't dare ask again.

I went into my room and made up my bed, making sure that all the laundry was carefully sorted so that Åsa could take care of it for me while I was stassed. Then I organized my paints so that they'd be neat and ready for me when I got out. I frowned at the oil painting I had started, a tortuous glowing mountainscape under a night sky. It was almost alien, except for the plant life I'd begun to fill the painting with, which looked more aquatic than terrestrial. I was very proud of it so far, but I knew I'd probably forget the vision I had for it by the time I got out. My artwork always evolved a bit during long periods of stasis.

And Xavier might have evolved beyond me. Maybe he'd go back to that Claire girl, or maybe he'd find someone new. Tears coursed down my face, and I tried to force them back in. Mom and Daddy couldn't see that I'd been crying. They were right; I was too high-strung. Far too emotional over the littlest things.

Åsa opened the door to my room, with a basket of clean laundry under her arm. "Oh, so sorry, miss," she said with a little bob. "Thought you were out with your young man."

Xavier! He didn't know I was going into stass tonight! I flew to the nearest sketchbook and scribbled out a letter as fast as I could. "Åsa, I need you to do something for me!" I said.

"What?"

"I need you to give this message to Xavier tomorrow. Can you do that?"

"Of course, miss. But can't you give it yourself?"

"No, I'm going into stasis tonight."

"Stasis? Whatever for?"

"Mom and Daddy are going away on business," I said. "Please, just give this to Xavier?"

Åsa blinked at me a few times and then nodded. I signed the letter, *Love always, Rose,* and tore it from the sketchbook. I pressed the folded sheet of paper into her hand.

"Why stasis?" Åsa asked. She was new to the dynamics of our household.

I sighed, disgruntled. "It's hard to explain."

Åsa's face turned hard on me suddenly. *"Ja, flicka,"* she said. "I'll do what you ask."

After our farewell dinner, Daddy gave me a hug before Mom led me into my big closet, where we kept my stass tube. She helped me inside and kissed me. "You make me very proud. You know that, honey? You always make the right decisions in the end."

"Thanks, Mom," I said. "I love you."

"I love you, too. See you in a few months."

"Have a nice trip."

"Good night."

"Good night."

The music started, and I could smell the sweet perfume of the stass chemicals as the hatch slowly closed over me. Mom was right. This was the right decision.

I tried not to think of Xavier.

.   .   .

I kept my eyes closed, at first, and tried to hold on to my stass dream, which involved sailing on the surface of glowing molten lava. The lava should have been hot, but was as comfortable as a relaxing bath. Someone held my hand quietly, and I was surprised. Mom usually kept shaking me until I gave up on my stass and my dream. The quiet presence woke me more quickly than Mom's prodding ever had. To my surprise, when I opened my eyes, the face smiling down on me was not Mom's. "Xavier?"

He grinned as wide as a church door.

"How did you get in here?"

He jerked his head behind him, and I saw Åsa standing by the door. "Morning, miss."

"What's going on?" I asked, and the answer made me feel both elated and guilty.

Åsa had delivered my message to Xavier and asked him why I was going into stass. Xavier told her the truth, that they put me in regularly. When he'd admitted that he'd known me since I was seven, Åsa said nothing. But the morning after my parents' departure, she'd knocked boldly on Xavier's door and asked him if he knew how stass tubes worked. Xavier was a rather accomplished hacker, and within a few hours, he'd figured out a way to change the chronometer on my stass tube so it would read that I was still inside.

Åsa had decided she could take care of me while my parents were away. I could keep going to school, keep living my life, and keep Xavier. It wasn't as if my parents looked at my academic achievements, and schools don't complain when the children show up—only when they don't. Mom and Daddy would never know. The day before they were to come home, I'd pop back into stass, and because of Xavier's hacks on the tube, they'd be none the wiser. When I asked Åsa why she was doing this, she said only that it wasn't her place to argue with my parents, but that she had been told to manage the household as she best saw fit while they were gone.

I felt guilty deceiving my parents like this. If it hadn't been for Xavier, I'd have told them to put me back in and I'd dutifully wait for Mom and Daddy to return. But there *was* Xavier, and I wouldn't give up this chance.

And so began the best year of my life. My parents did, in fact, come back two months later. I slipped happily back into stasis, and within eighteen hours they let me out for my champagne breakfast.

A month and a half later, when my parents were leaving again, I went into stass without a complaint. And when they came back after two weeks, they had no idea I had spent that time living my life. This happened again and again, all through that year. I would have missed my sixteenth birthday but for Åsa and Xavier. They held a private party for me, and Åsa sang me a birthday song in Swedish. For the first time, I watched the seasons change from summer to autumn to winter, and back to spring.

On the first clear, warm night that spring, Xavier and I sat out in the garden, wrapped in a blanket, watching the moon as it rose over the courtyard.

"I truly love this," I whispered.

"I truly love you," Xavier whispered in my ear, causing

shivers to run down my spine. "I'm so glad I don't have to lose you again," he said, with a kiss on my temple. "And again, and again." Each time he kissed me someplace else. "Every time, it's like you've died."

I looked up at his face, pale in the moonlight. "Does it really feel that way to you?"

"I grieve every time," he said. "I'm always afraid I'll never see you again."

I shuddered, a memory of the dying winter around us. But Xavier's arms kept me warm. "That won't ever happen," I reassured him.

"How can you know?" Xavier asked. "You'd have missed seven out of the last ten months if it weren't for Åsa. You'd still be fifteen."

"And you'd have left me behind again," I whispered.

"You're the one who keeps leaving me."

"And until now I've been . . . waiting for you. But now you've gone so far. I'm starting to fall behind."

Xavier touched my hair and stared into my eyes. "Do you think we should tell anybody?"

"Tell anybody what?"

"How much you get left in stasis. It can't be good for you."

"I'm too high-strung. I need to mellow out sometimes."

Xavier scoffed. "I think your parents would be stassing any child they had, whether it was high-strung or not. I've never seen you be anything but sweet and compliant." He kissed me along my forehead. "You're almost inhuman, you're so angelic."

"That's only because I know I can get away from it all if I need to," I said.

"I'm inclined to believe it a fortunate accident of character," Xavier said. Then he sighed. "Or maybe not so fortunate. Maybe if you weren't so biddable, you wouldn't let them keep you a child."

I pulled away. "Don't put it like that!" I said. "Besides, if I hadn't been in stasis, you and I would never have gotten together."

He smiled, running his fingers along my eyebrows. "Seven years isn't an impossible age difference," he said.

I didn't say anything, but I started doing calculations in my head. According to my birth certificate, I should have been thirty-eight. I must have lost more years than I'd been aware of when I was very young. Mom and Daddy didn't look so old to me, but then again, they did a lot of interplanetary travel. They spent lots of time in stasis, too. I looked at Xavier. If I'd never been put into stasis, I'd have been twenty-two when he was born. I could be his mother.

The thought made me uncomfortable. I snuggled in closer to him. "I love you," I whispered.

"I love you, too, Rose," he said. "Always."

Always. I wondered if his spirit still watched me, from wherever dead spirits go. Did he still love me now?

I drew the finishing touches on my newest Xavier sketch. It was a morbid, probably borderline obsessive way to spend my time, but it took my mind off Bren and Guillory and being hunted by an assassin. Xavier was still my touchstone, if only in my mind.

I never did ask where we were going, but by midafternoon Guillory's hover yacht was skimming south over the ocean. The yacht had everything. Like a magician, he conjured a caviar luncheon shortly after midday. He even offered me a shower in the tiny yet elegant bathroom, which I declined. Instead I concentrated on my portraits of Xavier. I'd decided to fill this sketchbook with a progression of him from a small baby on up. I had just finished a portrait of Xavier at twelve when Guillory perked up, looking out the window.

He had spent most of the trip talking on his cell or working with his notescreen. Now, as the setting sun began to turn the sky to gold, he said good-bye to his secretary, turned off his cell, and pointed out the window. "Here we are," he said.

I had half expected that he would take me to a private island. I wouldn't have put such an extravagance past him. But it was an inhabited shore we were rapidly approaching.

"Where are we going?"

"I have an incognito suite at the hotel here," Guillory said. "Useful when I want to escape for a few days. Most people know me as Mr. Jance here, so please call me Reggie, not Guillory."

The hover yacht pulled into a hover bay at the coastline, rather than in a parking garage. Around the edge of the beach, a wide industrial magnetic strip bordered the entire island.

No skimmers were allowed. That struck me as strange. Not to mention expensive. The magnetic strips weren't exactly cheap. "Where are we?"

"Nirvana," Guillory said.

"Excuse me?"

"Oh, sorry, you wouldn't know." Guillory laughed his annoying comradely laugh. "UniCorp created a series of man-made islands just north . . . oh, I forget. Doesn't matter, really. Truly beautiful, this place. They moved sand from the bottom of the ocean, built this little archipelago. When you look at it from above, the islands form the shape of the UniCorp logo. This one is Nirvana; it forms the head and horn of the unicorn. There's a great beach just under the throat. Only the most elite can afford suites here."

I was a little confused. "Man-made islands?" It wasn't an unheard-of prospect, but all the previous attempts at the dawn of the second millennium had eventually failed quite abysmally, creating stagnant dead spots in the ocean and resulting in barren, poisonous sandspits, not luxury resorts. "What's wrong with resorts on a natural island?"

"This place is assured to be secure. We're in the safest part of the ocean—virtually no risk of hurricanes or earthquakes. And there are no natives, so we didn't steal the land from anyone."

He said that as if it were a virtue, and maybe it was. But if I understood it correctly, the population of the world was substantially reduced already. To dump a vast amount of the planet's financial resources into resorts on a man-made sandspit in the middle of the ocean—rather than bolster the economy of some tropical island, or, better yet, do without the wasteful resort at all—struck me as a rather selfish way of looking at the planet. The history class I was taking with Bren had an entire unit on economics of the Reconstruction, and this flew in the face of all of it. Not to mention the devastation such a project would have caused to the seabed. Did they even know how many plants and animals had been thoughtlessly dispatched just to move the sand? Because UniCorp had vast amounts of money, did ocean ecology suddenly not matter any longer?

But what did I know?

I was struck again by how powerful UniCorp was. It owned people and colonies, and even the earth itself had to shape itself to its whim. What else was UniCorp trying to shape? I thought of Otto and shuddered.

Porters appeared out of nowhere and collected my bag. I took a deep breath and followed them into the resort.

Mr. Guillory signed us in, and we both had retinal scans recorded before the doors would even open. Mr. Guillory's name showed up as Mr. Jance when his retina was scanned, and at my scan, he entered my name as Rose Sayer. I hoped that would be enough to keep the assassin from guessing my whereabouts.

The constant scan on the net tickled. It wasn't the name that caught him this time; it was the actual retinal scan, which flared in bright colors across his plasticized processors. The name attached to it was inaccurate, but his programming was flexible enough to believe in human error.

TARGET IDENTIFIED: RETINAL MATCH CONFIRMED, ROSALINDA SAMANTHA FITZROY.

LOCATION KNOWN: NIRVANA.

DIRECTIVE: RETURN TARGET TO PRINCIPAL.

He looked up the location of the Unicorn Islands and assessed ways to get there. It would not be easy. He eventually determined he would have to commandeer one of the new hover vehicles whose specs were all over the net. While one section of his processors was calculating that, another was going through the now familiar routine of searching the net for the principal.

SCANNING . . . SCANNING . . . SCANNING . . . SCANNING . . .

PRINCIPAL UNAVAILABLE.

SECONDARY DIRECTIVE REINSTATED: TERMINATE TARGET.

INITIATE.

His processors predicted it would take him approximately ten hours to make it to the Unicorn Islands if he was able to procure a hover vehicle quickly. He was in luck. One hit him as he stepped onto the street.

He was knocked over by the skimmer's superior weight, but the driver slammed on the controls and it slowed and veered, bouncing back and forth across the road like a tennis ball. He predicted the inertia of the machine and stood back up, grabbing the skimmer to keep it steady. The momentum spun it in a circle, and then it stood still. Twenty more vehicles milled about behind the one he had stopped.

He ripped the door off the skimmer and dropped it on the road with a clang. The operator cowered inside the vehicle. "My directive requires transport," he announced. "I am commandeering this vehicle." He climbed in without further preamble.

The Plastine ignored the terrified occupant as he slid out the open door under his elbow. There was no reason to terminate a bystander who was not trying to hinder him.

—chapter 18—

Mr. Guillory's cell beeped the moment we entered the hotel room. "Reggie," he said, switching it on.

"Mr. Guillory, I thought you'd like to know," said the voice I recognized as his secretary. He'd been talking to her on and off the whole afternoon. "They've located the Plastine. I'm downloading the report into your screen now."

"That's wonderful," Guillory said, and he opened up his screen.

I crept behind him to see. A holorecording, looking distorted and strange on the flat screen, showed my shiny plastic attacker jumping into the middle of a road. While the hover skiffs behind the Plastine bounced back and forth between the magnetic pedestrian strips, like pucks on an air hockey table, the Plastine ripped the door off a now rather battered skiff and drove off. Another shot from a different angle showed the occupant of the hover skiff falling onto the road, rolling, and keeping flat as half a dozen hover skiffs passed harmlessly over his head.

Then the scene changed. I couldn't hear the newscaster's voice, but someone was interviewing the man, who had a scrape on his cheek from his high-speed fall onto the road.

Mr. Guillory's secretary continued. "The police say the Plastine is hard to track, and he appears to have disabled the satellite link in the skimmer, but they should have him apprehended within the hour."

"Thank you, Stella. Keep us updated." He turned back to me. "Well. See? I told you it would all be all right."

I took a deep breath. If nothing else, I was now certain that this thing existed. Guillory poked at his screen to check the time. "There's this great open-air restaurant down by the base of the horn," he said. "Care to join me?"

I shook my head. "I couldn't eat," I said.

"Suit yourself. This whole suite is ours. Your room is down that corridor; mine's just off here. You can turn the music or the holoview as loud as you like. All the rooms here are soundproof. Anything you need, don't hesitate to contact room service. You have my cell code?"

I nodded, and Guillory left me to my own devices.

I felt uncomfortable in this room. I'd been in rooms like it, usually at charity balls with my mother. I was always on display at those balls, more a prop than a person. Just as Guillory reminded me of a golden statue, this room reminded me of a jewelry box. Just the thing to house that golden statue. I sighed and went to find the bathroom.

Since the bath had done me such good the night before, I drew another in the opulent bathroom and sank into the purified and imported water. I knew the source of the water shouldn't make a difference, but it all felt false to me, like drawing a computer image instead of using oil paints. After my bath I climbed into a fresh uniform, leaving the bag and everything else in the bathroom.

I went into the central room of the suite, automatically scanning the room for my notescreen. It wasn't near ten yet, but Otto might be worried. Then I remembered that I didn't have my notescreen with me. I could probably have used Guillory's, but he hadn't left it available, and I wasn't about to go poking through someone's screen without their permission. So much for talking to Otto. For today, anyway. I idly wondered if Guillory's secretary had called yet, to confirm the Plastine's capture. Perhaps I could go home tomorrow? I really did want to talk to Otto. He'd find this place hilarious. UniCorp playing god, with their man-made islands and their man-made people. I wondered about Dr. Bija, too, if Guillory or anyone had bothered telling her where I was. I was afraid I might miss my next appointment. Otto, Dr. Bija, Zavier, my studio . . . I hadn't realized it until this moment, but I really had created something of a life. Now I was worried—what if this attacker meant that I would lose my new life, too?

I debated turning on the holoview I saw in the corner, but decided against it. I glanced at the clock. I opened the window to the balcony, and the sound of the ocean washed over me. Despite being gilded and expensive, the room was fairly comfortable. I curled up on the chaise longue with my sketchbook, but I soon found myself nodding. With a hint of relief, I let myself fall asleep to the sound of the surf outside.

My rest was interrupted. Mr. Guillory burst loudly into the room. "Rosalinda! I'm glad you're up!"

I blinked, bleary-eyed. It was pitch-dark outside, and the scent of the air had that peculiar lightness that occurs sometime after midnight.

Guillory had changed from his blue suit into a yellowish brown lounge suit, obviously his idea of casual wear. He glanced at the open patio for a moment before sliding the glass door closed, shutting out the sound of the false surf. He headed over to the bar and poured himself a drink. "I was half-afraid you'd have gone to bed."

"I fell asleep here," I mumbled, trying to figure out a way of saying, *I really should find my room now.*

"Good, good," Guillory said, not really hearing me. He turned around with a drink in his hand and pulled one of the gilded chairs a little closer to my chaise, sitting down rather heavily. In his brown suit, perched in the golden chair, with the glass of amber fluid in his hand, he looked like a statue of an Egyptian pharaoh, half-god, overlooking his domain. The ice in his glass glinted like diamonds.

"So," he said. "Rosalinda. You know, I've been thinking. It was such a surprise when you joined our little UniCorp family. *Re*joined, I should say. When I first met you, I thought I really knew you. I thought I had you pegged. But I realize I don't. I just made up some image of you. You're not very much like your parents, are you."

I sat a little straighter and gripped my sketchbook. "I don't know."

"Well, I know," Guillory said with a smile. "I'm running their company, after all. Quite a legacy, that is. You know, Jackie was real heavy into charities. Balls and such, that kinda thing."

"Yes, I know," I said, put off by the casual way he'd called Mom *Jackie*. "We'd go shopping for matching dresses and she'd take me to charity galas, balls, dinners, poker tournaments."

"That must have been a lot of fun," Guillory said. "Must have gotten a lot of attention, two beautiful women walking in like bookends. Your mother, she was a real hot-looking woman back in the day. I've seen pictures. Looked a lot like you, you know."

I swallowed. This was making me uncomfortable. "Thanks," I whispered.

"No wonder she landed your dad, huh? Most powerful man in the world."

"I don't know about that," I said.

"No, really," Guillory said. He leaned forward in his chair, as if telling me a secret. "Forget what anyone says. Forget the elected officials and the world leaders and the religious icons. They're all well and good, but power—the real power—lies with people like you and me."

I wasn't sure I was glad he'd included me in that statement.

"Your father knew what he was doing," Guillory continued,

leaning back in his chair again. He took a sip of his drink. "Think about it. Multitier the company so that if any one section folds, the others can compensate. I mean, they got their NeoFusion, but then they just got their fingers into *everything*. Handpicked a selection of truly remarkable people to rule. They're the true royalty of the worlds, mark my words. And quite a legacy they've left behind, too: the company, the colonies, ComUnity, that school of yours."

That thought seemed to derail him. He took another sip of his drink. "So tell me. That school. When I put you in Uni Prep, I was hoping you'd only be around the *best* people. How's that working for you?"

The best people? "Um . . . good, I guess."

"I've been looking over your report cards," he said, and my eyes widened. My report cards went to *him*? *I* hadn't even seen them yet! Unless he had access to the school's records. If he had access to the school's records, did he have access to Dr. Bija's? Weren't school grades supposed to be confidential between you and your guardian? Which should mean Barry and Patty, right?

I didn't have time to fret over that too much, because he continued: "Not very impressive. I've been wondering if there's any better place for you." He frowned at me. "Had you ever thought about boarding school?"

"I—I thought Uni Prep was a boarding school," I said in a panic. I'd never been to a boarding school, but the few times I'd asked my parents about them, they'd told me nothing but horror stories: how the children were whipped and starved by the teachers and sexually molested by the other students, how the prestigious children were frequently kidnapped and held hostage. They could take much better care of me than any boarding school. Now they were gone, and Guillory was going to send me away?

"Well, maybe," he said, looking down at his drink. It had nothing but ice in it. He stood up to go to the bar to pour another. "Too soon to think about changing you now, anyway," he said. "You've only been alive, what, two months?"

He couldn't send me away. I'd make my grades look better. I had to study harder. I swallowed as he fell back into his chair.

"You know, Rosalinda, I remember when I was a kid, my parents always used to ask me about my dreams and aspirations."

I frowned. Where was this going?

"You got any dreams and aspirations?"

"Um . . ." I didn't know what I was supposed to say. At the moment, my biggest dream was sleeping through the night without a nightmare. My fondest wish was not to be hunted by a militant animated corpse bent on my termination. I also had an aspiration to get out of this conversation, but I couldn't quite see how I could do that. "I used to have some," I said. "But the world has changed a lot."

"Yeah!" Guillory said, raising his glass as if to toast. "It sure has." He looked up at his glass and frowned, suddenly realizing that might not have been the best tack to take. "I'm real sorry about your folks, honey," he said, lowering his glass. I was about to say thank you when he continued, "But in the end, come on. Aren't you having more fun now?"

I stared at him, appalled. My world had died around me, and he thought I was having more fun?

"I mean, when I was a kid, I would have given my left arm to not be supervised all the time. Able to do what I wanted to do. But, nope, had to have parents on me all the time. Didn't even have any brothers or sisters to take the pressure off. Did you have brothers or sisters?"

"No," I whispered.

"Me too. I was an only child, just like my son. Only had the one son. Hank. I always *wanted* to have a daughter," he said.

I wasn't sure if he was saying he hadn't wanted his son or not. He took another sip of his drink and tilted his head at me. "Hank's in college right now. Sure wish you could meet my boy. He'll be home for the holidays. We'll have a party so you two could get together." Here he snickered with a certain lascivious tone. "Never know what might come of that."

I couldn't suppress a shudder.

He stood up and headed back to the bar. I hadn't noticed that he'd drained his glass. How many had that been now? The third, at least, and I was pretty sure he'd had more than a little before he'd woken me up. He shoveled some ice into a second glass and filled it. "You want a glass?" he asked, holding it out to me.

"No."

He shrugged and poured my half glass into his own. "You know, speaking of your parents," he said. We hadn't been. "You know, at the end there, your dad was real messed up. He just couldn't cope. Probably just as well he passed on. If he'd continued, he'd have left the place in a hell of a mess. And at least he didn't go alone! They both went together; left the company in *good* hands." He was waving the glass around as he stood there, and I felt completely trapped. I was trying to figure out how to excuse myself when he said, "Dark Times and all. What happened was probably the best thing for everybody, all in all."

My body seemed to melt, in pure shock. The blood left my face. All I could do was stare at him. How could he possibly say that? How could he say that the death of more than half the people on the planet was the best thing for everybody?

"I always felt that way," he continued as if he could hear my horror and was defending his stance. He took a big swallow from his glass before heading back to his chair. He nearly tripped when his feet got to the carpet, but he righted himself and plunked down heavily into his golden crushed-velvet chair. "It was amazing what your dad tried to do, though. Hold the company together like he did. You know, with so many folks gone. So many of UniCorp's employees died during the Dark Times that we didn't have to lay too many off. Not like *some* places. Not that we haven't had our own little Dark Times, too, you know. Hell, the company had its ups and downs, like I told you. Lost a lot of money, now and then. Ten years ago, when the stocks were down, we had to let so many go. Lost a lot of good people. Hell, I was working so many hours, I nearly lost my own wife, too."

I did not want to hear this. I did not want to hear this.

"I found a little friend in the office that helped me a lot," he continued doggedly. "She's the hardest worker, you know? She makes me feel young again."

I flushed. This was a piece of information I did not need, did not want, and wanted to forget—now. What was I supposed to *do* with this knowledge? It wasn't any of my business!

"Feel almost as young as you," he went on, and I turned rose-red again. "You know, we're just going to have to set you up with someone. What's going on with you and that Sabah fellow? What's his name?"

I didn't want to open my mouth, but I was afraid if I didn't supply him with the name, the rest of the conversation would just get worse. "Bren," I whispered.

"That's it! Bren! Good boy, Bren. I beat him at tennis a few times."

I suspected that was a lie, unless he'd played him when Bren was only eight. "His mom and dad are good employees. I like Sabah; he's got class. But opposites kind of attract, you know. I know that's why Sabah married Annie." What was so opposite about Annie and Mr. Sabah? "Opposites attract no matter if you want them to or not. You can't be too careful who you hang out with. I never did approve of Bren hanging out with that Europa kid."

No. No, please, don't bring Otto into this!

"I just don't get it," he said, his voice slurred over. "Everyone tells me that kid's so smart, all those scholarships and tests and things, but I just don't see it. They're just trying to improve their diversity or some such. He looks good on their records, but he's just a dead-faced zombie. Can't even talk!"

I wasn't surprised that Otto had never, ever touched Guillory, even if he'd had the chance. Touching that mind would make you need a mental shower. I wondered if that was why Otto saw Dr. Bija—not for his own problems, but for everyone else's.

"They should just accept it. The kid's just gorked, and there's nothing anyone can do about it." He shook his head and took another slug of his drink. "I think we should just give up on that whole failed experiment."

Was he saying what I thought he was saying? The blood left my face again, back to the white rose. Give up? That meant, what? Kill him? My hands clenched in either horror or rage, I wasn't sure which. I rather wished I had accepted that drink he'd offered, so I could throw it in his face. I could feel my skin trying to crawl off me, trying, I supposed, to get away from this odious gilded creature before me.

He stared at me, his eyes unfocused. "You know, you're a really cute kid," he said. "A really cute kid." Oh, God! He wasn't about to . . . grab me or something, was he? I tried to remember where I'd left my cell. Damn it, it was still in the bathroom! He was shaking his head. "It's a real shame what's gonna happen to you."

I tilted my head. "What . . ." My words came out in a raw whisper of horror. "What do you mean?"

And at that moment I found out.

The door fell open, startling Guillory not a millimeter. "You are Rosalinda Samantha Fitzroy. Please remain still for retinal identification."

"You!" I screeched at Guillory. He lifted his head to look at me, but I couldn't read his drunken eyes. It all made perfect sense. Of all the people in the world who might want to kill me, Guillory was at the top of the list. And how else could the Plastine know where I was?

I backed up, my hands gripping my sketchbook like a lifeline. I couldn't run. My body still hadn't recovered from yesterday's attack. It would do no good to scream. Guillory wasn't going to help, and the hotel room was soundproof. I ran through my parents' teachings. Run, scream, fight. I was down to option three.

The Plastine no longer had a stumble stick, but he still carried the control collar in his left hand. He reached for me with his right. I grabbed him by the wrist and twisted. I ducked backward under his arm and elbowed him in the side, to incapacitate him and give me a chance to get away. Or that was the plan. Instead I elbowed him in the ribs and nearly broke my arm. Pain shot up to my shoulder before the whole arm went agonizingly numb. I feared I'd permanently damaged something, and I cried out at the pain.

Meanwhile my head was whirring. The damn thing was built like steel. But I remembered what had happened in my studio. I switched from defense to evasion tactics, though I knew I couldn't keep those up for long.

I danced behind the Plastine and ducked and dodged, trying to be as slippery as an eel. I was already losing my breath. I was so intent on avoiding the Plastine, I didn't remember Guillory was behind me. He stumbled into me, nearly knocking me to the ground. I was surprised he didn't shout, "Come and get her!" Instead he glared, wild-eyed. Maybe he hadn't intended to actually be present at my death. Blasted coward.

The Plastine swung at me, catching me in a backhand meant to knock me out. I went with the blow instead of fighting it and cracked my head against Guillory's. His hand tightened on my arm. He tried to pull me, but I wasn't having that. I stomped as hard as I could on his casually sandaled foot. He groaned, releasing me, and with a mule kick, I raised my heel into his groin. He dropped like a deer, moaning in pain.

I'd neutralized Guillory in the time it took the Plastine to compensate for his backhand blow. He stood before me again, control collar at the ready. I twisted, spun behind him, and kicked the Plastine in the buttocks. It was like kicking a statue, but like a statue, he could also fall. The Plastine tilted, fell, and landed full on Guillory.

There was my chance. I bolted for the door.

One of the lifts was just opening its doors. I jumped inside and stabbed the ground floor button. "Down, down!" I told the thing, in case it had a voice control, too. By this time I was pretty sure the Plastine worked alone, but I was still relieved when the lift opened its doors on the lobby, and there was no one there but the porters and the desk clerk—unless Guillory had paid them off, and they were working for him, too. But no one tried to stop me as I ran through the exquisite lobby and out into the tropical night. *Coit. Now what?* I had no idea where to go from here. I had no money, and my credit tick was cached inside my cell, which didn't help me, because my cell was still in the bathroom upstairs, with the assassin and the man who had commissioned him. What did I have? Nothing! I was, thank heavens, in my school uniform and not my pajamas, but that was it. My assets were my ill-equipped body and the clothes on my back. I looked down at my hands and suddenly smiled.

I still had my sketchbook.

—chapter 19—

"Bren?" I asked.

I'd used my last coin to buy this time in the holobooth. The holobooth was dingy, with unpleasant substances dribbling down a few of the walls, and I wished I still had my cell.

It took seven chimes before Bren fumbled his cell from his bedside table. His face, half awake, appeared sideways in the holobooth, still on his pillow. He looked sleepy and vulnerable, like a little boy. "Rose?" he muttered, still half asleep. "Rose, it's after midnight, and I've school. What's wrong?"

"I'm sorry," I said. "Just five minutes, then you can go back to sleep."

Bren blinked once or twice and then sat up. The cell adjusted and righted his holoimage. "What?"

"I need you to send my limoskiff to come and get me. Can you do that? Then you can go back to bed."

"What?"

"I need you to send me my limoskiff. It's down in the garage. I know you have the key. I haven't locked the codes—all you need to do is tell it where to go and it'll go there."

"Where do you need to go?"

"I'm down at the hover-bus depot. I need it to come and get me."

"What are you doing at the hover depot?"

Trying to explain my predicament to a boy who was half-asleep was more difficult than I'd imagined. "I bought myself a ticket home," I said. The words came out triumphant. Though it had taken ingenuity and twenty-four hours, I had made my way back *all by myself.*

The busker I had seen on the way to Nirvana had given me an idea. With a story of a funny uncle I wanted to avoid, I'd coaxed my way onto a ferry from Nirvana to one of the more commercial Unicorn Islands, this one called Shangri-la. Tourists and travelers were everywhere, even after midnight. I'd situated myself outside the hover-bus depot, drew up a sign, and started sketching publicly. After an hour of advertising my portraits, I'd gotten my first customer. She paid me for a sketch of her boyfriend. People will pay a lot for a decent sketch as a souvenir, particularly at a tourist's paradise like the Unicorn Islands. Three more sketched portraits had earned me the price of a bus ticket back to ComUnity and a greasy meal I actually managed to keep down.

I was inordinately proud of myself. Mom and Daddy always told me that I wasn't able to take care of myself, that if left to my own devices I'd be completely helpless. Maybe that had been true *then,* but I didn't feel helpless now. With no assets at all, I was able to quite literally make my way through the world.

I finally got Bren to understand what I wanted, and he told me my limoskiff would be down to get me within half an hour. I thanked him and then resumed my nervous pacing in the shadows.

I was ambivalent about those shadows. They made it harder for anyone to see me, surely, but that also meant that if the assassin did attack, no one would see him, either. Not that that would stop the plastic corpse. Secrecy wasn't exactly in his programming. I was surprised he had managed to elude the police. But of course, now I knew whose help he had been getting.

The Plastine wasn't the only thing eating at me. Earning my way onto the bus had been exhilarating, but halfway home it had started to depress me. None of the UniCorp officials ever entered ComUnity by hover bus. The only people who had shared the seats beside me were the families of the working class, the servants, the waiters, the kinds of people who catered to *my* kind of people. It wasn't that I didn't like these people. In fact, they seemed considerably more genuine than any of the upper echelons. They were like Åsa. But as I sat there in my Uni Prep uniform, I realized what I must seem like to them. A leech. I probably seemed as odious to them as Guillory had seemed to me, even before last night.

Finally I spotted the shiny black outline of my limoskiff gliding to the curb. I stepped over the red-striped pedestrian warning strip to open the door. I'd planned to just tell the skiff to circle round and round ComUnity until I figured out what to do. My plan was thwarted.

"Are you going to tell me exactly what's going on, now?" Bren asked as I stuck my head inside.

"What are you doing here?"

"You think I'm going to let you go off alone in the middle of the night? My mom would murder me." He took my sketchbook from my hands in a kind of proprietary gesture and set it on the seat beside him.

"Won't she murder you for sneaking out?" I asked.

"Probably. So it had better be worth my time. What's going on? What happened to the Guillory-sanctioned witness protection?"

I took a deep breath. "Guillory took me down to Xanadu. Or . . . Nirvana, whatever it's called. Did UniCorp *really* waste so much money on that folly?"

Bren twitched his head in contemptuous acknowledgment.

"And while we were there, the Plastine came."

"What?" Bren stared at me. "Again? But you were incognito!"

I sighed. "I think someone told it where to find me."

"How did you escape?"

"Distracted it. Tried to fight it. Nearly broke my elbow. Ran. Then I worked my way back here with my sketchbook, keeping out of sight of anyone from UniCorp."

Bren was horrified. "*That's* it." He pulled his cell out from under his shirt.

"What are you doing?"

"Celling Guillory and then the police."

"What are you doing that for?"

"Because I assume you didn't. Am I right?"

He was.

"You just let atrocious things happen to you and don't tell a soul. You didn't complain the first day of school when you were being tortured by your history class, you didn't tell Barry and Patty about the first assassination attempt, and you haven't told anyone about Barry and Patty, either."

"What are you talking about?"

"I'm talking about the fact that those are two of the most mercenary pseudoparents that have ever been put on this planet, and I haven't heard one word of complaint out of you."

"They're all right," I said sheepishly.

"They're all right in that they leave you alone, I guess," Bren said. "I'm celling Guillory."

"Don't!"

He stared at me, his face hard. "Tell me why not."

"Don't tell him where I am! Don't tell anyone!"

Bren frowned. "Rose, you can't handle this alone."

"Yes, I can! Don't! Please, *please,* don't cell Guillory!"

"Why not?" Bren snapped. "Tell me. Whatever you're keeping secret, tell me!"

I blinked. Why *was* I keeping this a secret? Why did I want to protect Guillory? I didn't know. It was almost as if it were habitual. It just seemed to me like the proper course of action, as if I'd kept secrets like this before.

I was puzzling over this when Bren muttered, "Burn this," and lifted up his cell again. "Guill—"

I put my hand over his cell. "I think Guillory's the one who set this thing on me," I said.

Bren hesitated and then slowly lowered the cell.

"Why?"

I swallowed, unwilling to voice my suspicions. Besides, I wasn't sure if he was asking why I thought that, or why Guillory would want to.

"I wouldn't exactly put it past him," Bren mused, "but it isn't quite his usual style."

"What do you mean?"

"I mean, when he kept you a secret in the hospital; that's more his style. When he signed up Barry and Patty, who worked for him in Florida, as your guardians; that's his style. He's . . . more of a worm, less of a snake. He'll lie, undermine, and manipulate, maybe even steal to get what he wants, but . . . an assassin?" He blinked. "I don't know. I'd have thought that's about where he'd draw the line."

"I don't think he has any lines drawn," I said. "He wants to kill Otto. Said we should give up on the whole failed experiment."

Bren grunted in disgust. "Coiting ass." Then he looked at me, realization on his face. "Was he drunk?"

I nodded.

Bren sighed. "Yeah, Guillory becomes the world's biggest prick when he's drunk. Which is most evenings. Guess I should have warned you."

"Bren," I said. "It wasn't just that. He knew the Plastine was coming, and he didn't even try to stop it, or cell security, or anything. He just sat there. Then he tried to knock me down so that the Plastine could get me. I'm just like Otto to him—a mistake that should never have happened. If I weren't around, he wouldn't have to worry about losing the company."

"That is a pretty big motive." Bren tapped his finger on his knee. "If he'd arranged to program a Plastine, there'd be a record of it on his computers."

"Would there?" I asked. "He had a pseudonym on Nirvana."

"Those have to be registered, or he'd be arrested for tax evasion," Bren told me. "Building, shipping, and programming a Plastine is a highly expensive proposition. To arrange it in the time he's had since you've been out of stass, he'd have to use company funds to do it. Any pseudonym he used would have to be filtered through the UniCorp system." He frowned. "My grandfather would know."

"You think?" I asked.

"Yeah, he's only one rung down from Guillory. Could have had Reggie's job, actually, but he didn't want it. He knows everything about that company."

I swallowed. "But if Guillory's trying to kill me"—I didn't want to say this—"might not your grandfather and Guillory have . . . the same agenda?"

Bren's head snapped up and he stared at me. "If he did, Mom and I would arrest him ourselves. No, Granddad's got principles. Besides, I doubt he cares enough about you to hate you. Granddad's kind of a 'let the chips fall where they may' kind of guy."

He hadn't struck me as such from what little I'd seen of that scowling, angry old man, but I guessed Bren knew him better. "Okay," I said. "So, what do we do?"

Bren checked the time. It was one AM. "Granddad's probably in his office; I'll cell him," he said.

"Don't say my name," I said. "If the Plastine is being run through UniCorp, then the UniCorp switchboard might have a voice scan on cell calls, which would be triggered if my name was used."

"Good point," Bren said. "You're clever."

"Not really. Daddy used to do that when I was a kid," I said. "Kept an ear on gossip about all kinds of things, dozens of keywords."

Bren pulled his cell back out. "Granddad," he said.

The cell hummed for a moment and then the white-haired scowling image appeared in Bren's lap. "What's wrong, Bren? It's late."

It might have been late, but the head in the hologram did not appear asleep. I could see the suit collar around his neck. Bren was right; he was still up. A workaholic. Just like Daddy.

"I've got a serious problem here, Granddad. Can we come see you?"

"We?"

"Yeah, I've got an *old friend* here," he said, with just enough emphasis on the 'friend' to indicate that it probably wasn't just Anastasia or Nabiki. "She's in a bit of trouble."

The hologram turned still for long enough that I suspected a glitch in the connection. "I'll be at my office," he said finally, and the hologram turned off.

Bren nodded. "All right. Let's turn this thing around." He leaned forward and tapped on the dashboard of the limoskiff, activating the location control. "Uni Building, please."

My skiff slowed, turned in a slow arc, and headed back toward the center of ComUnity. "We should be there in twenty minutes," Bren said.

I had gotten distracted when Bren leaned forward to tap the dash. He was wearing a soft tennis shirt—he'd probably been sleeping in it, as it looked a little rumpled. The sleeves were short, and the muscles in his arms rippled like water. *Holy coit,* as they said now. How could he be so damned gorgeous after just waking up? He sat back, and silence descended upon us. The silence grew heavier and heavier, until even breathing seemed awkward.

Burn it. I'd ruined it. Me and my wretched infatuation had broken the easy camaraderie we'd shared since I started school. He'd always been the one to talk—tennis, his friends, school—but my infatuation had killed a certain branch of his enthusiasm, and it was the branch that he used to share with me.

"You must hate me," I said.

Bren looked at me, more bemused than anything else. "Why do you say that?"

"All I do is cause you trouble," I told him. "The moment you meet me I faint at your feet. I drag all these reporters into your life. I hang on you at school like an albatross, and then

I go and fall in love with you. You know, just to hammer the nail in the coffin."

Bren laughed. "I actually like you, Rose."

I realized what I'd said. "I'm sorry. I wasn't fishing for a compliment. I was just trying to say sorry."

"I know," Bren said. "You don't ask for compliments. Or attention. Or sympathy. Or even for a glass of water, I suspect." He sighed. "You know, when Granddad told me to look out for you, I was petrified. I thought I'd have to deal with some princess used to getting her own way every day of her life. I thought you really would hang around me like an albatross. I thought you'd be arrogant and . . . haughty. And you weren't. Aren't. It surprised me that I actually kind of liked you."

I was confused. "You do?"

"Yeah. You're a lot nicer than I would ever have expected someone in your position to be. I mean, look at how you treat Otto. I've never seen anyone warm up to him so quick. You're sympathetic and kind and understanding and beautiful and you're . . . pleasant to be around."

An annoying thrill passed through me when he said that I was beautiful. Where was this coming from?

"You aren't very fun, really, but that's hardly a requirement. Instead, you're easy. You're . . . a very relaxing person, just easy to spend time with." He shrugged. "It surprised me."

I should have left it alone. I should have held my tongue, but I couldn't help it. The perverse imp of my infatuation just had to twist the knife. "Then, why . . . ?" I took a deep breath and swallowed. "I'm not trying to change your mind or anything, but if that's all true, then . . . why not?" I finished lamely. I knew I was bright red by the end of that little speech, but I needed to know.

"Why not go out with you?" Bren asked.

I nodded, unable to speak.

"Well, first you just surprised me. Since then, I've been thinking about it." He sighed. "It's hard to explain."

"Just . . . no spark, or . . . ?"

"That's not it." He shook his head. "You don't wanna hear this."

"I think I do," I whispered.

He hesitated, then said, "Okay. Okay. The thing is . . . The thing is, I know that I have it in me to give everything of myself to someone I might come to love. And you are very easy to spend time with. But that's part of the problem." He looked at me then, and I swallowed as he searched my face. "I look at you . . . and I get a sense of what Otto sees when he touches you. Gaps. Or worse. This unfathomable abyss inside your soul."

The words were painful, but I'd never realized before that Bren had the heart of a poet.

"At least that's the way he put it."

Oh. It was Otto who had the heart of a poet. Well, okay, I could see that.

"And I know that I could. I could like you, let myself really care for you. But if I did, I just know that I'd throw more and more of myself down into that abyss, and it wouldn't begin to fill it. Rose, you just *need* more than I have to offer. There's so much pain there that I could never heal. And I'd want to. I'd shrivel up and wither long before anything started to get better for you. It would just be worse for both of us, in the end."

I sighed. He was right. What I felt for him wasn't really love, but it was more than mere desire. It was a need. And it wasn't even a need for him, it was just a need for *something*. Anything. Everything.

Everything I lost.

"I'm sorry I put you in that position," I said.

"Stop apologizing for living," Bren said. "It's like you think you shouldn't have been born." He shook his head. "You're allowed to get a crush on anyone you want. You haven't done one thing wrong since I've known you. None of this is your *fault*, Rose."

But it was. It was my fault for existing in the first place.

We arrived at the Uni Building a little after that.

The Uni Building was a massive sky-piercing monolith based on the premillennium Art-Deco skyscraper the Chrysler Building. Almost everyone who lived in ComUnity had a family member who worked in that building, if only in custodial services. It stood all by itself in the center of a grassy park, standing so tall over the rest of the area that I'd always thought it looked a little silly. However, space had been at a premium before the Dark Times, and it was easier to get permits for a skyscraper than for a sprawling decentralized megacomplex, which had been the alternative for UniCorp's expanding business. It was also a prestige thing.

Bren knocked at the rocket-proof NeoGlass™ gate. Across the vast marble foyer, a bored-looking security guard looked up from a dimly lit alcove filled with security screens. He smiled when he saw Bren. "Here to see your granddad?" he asked as he opened the door.

"Yeah, he's expecting us."

"Check in at the ret scan on your way up," he said. As if we could avoid it. The ret scanner automatically recorded everyone who entered or exited the building.

TARGET IDENTIFIED: RETINAL MATCH CONFIRMED, ROSALINDA SAMANTHA FITZROY.

He perked up. He'd suspected he'd lost his target forever.

LOCATION KNOWN: UNICORP BUILDING.

He went through his little programming dance of searching the net for the principal, and eventually reinstating the secondary directive when the principal couldn't be found. The skimmer he had commandeered to get to the island had probably been taken by the police, but his plasticized mind had grown more flexible with use. He knew that he now had access to a new hover yacht. Before he stood up for pursuit, he set his nanobots to cleaning up his body again. Blood stains tended to frighten the surrounding humans and delay his search for the primary target.

—chapter 20—

It was strange being back in the halls of the Uni Building. While everything around me had changed, UniCorp was a constant. The building had not altered in any significant measure. Bren and I stepped into the lift, and Bren pushed the button for the top floor. I ran my fingers gently over the polished granite sides of the lift. There were a few flaws in the stone, nicks and dings from decades of movers redecorating offices, but otherwise there was no difference between then and now. I could almost imagine the lift doors opening to reveal my father, waiting to welcome me with a brusque smile and a secretary to keep an eye on me.

Instead it would be Bren's scowling grandfather. "I don't like this," I said. "Disturbing an old man in the middle of the night."

"We aren't disturbing him. I told you—he's in his office. Practically lives there. Actually, he's got a suite just across from it. He used to live in our building, but he spent almost no time there. When Guillory asked him for the apartment, he just let him have it."

My ears pricked. "When Guillory asked?"

"Yeah, so you could have your old condo back."

I swallowed. "You mean I stole this guy's house?"

"Not really. You took an expensive empty white elephant off his hands, which he almost never set foot in. It didn't help when Gramma died. He didn't have much reason to come home after that. Man's a complete workaholic, except when he's on vacation."

"Is he different when he's not working?"

"Yeah, he's much nicer with family than he ever is working."

"Good," I said. "'Cause he kind of scares me."

"Used to scare me, too," Bren confessed. "Until he saved me from a bad fall while we were skiing when I was ten. Broke his leg keeping me from falling off a cliff. I didn't know it was there. The signs warning about it had been snowed over. Never seen anyone move so fast. He's"—Bren shrugged, trying to think of the right words—"abrasive and dour and taciturn, but he's always there when you need him."

"I hope so," I said, "'cause I definitely need someone."

The lift came to a rest, and the door opened onto the familiar atrium on the top floor of the Uni Building. My mother had designed the atrium based on a traditional Roman garden, complete with columns and mosaic. A bright fountain splashed in the center, a mock waterfall surrounded by imported tropical plants. The plants had changed, and I saw that several of them were now fake, a degeneration that my mother would never have stood for had she been alive.

Daddy's office had been on the upper floor of the atrium, so I expected Bren to lead me up one of the spiral staircases, but instead he led me behind the fountain to what had once been the enclave of assistants and personal secretaries.

This had changed dramatically. These offices had been opened up and made into a second atrium, with a different collection of plants. At the far end, a glass-fronted waiting room looked over the foliage, with a welcoming receptionist's desk, now empty. Behind this, through a copper-plated door, was what must be Bren's grandfather's office. Without much preamble, Bren opened this imposing door and ushered me inside.

The CEO's office was earth-toned, with landscapes on the walls, and I recognized the same hand that had decorated my condo. The desk was wood, large, but with only one screen. I found it in stark contrast with my father's old desk, more of a command console, really, with its half a dozen screens linked through to the net, keeping him updated on a thousand different projects and accounts. This desk spoke of a tidy mind, a man who didn't need to keep everything at his fingertips, because he always knew where to find it.

A leather chair turned away from the screen and revealed Bren's grandfather, waiting for us. I realized now that I had never really looked at the man when I wasn't half-blind from stass fatigue or drugged and in shock from the stumble stick. He'd frightened me both times with his irate rantings and unpleasant scowl. Now that I looked at him, the scowl seemed less angry than sad. This looked like a man who had seen all the horrors the world had to offer, and they weighed too heavily on his heart for him to lighten his bearing. My fear melted a bit.

He regarded us as he sat back in his chair.

Bren did not look the least chagrined about interrupting his grandfather in the middle of the night. "Hey, Granddad. You've met Rose."

"Yes, I have," he said with a bit of a formal nod. "Nice to meet you again, young lady."

"Nice to meet you, Mr. Sabah."

"He's not a Sabah. He's Mom's dad," Bren corrected me.

"That's all right," he said easily, cutting Bren off. "Just call me Ron. Please, sit down." He gestured me to a moss-green sofa against the wall and turned to his grandson. "What seems to be the trouble?"

"The assassin tracked her down to Nirvana, and Rose thinks Guillory set it on her," Bren said without preamble.

A flash of dreadful anger clouded Ron's face. His eyes burned as he stared at me. "You what?"

I cowered. "I don't know," I said. "I—I guess I don't have any proof. . . ."

He stared at me for another moment. Then he spoke, so quietly I barely heard him. "I'll kill him," he said with a terrifying, grim smile. He turned back to Bren. "Tell me everything."

Bren shook his head. "I can't. She hasn't told me anything, yet. Just that he was being his usual drunken sped self."

Ron turned his scowl back to me. "What makes you think Reggie's behind this thing?"

I couldn't speak. Something about his glare was making me feel ill, and all I could do was stare at him. Ron seemed to realize this and turned away from me. He pulled off his glasses and pinched the bridge of his nose. "Bren, you ask her," he said, then put his glasses back on again.

Bren sat down beside me on the sofa. "It's okay, really. Just tell him everything. What's the first thing that made you think it was him?"

"When the Plastine came in, he didn't cell security or anything. But then, he knocked me down, so I couldn't run away. And he seemed to know just when the Plastine was going to come."

"He did?"

"Yeah. He said I was cute and that it was a shame what had to happen to me."

Ron cursed under his breath. "All right." He turned to his screen. "I'll start a search program right now to see if he's been siphoning funds." His fingers tapped deftly over his pad, and his brow furrowed. "There." He turned back to me. "That'll take a while; there are a lot of files to cover. In the meantime, tell me everything you know. Is there anything else that makes you think he may have done this?"

I wanted to cry, remembering the words he'd been spilling at me. The conversation had been so appalling that the assassin had almost been a relief! "He was so awful," I whispered. "He was talking about Otto and how he thought they should just give up on him. He was kind of . . . hitting on me. And he was so callous. He was saying that the Dark Times were the best thing that had ever happened for everyone."

Bren's brow furrowed. "Are you sure?"

"I'm not making it up."

"I didn't think you were, but did you hear him correctly? I mean, Reggie's an ass, but I didn't think even he'd stoop to that kind of statement. It's like saying that holocausts are a pretty neat idea."

"Well," I amended, "he didn't say the Dark Times specifically. He said that the best day for everyone was the day my parents . . . died." It was very hard for me to get that last word out. "And that's . . . well, the only reason I was left so long. If they hadn't died—"

Ron cut me off with a groan. "Ahh." He sat back in his chair, which quietly leaned a bit backward to accommodate his more casual posture.

Bren frowned. "But the Fitzroys died—"

"Bren," his grandfather warned. There was a long silence as Ron seemed to regard his hands. He tapped his thumb pensively against his wrist. "I don't suppose it would have occurred to Reggie to tell you. His thinking tends to be self-centered. And it isn't really the role of the police." He sighed. "Leaves me," he said, almost under his breath. He turned back to me. "How much do you remember of your life, young lady?"

"All of it," I said, surprised. "What has that got to do with this?"

"Just listen to me. Bren has admitted a secret to me, that you told him you and your parents would frequently use stasis as a . . . coping mechanism?"

I wasn't sure if I should feel afraid or indifferent. Before Bren had told me about the "maladjusted" label I'd be saddled with, it wouldn't have bothered me in the least. The one thing I didn't feel was shame. I shot a questioning look at Bren.

"Granddad wouldn't tell anyone," Bren said. "I just . . . I couldn't understand it."

My questioning gaze turned exasperated. I suppose the peaceful, calming fearlessness of stass would be hard to explain to anyone who never used it regularly. I turned back to Ron. "Yes," I said. "Bren told you the truth."

Ron nodded. "Has Bren also informed you that such treatment, particularly of a minor, has been constituted a felony?"

"Yes," I said, "but I don't get it. It's not an assault. And if stass is illegal, why have stass chambers at the hospital? I saw them there."

"Hospitals have special dispensation. Victims of certain diseases or those in need of transplants who can't afford to wait can be scheduled stass time. Stass is still used for interplanetary travel, rotating the passengers who are awake with those who remain in stass, but that is only because of the many years it takes to travel to the outer colonies. Interplanetary travel would be impossible if we had to keep all the passengers awake. We couldn't build vessels with enough space for living quarters, supplies, or even oxygen and still afford to send them across the solar system. But despite being safe and effective, all stass is strictly regulated and even prohibited in many cases."

I really didn't understand. Why couldn't someone just take a break from the world? "Why?" I asked.

"It's a little hard to explain," Ron said. "Particularly given your background. When I was young, there were no laws regarding stasis. I remember various cases that made the instigation of those laws an imperative."

I rolled my eyes. The legalese was driving me a little nuts. "Such as?" I asked.

"Let me put it this way," Ron said, putting his two forefingers together to form a steeple. "Imagine you had an illness, appendicitis, something easily cured with surgery. Now imagine that your doctor hasn't had lunch yet. Rather than perform the surgery, he puts you into stass until after lunch." He shrugged. "Doesn't seem so bad.

"Now imagine that your doctor, instead of missing lunch, has a date with his wife that evening and doesn't want to be tired. So instead of performing your surgery, he keeps you in stass until the next day. That's twenty-four hours. Probably there would be no noticeable difference in your perception.

"But now imagine that the doctor has scheduled a vacation, so he arranges for you to be kept in stass for the next two, three weeks, while he heads off to Acapulco with his family. It is considerably more convenient for him to stass his patient than to perform the surgery. So, basically, for his own convenience, this doctor has stolen three weeks of your life, when all you really needed was an hour of his time. He could have delayed his vacation, he could have referred your case to another physician, but because he wanted to be the one to do the surgery — just not right then — he has assaulted you. He has taken from you something very precious and irretrievable. He stole your time."

I felt ill. I didn't like how he'd phrased that. "I . . . never thought about it that way before."

Ron smiled rather ruefully. "I know," he said, and it sounded much more sympathetic than I would have expected. "For a parent to place a minor in stasis today, there has to be an application to the government, an assured affidavit from a physician explaining why the stass is absolutely necessary, and oftentimes a filing fee, just to keep parents from doing such things lightly. Children with debilitating chronic illnesses have sometimes been stassed in the hopes of keeping them alive till a cure can be found. Only for those cases, and for children who are transplant patients, has earthbound stasis ever been permitted for a minor."

Something had begun to flutter within my chest, a frightened sparrow. My hands were shaking. "I still don't understand," I said.

The voice of Bren's grandfather continued, unyielding. "Imagine," he said, "that a parent feels overworked. The baby has been crying all day. All they want is a half-hour nap. Every parent has felt this way. They put the child into stasis until they feel more able to handle the situation. They do this instead of getting a babysitter, instead of organizing their schedule, instead of admitting they need help. For their own convenience. *Once* may seem better than abuse, I grant you. It just *doesn't seem so bad.*

"But imagine now that the child is two, three. The parents want to host a holiday party, but the child would be a hassle if she were underfoot. Put the child into stasis until after the party. Won't take too long. For their own convenience.

"Now they want to go on vacation."

I wanted to leap up and stop him, but I was afraid my legs wouldn't hold me.

"A romantic second honeymoon," Ron said. "Can't have a five-year-old along to spoil the mood. Back into stass. The child is thirteen. She wants to go on a week-long field trip, and she fights with her mother about it. Can't have that. Stass her until the trip is over. Problem solved."

He laid his hands carefully on his desk and leaned forward, just a little. I couldn't meet his eyes, but his voice would not stop. "Stass her when you're tired. Stass her when you're busy. Stass her when she's fretful. Stass her when you're bored. Stass her when she isn't doing exactly what you want her to do. Before you know it, the parents have aged ten, twelve, twenty years . . . and the child is still a child."

I couldn't look at him. He was telling me my life. I wanted to hit him. I wanted him to hurt. I wanted this feeling inside me to go away. I couldn't breathe. I felt as if I were standing on the edge of a high cliff, and I couldn't stop shaking.

"Rosalinda." Ron's soft, dark voice wavered with age, but it sounded very kind. "The helicopter crash that killed Mark and Jacqueline Fitzroy took place thirty-two years ago, more than nine years after the Dark Times officially ended." I looked up at him then, unable to understand what he was saying. "It wasn't to save your life. They never came to get you," he said, his voice barely a whisper. "They never let you go. They never let you grow up."

There was a moment of stillness, of darkness, and in that moment I could have sworn I had died.

"No, no, no!" someone shouted in my ear. "No one knew I was there! Everyone died!" I wished she would shut up; I was trying to understand where I had gone in the darkness. I opened my eyes, and I saw a strange-looking young woman below me, standing on the parquet floor, her fist raised in defiance. The old man sat at his desk, his eyes serious, watching her intently, and Bren stood backed up against the wall, almost in fear, his face so pale his mahogany skin looked like milky coffee. Only then did I realize the voice was mine. "They loved me!" the girl shouted. "They wanted to protect me! I don't believe you!"

Bren's grandfather stood up and marched out of the room. Hovering near the ceiling, I watched him go with detached interest. Did the girl frighten him as much as she frightened me? That little girl down there looked like a phantom — much more like a walking corpse than the Plastine. There were bright-red spots high on each cheek, and her ears were red as strawberries. She was so thin I could see each individual muscle as it clenched in fury, as she waved her fist impotently at the empty desk. Her brown eyes were empty, dead holes. Gaps. What was it Otto had said? *This unfathomable abyss inside your soul.* It frightened him.

It frightened me, too.

There was more to it than that, though I thought I was the

only one who could see it. I could see the girl burning with a bright, ghostly fire of rage, fierce enough to engulf the whole room. More than fierce enough to burn her to a cinder. I hovered near the ceiling, but I wondered if I was only part of that fire—a burning spirit of rage and disbelief.

Something about that thought brought me back to myself, and I couldn't see the fire anymore, or myself, just my clenched fist before my face, and Bren against the wall. He looked positively stricken. "I don't believe it," I whispered to him.

Bren opened his mouth, but then closed it again, as if he were afraid to say anything.

And his grandfather walked back into the room and held a framed photograph out for me to see. I took it with the hand that wasn't still clenched.

He must have taken the picture from Guillory's office. I recognized the room before I recognized the people—the ballroom on the ground floor of the Uni Building. The photo showed wealthy people in expensive clothes mingling. I noticed a shadowy figure in the back corner that might have been Bren's grandfather, closer to his prime. This must have been taken at the yearly company party. The traditional unicorn ice sculpture was melting in the background. Mom and Daddy were older, much older, but I recognized them.

Mom still had her beautiful blond mane of hair. She must have dyed it, because Daddy's hair had gone completely white. Mom looked younger than she should have, and different, and I recognized the effects of plastic surgery. I'd seen enough of it in friends of the family. Daddy was still well dressed, and his

eyes were still distracted. His smile was still brusque and insin-
cere, and he seemed to be focusing on something other than
where he was. They were old—it had clearly been decades
since I'd been put into stass. But the most damning thing was
the figure standing between them, holding a champagne glass
and grinning from ear to ear. A young man, midtwenties, clearly
fresh out of business school, looking just a little in awe of the
two figures who were posing with him. Reggie Guillory.

Reggie Guillory, who wasn't even born when I was put
into stass. No wonder Guillory had spoken as if he'd known my
parents. In this picture he wasn't much more than twenty-five,
his hair still a natural gold, his expensive tan somewhat darker,
looking even more like a golden statue, as he had that unnatural perfection that sculptors always strive to achieve.

It was proof in my very hands, and I still didn't want to
believe it. I lifted the photograph and threw it with tremen-
dous force against the far wall. The glass splintered, and the
frame split in two.

It wasn't enough to destroy the proof. I needed to wreck
everything. If my stass tube were there, I'd have taken my fury
out on it, but it wasn't. Instead I ripped down one of the landscapes that graced the wall and flung it like a Frisbee across the
room. Bren ducked. I threw knickknacks. I hurled heavy paper-
weights, which left gratifying dents in the walls. My hands closed
on glasses from the bar, and I hurled them against the windows,
where they smashed satisfyingly, leaving delightful-looking
broken shards.

I realized after a little while that no one was trying to

stop me. In fact, Bren's grandfather had somehow sidled up beside me and was patiently handing me objects to throw. Bren stood in the doorway, out of the way of any shrapnel, with a look on his face that I can only describe as a serious smile.

I dropped the last item—a metal tumbler from the bar. It landed with a clatter on the floor, and I followed it. I felt better.

A gentle hand caressed my hair. "I'm so sorry, Rose," said Ron. Then he stood up, and I saw him go and touch Bren's shoulder.

Whatever he said to him, Bren came up and rubbed my back. "You're okay now," he said, more to reassure himself, I think. "No one'll let anything like that happen again. We won't let it happen. Me and Mom and Granddad, we'll make sure of it."

I looked up at him. I felt hollow. "I'm tired," I whispered.

Bren smirked a little and helped me sit up. "I'm not surprised. I should take you to play tennis—you've got a great arm." He helped me to my feet and let me rest my weight on his shoulder while he led me to the couch. "Here," he said.

I curled up on the sofa and took a deep breath. Ron disappeared again and then reappeared with an afghan. He tucked it gently around me. "Nothing will hurt you here. I promise," he whispered. "You rest now." He had the most relaxing voice.

I think I might have smiled a little, but I was asleep so quickly it was almost like stasis. Just as sweet, too. My fear had left me. I'd already lost everything. What else was there to fear?

—chapter 21—

I couldn't have been asleep long, no more than an hour or so. When I woke, it was still dark, and Bren was clearing some of the debris from my tantrum, throwing it into a big garbage can. I took a deep breath and stretched. I felt good, almost satisfied, as if I were settled into a hot tub after a long day. The afghan over me was warm and smelled of cologne, probably Ron's.

Bren and I were alone in the room. "Where's your granddad?"

"Still examining Guillory's accounts," Bren said. "He didn't want to wake you, so he left to make some calls. Even if Guillory didn't sic this Plastine on you, Granddad's gathering some pretty shady stuff. He says he hasn't been paying enough attention the last few months. He's getting angrier and angrier as he sorts through it all."

"I'm surprised he isn't angry at me," I said. I threw the blanket off and knelt next to Bren to help him pick up the detritus. "Look what I did to his office."

Bren grinned. "He helped you do it! I kept trying not to laugh."

"I can't remember the last time I got angry like that. If I ever have."

"You probably haven't," Bren said.

I considered this. He was right. I didn't get angry. I didn't complain. I didn't even draw attention to myself. Because if I had . . .

I tried to put the thought away. Oddly, I had the feeling I'd been doing that for years.

"I know I've never totally trashed a room," Bren continued.

I carefully picked up another shard of glass. "They probably have janitors for this kind of thing."

"I don't want to leave Granddad's office like this," Bren said. "He's usually pretty fastidious."

"But they probably have brooms," I pointed out. "This is broken glass."

Bren frowned, then shrugged and kept picking up shards. "I'll be careful."

We cleaned in silence for a while.

"I'm sorry I didn't tell you," Bren said awkwardly. "It didn't even occur to me that you didn't know. Everyone knows. It's one of the reasons Otto was so drawn to you. He feels just as abandoned."

I closed my eyes. "Do you really think they meant . . . to leave me there?"

Bren hesitated. "I didn't know them. The Dark Times were

so horrific, I could see someone keeping their child away from all that. Even if it was dangerous."

Twenty years in stass would have been dangerous, too. Not as bad as what I suffered after sixty-two, though. If I'd been released only twenty years after I was stassed, I would probably have been able to eat normally after two months. As opposed to now. "But . . . he said nine years. . . ."

"Yeah," Bren said, his tone soft. "Granddad says they were very careful to make sure no one knew, or cared, that you were staying young while they raised you. That's why I couldn't find your birth records. They did everything they could. Changing your schools. Erasing your image from the public record. Keeping you secluded, except for specific functions." He looked down. "Keeping you scared. Maybe they meant to come get you in the end, but . . ."

"Another nine years." I couldn't fathom it. "Was I really *that* awful?" I whispered.

Bren dropped another shard of glass into the bin. "No one can be that awful."

"I shouldn't have yelled at Mom," I said.

Bren skirted the broken glass and came to sit a little behind me. "I yell at my mom all the time," he said. "I get sent to my room. Somehow, I don't think stasis is an equivalent punishment."

"It wasn't a punishment!" I said, turning to him.

Bren's face was impassive. "Wasn't it?" He took my hand and helped me stand up. He led me back to the couch and sat down with me. His arm wrapped around my shoulders and held me securely. Spiders entered my flesh where he touched me, warm, delicate spiders, with many tingling legs.

"Don't," I said, trying to pull away.

"I can't be your friend?" Bren asked.

"You are, it's just . . . I haven't gotten over you yet, okay? It's distracting."

"Oh. Sorry." He let me go.

I gripped the sides of my head. "Oh, God, this is embarrassing!"

"What is?"

"You know all this *stuff* about me. It isn't fair. Tell me something."

"What?"

"Anything," I said. "Tell me something personal. I barely know you."

Bren gave a soft chuckle. "There's . . . not a lot personal to say," he said. "The most important aspect of my life is tennis . . . and I fully intend to give that up after high school. Tournaments, at least. I've never been in love, 'cause the whole idea kind of scares me. I've never spent more than two weeks outside ComUnity, and I'll probably end up coming back here after college, just 'cause there's nothing strong enough in me to keep me away." He sighed. "Kind of depressing, now you ask me about it. I tend to follow the path of least resistance. The most exciting things that have ever happened in my life have been in that subbasement."

I frowned at that statement. "You mean, *I'm* the most interesting thing that's ever happened to you?"

"Yup. But that really isn't surprising, Rose—you're the most interesting thing that's happened to humanity since they discovered life on Europa."

Echos of Otto again. It was like we were bound together.

"Even if you weren't Mark Fitzroy's daughter, finding someone in stasis after that long would be worldwide news. Being who you are . . ."

I sighed. "I knew I was a freak."

"You might be right," Bren's grandfather said, striding into the room. I thought at first he had been listening to me, but he went on. "Reggie has taken out a considerable sum of money from one of the company accounts recently. It wouldn't be enough to pay for a Plastine, but that doesn't mean he hasn't combined it with other funds. I'm still looking."

Bren stood up to get back to his cleaning. "You think you can trace it all, if he did it?"

"I hope so." Ron looked right at me. "Don't worry. It'll all be all right."

For some reason, I believed him.

Part of me wanted to go back to sleep again, and part of me didn't want to stay still. I looked over at Bren and considered getting up to help him clean, but something in his demeanor told me he wanted to think, and I'd get in the way.

I returned to my sketchbook. I'd finished my time-lapse sequence of Xavier and needed to start something new. I wasn't in the mood for one of my landscapes—too agitated. I didn't want to sketch Bren—too complicated. So I turned to sketch his grandfather instead.

Ron sat at his desk, having turned off the holo on his cell and inserted it in his ear, so he could have a more private conversation. "No, I understand that," he was saying. "I'm afraid, it is urgent. Very much so. . . . Well, I wouldn't want to have to tell that to the board. . . . I'd only do that if I had to. . . ." He sounded quietly intimidating. I was glad he was doing it *for* me, and not *to* me. I would never want to cross this man.

He was very easy to sketch. My charcoal flew down the lines of his nose, up over his cheekbones, along his jawline. His throat gave me some trouble. I hadn't had much opportunity to sketch older men, and I wasn't used to the folds of skin. Once I had the general line of him, I went back to concentrate on his brow, to make sure I had captured his eyes behind his glasses. He was very easy to draw.

Too easy.

I knew these lines. I looked again up at the old man who was leaning back in his chair with the easy practice of many decades at this desk. No way. I was just obsessed and seeing things.

I turned back to my sketchbook. I sketched out the line of him again—cheekbones, chin, jawline, nose—but ignored the folds of his skin, his glasses, the cut of his hair. I drew his eyes again.

It couldn't be. I had to be imagining it. I closed my eyes for a moment, then looked again.

I knew this face. I knew it very, very well.

Ice crept through my blood. There was a sickly taste of acid in my mouth, but for once I didn't feel nauseated. I simply sat there, staring mutely at the old, old man.

Bren's grandfather turned off his cell and stood up, turning toward the door. I bolted from the couch, scrambling to get there ahead of him. My movement startled Bren, who knocked over the trash can with a bang.

Bren's grandfather raised an eyebrow as I stood before him. "Yes?"

The words fell flatly from my mouth. "What's your excuse?"

A flash of nervousness passed over his face. "About what?" he asked.

I passed him the sketchbook. He frowned as he looked at the charcoal sketch I had done of him, and the other half-formed line drawing beside it. I reached forward and turned to the previous page so that he could see it.

It was the last image of my sequence of Xavier: Xavier at seventeen, his fond smile, his sparkling hazel-green eyes, the little goatee, the look of hesitant self-effacement, which always kept his arrogant streak from overpowering him.

The old man blinked at the drawing, his already sad eyes turning sadder. He flipped back another page, and there he was at fifteen, not yet grown into his nose, just a hint of downy fuzz touching his chin, his self-consciousness more pronounced. Back again to twelve, with the glimmer of mischief behind his eyes. He skipped a few pages, closing the book at the drawing of when he was three, a chubby-cheeked cherub with chocolate on his nose. "I'm surprised you remember," he said.

I stared at Xavier, my Xavier, grown into his seventies, skin sagging, yellow hair turned white, bright hazel eyes cloudy with age, a barely concealed tremor in his right hand. My Xavier. I wasn't sure if I wanted to laugh or cry. The dead, hollow feeling had returned. "It wasn't so long ago," I said.

Xavier smiled ruefully. "Yes, it was."

He was right. It had all been so long ago—in another life, when I was another girl. A chosen princess of UniCorp, champagne queen every time I opened my eyes, fashionable, sedate. A girl whose devoted parents would never abandon her to a slow death by stass fatigue, a girl who had a best friend who loved her and would always be there for her. I'd been trying to hold on to that life, to convince myself that I was still that girl, and I wasn't. I was someone new, lost and alone, a child out of time, a burden to Guillory and Bren and everyone else who only suffered because of my reappearance. A burden to *him*.

"You arranged for my studio," I said, all the mysteries falling gently into place. "And Desert Roads. And Bren . . ." My voice caught on the name, and I glanced at my Prince Charming. Bren stood, bewildered by our exchange, frowning, his hazel-green eyes narrowed in confusion.

I could see it, now that I let myself. I'd let the dark skin and the textured hair and the Eurasian eyes mask the line of his jaw, the shape of his nose, the color of his eyes. No wonder I had fallen for him like a rock off a cliff.

I turned back to Xavier. "'Call me Ron'?" I closed my

eyes. Ron. Ronald was his middle name; he had taken to using Ronny in school because of the kids teasing him about the *X* in Xavier. It wasn't surprising he used it for business. The tears were falling now, but no sobs wracked my chest. Water simply streamed unchecked from my eyes. "How could you?"

Xavier closed his eyes for a moment, then shook his head, his face a mask of sorrow. "I didn't know," he whispered.

The lameness of his excuse boiled the river of tears inside me. My hand came up and I slapped him hard across the cheek. He turned his head with the blow, pulling away so that he didn't feel the full force of it.

I was horrified the moment I'd done it. That was something I could have done, even justifiably, to my Xavier. But an old man deserved more respect from me. I didn't know what to say, how to feel, or whom to turn to. I did the only thing I could. Before Xavier even had time to turn his face back to me, I bolted.

I hadn't even run so fast from the Plastine. My footsteps echoed like thunder through the atrium. I heard someone shouting after me, but I didn't even pause. I stabbed the down button for the lift. It was still on the top floor, waiting for me. I jumped inside and pounded on the close door button. Through my tear-blurred vision I could see a dark form running down the atrium after me. Xavier couldn't possibly run so fast—that had to be Bren. I didn't wait for him.

The door closed and I rode the eighty floors down to the ground level. My hurried exit frightened the security guard, who leaped from his alcove, weapon raised. "What's the trouble?" he asked, only half-reassured at seeing it was only me.

"Just open the door." I was surprised I could get any coherent words out at all.

The security guard opened the door for me, and I fell out into the teal-blue light that lifts the darkness into morning. My limoskiff had moved in the night, and I didn't know how to call it. It always just knew when I got out of school. I panicked and started to run. I didn't know or care where, just anywhere.

"Rose!" I stumbled at the voice and fell onto the grass. I'd ended up in the decorative park garden, just to the left of the building. "Rose!" Bren caught up to me, panting. I was gasping like a fish, my muscles burning, my lungs bursting. Bren's endurance was far and away better than my slowly recuperating body's.

He caught my shoulders and forced me to face him. I didn't want to look at him. I didn't want to see my Xavier looking at me through those almond-shaped eyes. I gasped and wept, trying to find myself amid the torment. But I couldn't find any part of me that seemed to be working. I couldn't make myself get up again, couldn't make myself pull away. Too much of me had been stagnant too long.

"Rose, what is it? What is it?" He sounded so concerned, and his warm brown hands smoothed some of the tears from my cheeks. "Talk to me; you look like you've seen a ghost! What happened?"

I pulled my head away, furious with myself. Bren frowned a moment and then wrapped his arms around my shoulders, pulling me to him. I wished I wanted to pull away. But I didn't. I still wanted him—or someone, anyone—and I couldn't bear it. I let him hold me while I fought the tears. I pulled away as soon as I could force myself into composure. My lungs didn't seem to want to work, and I coughed a few times to try to clear them. "I'm sorry," I said when I could. "I'm sorry for all of it. I'm sorry I threw myself at you. I . . . didn't realize . . . why."

"What do you mean?" Bren asked.

Xavier hadn't explained it to him? No, I supposed he wouldn't have had time. I looked at Bren. Why hadn't he told me? Why hadn't he guessed? He must have pictures of his grandfather as a young man; why hadn't he connected those to my portraits of Xavier?

As if thinking of my sketches had conjured it, I spotted my sketchbook on the ground by Bren's knee. He must have brought it with him. Kind of him, really. I guess he'd noticed I never went anywhere without one. I pulled it from the grass and opened it to the telling page, comparing the old man with the young one. "How could you not know?"

Bren stared for a long moment at the sketches, and then, like his grandfather, he leafed through my age progression of Xavier. His mouth opened in astonishment. He turned back to the picture of Xavier at seventeen, smiling fondly. "I didn't know, because this boy is smiling," Bren said. "Granddad doesn't smile."

"But the name . . ."

"I always thought Granddad's name was Ronny. I mean, I

know, I guess I've seen Xavier before, it's in some records we've got, but it's not a name he uses anymore. I've seen it referenced maybe twice in my life." He turned back to the portrait again and exhaled through pursed lips, almost a whistle, as if trying to figure out what to say.

"I must have . . . seen him in you," I said quietly. "Made me act a little stupid, I guess."

"Not stupid," Bren said. "This is a situation I don't think human beings are genetically geared to handle. Sometimes I worry technology's screwing with us. It has definitely screwed with you." He reached forward and took my hand. "I'm sorry."

I pulled my hand away. This was aggravating. I'd been trying to get over how Bren made my guts twist and my heart race; now I felt a weird protectiveness toward him, like I had for Xavier when he was still a child. But he was still just as gorgeous as he had been from the beginning, and the two feelings blended and confused me, and I didn't know how I felt. It was all too much. I wondered if falling in love with my boyfriend's grandson officially put me above Otto on the weirdness scale.

"Did he send you after me?" I asked.

"No," Bren said. "I grabbed your sketchbook and on the way out the door asked him, 'Should I . . . ?' And he nodded. I don't think that quite counts as sending me."

"No," I said. I felt a little better about that.

He shook his head. "This is just weird. You could have been my *grandmother*."

"That was always true," I pointed out. But he was right. I could have been. Or the grandmother of someone very like him, anyway. But I wasn't. And I should have been. I *should* have been. My life had been stolen from me. I hadn't felt really together since I'd woken up from stass, but it had never seemed so final before.

I could see the lights of my limoskiff slowly inching up the road. It must have had a proximity monitor. I frowned at it, but was distracted. "Holy coit," said Bren. Something had just occurred to him.

"What?"

"Mom's name is Roseanna," Bren said. "Rose. Like you."

As he said that my heart twisted. I surged to my feet. "If he cared so burning much for me, why the coit did he leave me to rot!" I shouted. I pelted for my limoskiff and closed the door before Bren could collect his wits. His hand thudded on the window, but I'd already told the skiff to go. I left him behind me in the slowly growing light. I frankly didn't care if the Plastine caught me anymore. But I didn't know where I was going. I really had nowhere to go.

—chapter 22—

The skiff circled ComUnity seven times in the pale rosy dawn.
I couldn't think. I tried to sleep but just got hit with dreams:
dreams of Bren turning into Xavier, Xavier turning into
Guillory. I wanted to go get my dog, but I was afraid to go home.
I wasn't afraid of the Plastine—death sounded like a joyride just
then—I was afraid of all the things that had been part of Xavier.
I could see it now. His taste was all over the walls. The paintings,
the landscapes, which looked a little like mine. The re-creation
of my bedroom. My studio. The prism. I closed my eyes.

Why had he bought my parents' condo? Was he really trying to hold on to me? Why couldn't he have looked in the
subbasement? Why didn't he spend every moment of his life
scouring the world for my tube? And if he wasn't going to do
that, why couldn't he just forget me? Why did he have to be
this half-haunting presence now?

I had lost my parents, I'd lost my time, and now I'd even lost my dream of my perished lover. All my grief for his death surged backward through me, undigested. It hurt worse than swallowing it had.

I didn't want the sun to rise. I didn't want the world to continue turning. I wanted the whole planet put into stasis until I could catch up.

A familiar beep sounded from near the dashboard of the limoskiff. *Ding, ding . . . ding, ding . . . ding, ding . . .*

I shook myself and crawled to the shadowed corner where the sound had come from. It was my notescreen. How had that gotten there? Then I realized I was the one who had left it in the skiff when I'd fled from school the day after I'd made my offer to Bren.

Ding, ding . . . ding, ding . . . I picked it up and opened the screen.

A page was already linked through the net. I pulled it up.

Rose. Rose, burn it, write back, already! Rose, if you've gone back into stasis, I'm searching the world over to wake you up again! Answer me!

I quickly pulled up a keypad, even as Otto continued, Come on! Where are you? Please, don't let that thing be after you again!

I'm here, I wrote, stepping on his notes. Still here, unfortunately.

Thank every god ever invented. Where are you?

Nowhere, I answered truthfully. I didn't know where I was, and it didn't matter.

No, really. Where are you?

I honestly don't know, I told him. Just skimming around ComUnity.

I was worried about you. You weren't answering your screen yesterday.

I forgot it.

I saw Bren in the quad just now and asked if he knew what had happened to you. He's worried about you. Can I tell him where you are?

No. You can tell him I'm okay, if you must.

Good. He went home and checked your tube after you ran off. When you weren't there, he got scared. His parents made him come to school, but he can't concentrate.

I'm afraid I don't care much, I wrote.

Hold on — Mr. Prokiov is on me about linking up during class. I'll be right back.

There was a long, long time when the screen went still. I curled up onto the skiff's seats and tried to force sanity back into my head. I couldn't.

My screen dinged again. There, I'm in the quad. Bren told me what happened this morning.

There was really only one thing I could say to that. Coit. Then I asked, How much?

You can tell a long story really fast in your mind, he wrote.

Coit, I wrote again. Could I ask you to employ your code of ethics and not share this story around? Like, not with Nabiki, not even your family? I actually cared what they thought of me, and this was too weird probably even for them.

I swear on 42's grave.

I was touched. Thanks.

Nabiki and I broke up, he wrote.

I wasn't sure why he was telling me this. What? Why?

Well. You remember that fiercely protective thing she had for me?

Yes.

Well. When you told me someone was trying to assassinate you, I kind of had the same feeling. I've spent the last few days hacking through the net, trying to find out anything and everything that might help. Nabiki didn't like it, said I wasn't getting enough sleep. She said you had plenty of people looking out for you, and you didn't need me. I nearly . . . well, it was only a thought, but she was touching me at the time. I wanted to hit her. I'm a bit of a pacifist, and I don't think that kind of thing very often, not even about guys who beat me up — and, yes, that has happened. Nabiki said that if I was thinking like that, then maybe I didn't need her anymore. She was right.

If Otto's compliments were as intense as he said they were, I hated to think what his anger was like. No. Go back to her, I wrote. Tell her you're sorry. I don't want to ruin anyone's relationships.

You haven't. One of the convenient things about my form of communication is that I can quickly convey and assimilate everything someone is feeling. What Nabiki loved was being needed. Now I'm the one who . . . Look, let me come to you. I was touched. Not that Otto could do much to protect me from a Plastine. You need family. Where are you?

I really don't know.

Tell your skiff to come to the school. We can talk in the dorms.

We're talking now.

No, we're not.

It took me a long time to understand what he meant. You don't want to be in my head right now, I wrote to him.

Maybe, Otto wrote back.

Otto, even I don't want to be in my head right now.

Maybe not, he wrote. **But you can't be alone. Someone's trying to assassinate you, Rose!**

I sighed. Okay, I wrote back. But I don't know how far I am.

I'll be waiting.

The link disconnected, and I told my skiff to head for Uni Prep. It turned, the machinery giving the more satisfied hum it had when there was a definite destination in its processors.

It took my skiff about an hour to reach the school. The ever-widening circles around ComUnity had taken me pretty far out of the way. The skiff stopped just outside the quad, but I told it to circle around the school to the dorms. I wondered how I was supposed to find him, but Otto was waiting on a bench under a tree, just outside the boys' dorm. As soon as he spotted the skiff, my notescreen dinged. **Right here,** he wrote. **I said I'd be waiting.**

I opened the door to my skiff and climbed out. I was able to construct a smile of greeting, but it was as forced as his own usually were. It fell apart almost instantly.

Otto jumped forward and put his hand on the small of my back, guiding me toward the school without touching my skin. It felt very different having him *here,* beside me. I'd almost turned the Otto I saw at school and the Otto I spoke to on my screen into two different people. I barely knew this Otto. I didn't know what to say. We walked in utter silence.

Otto watched me through his yellow eyes. He forced a smile and then held open the door to the dorms for me. I took a deep breath before I went inside. There was a brief hum as the security system registered our presence.

TARGET IDENTIFIED: RETINAL MATCH CONFIRMED, ROSALINDA SAMANTHA FITZROY. LOCATION KNOWN.

The target had not been at the last known coordinates, in the UniCorp Building, and he had resigned himself to returning to his station. He hadn't made it there yet when the information filtered to him through the net. He entered the new location into the hover yacht controls. Slowly, it turned toward UniCorp Preparatory School.

Otto led me to a kind of visitors' lounge. It was bright and impersonal, and it reminded me of my parents' style of decorating. I still felt awkward. "I really don't know what to say."

Otto shook his head telling me not to worry. He reached out a hand toward mine.

"No," I said, pulling away. I touched my forehead to hide my eyes. "Otto, you really don't want to know."

There was a long moment of stillness, and then my notescreen dinged. I looked up. Otto had moved across the room and was sitting in a chair facing away from me. I swallowed and looked down at my screen. **How are you feeling?**

I sat down, relieved. I'm okay, I wrote.

You don't look okay.

I haven't slept, I wrote. I ran for the third time from an indestructible assassin, worked my way back from the Unicorn Islands with only a sketchbook to my name, discovered that my parents had intentionally abandoned me for at least twenty-nine years in stasis, and then realized I'd fallen in love with my old boyfriend's grandson. I put down my screen and looked up at him. "My extremely old boyfriend, I might add," I said aloud. I sighed and buried my head in my hands.

I heard Otto shift, and then my screen dinged again. I uncovered my eyes. Otto had turned to face me, but he was looking at his screen. That's what's really bothering you, isn't it, he had written. This Xavier of yours.

"Sort of," I admitted.

That's what made you run away.

"God, Bren really told you everything, didn't he."

He recognized my concern as real.

I shook my head, relieved that for once he could see it. "Why?" I asked. "What do you see in me?"

He looked up from his notescreen, and his eyes searched mine for a moment. I could try to show you, if you'd like, he wrote, turning back to his screen. I'm not used to having to find words for this kind of thing. It isn't anything so simple that I can encapsulate it in a glib phrase. He paused before he wrote again. Or even in a heartfelt, serious phrase.

I didn't know what to say to any of that. He was right. Some feelings just didn't turn into language very easily. I thought I could paint a picture that would have the same impact, but even that wouldn't have exactly the same meaning. As I watched him, he started writing again.

Why do you keep talking to me? Maybe the answer is there.

I shook my head. "I don't know," I said. "You're interesting and different and anyone would be curious."

If you were just curious, you would have taken me up on my offer and looked up the medical records, he wrote. He wrote much faster than I ever did, but I supposed he had more practice. *That's what most people do. Much of my life is public record, down in a dozen science mags on the net. Not to mention all the UniCorp files, which I know you could access. You looked to me, not those.*

"True," I whispered. "I feel . . . I meant it when I said I'd be your family. I feel like I already am."

You don't have any other family.

"I did once. They loved me."

Otto looked up from his screen without writing another word. I could read it in his eyes, though. Yellow. Inhuman. His very DNA tattered and stitched together to form an alien monster, without a home, without a family, without a species. *Did they love you?* his eyes said. *Did they really? Or did they love you the way UniCorp loved me?*

"Why did you try for the scholarship?" I asked him, ignoring the unspoken question.

His eyes narrowed, perplexed. I supposed it did seem incongruous. He turned back to his screen. *To win my freedom.* He hesitated, then asked, *Why?*

"I won a scholarship once." The words were painful to say. "To the Hiroko Academy of Art, sixty-two years ago."

Why didn't you go?

"I went into stasis instead."

Is that what you wanted to do?

That was the question I'd been avoiding asking myself ever since I'd gotten out of stass. The answer made me feel ill. "Yes," I whispered.

Why?

I stood up, dropping my own screen. "Why do you keep asking why?" I demanded.

Otto glared at me, and his hands moved in an intricate pattern I couldn't read.

"What?"

He made an irritated dolphinlike noise and picked up his screen. He thrust it into my hands. **Because I care!** it read.

I hung my head. "Why?"

He moved his hands again. I didn't know the language, but it was beautiful. He did the same series of gestures again. He held his palm out to me, then pointed his two index fingers sharply together, patted the back of his left hand, and then held his hand against his heart. And I understood it, without a word. *Your pain touches my own.*

But our pain was so different. His was forced upon him. Mine I had embraced by choice. "I hurt Xavier," I whispered. "I broke his heart. I used everything I knew about him, turned his love for me into a weapon, to make him go. That's why I wanted to go into stass. That's why I got forgotten. That's why I didn't deserve to wake up, ever!"

Otto put his hand over his heart and held out his other hand. I could read the meaning in his eyes. *Please.*

I hesitated, then whispered, "I'm sorry." His face fell—not as expressionless as I'd thought, now that we were so close. But he'd misunderstood me. I was apologizing for what my mind was about to force upon him. The tangled briar of my own blame.

My hand reached for his.

—chapter 23—

It was sixty-two years, eight months, and twelve days earlier that my life had started on the path that led to this horror. It began as good news. I was leaving my art class when Mr. Sommers stopped me. "Could I speak to you for a moment, Rose?" he asked.

I swallowed, afraid I'd done something wrong again. You'd have thought that art would be the one subject in which I would have no troubles. No such luck. In my academic classes, my teachers regarded me with a quiet despair. In my art classes, I frequently had teachers who regarded me with either rank envy or open hostility. The hostility usually resulted from my constant presence in their classroom—early morning to late evening, and sometimes my lunch period—and the fact that I used ten times as many art supplies as any other student they'd ever had. I was pretty sure I was about to get another lecture about wasting the school's resources.

"Rose, I need to talk with you about something," Mr. Sommers began.

"I'm sorry," I said automatically.

Mr. Sommers raised an eyebrow. "What for?"

"For whatever I did," I said. "I'm sorry."

Mr. Sommers smiled then. "This isn't anything bad." I looked up at him in surprise. "You remember those extra-credit paintings you brought in for me?"

"Yes," I said. This school had a small art gallery, and they tried to hang some of the students' artwork, along with local professional artists' work. Three months ago, Mr. Sommers had offered extra credit to anyone who wanted to bring in a piece they had done outside of class, for possible display in the gallery. I'd brought in half a dozen oil paintings. None of them had been hung in the gallery, but I didn't mind. I got the extra credit whether they were chosen for display or not.

"I was very impressed by your skill," Mr. Sommers said. "So impressed that I collected some of the assignments you've done for me, along with those paintings, and shipped them to a friend of mine who is on the awards committee for the Young Masters Program for Artistic Excellence. Have you heard of them?"

I had. For the last ten years, they had been the premier world venue for serious art students. I'd known about them since I entered middle school . . . which, admittedly, was several years ago. "Did he like them?" I asked, more curious than hopeful. If his friend thought that I had the potential to enter the Young Masters Program in two or three years' time, I was well pleased.

"He liked them well enough that he sent me a message today, informing me that one of your paintings has been selected as one of the two winners of the painting category."

I gasped. "What?" That was impossible! Senior apprentices to famous artists entered the Young Masters Program. College art majors. Already established artists under twenty-one. For a high-school student to have won one of the categories was virtually unheard-of. "W-which painting?"

"The one you labeled *Undersky.*"

I nearly sobbed with happiness. It was the painting I'd felt sure I'd never get a chance to finish, the one with the tortured mountains and the undersky plant life.

"The awards ceremony is held in New York every year, and you've already won transportation to and from it for you and a family member. Winning one of the categories is an immense honor." I didn't need him to tell me that, but he went on. "This makes you one of ten individuals who might win the Young Masters Award. The portfolio I collected for you will be compared with the winners of the other four categories, and we'll find out at the awards ceremony whether you've earned the title of this year's Young Master. If you have, you'll be awarded a free place in the Young Masters Summer Art Tour through Europe, plus a full scholarship to the Hiroko Academy of Art once you've finished high school."

I had never thought about needing money before in my life. My parents were disgustingly wealthy. But I realized as he said it that my parents' money belonged to them. If I were to go to a college, it would be one they selected for me. If

I were to go on a tour of Europe, they were the ones who would have to send me. Since they had never allowed me to leave ComUnity without them, except to go to school, I was pretty sure they never would.

If I were to win the Young Masters Award, I'd be . . .

Free of them?

That was an odd thought. But that was what passed through my head. I'd be free.

And it all came crashing down the next second. "Since you are underage, I'll have to have your parents' consent for you to go to the awards ceremony. Can you arrange that?"

I faltered for a moment. "I . . . I wouldn't know what to say to them."

Mr. Sommers nodded. "Understandable. I'll call them this evening and discuss this opportunity with them." He smiled. "You should be very proud of yourself, young lady. This is an honor not many can achieve."

"I don't know how to thank you, sir," I said. I'd never noticed Mr. Sommers taking any particular interest in me. But now that I thought about it, this was the first time I'd had the same art teacher for more than six months. I'd always switched schools and missed months so often that I was never able to establish a rapport with any of them.

"You just keep up the good work, Rose. I'll see you tomorrow, and we'll make the arrangements for the trip."

I went home with a copy of the awards announcement gripped in my hand. When I got through the door, I ran to Åsa and told her all about it.

"Ah, *flicka*," she said. "I knew you would do well." She wasn't one for words or kisses, but she started making cookies. Since we usually ordered our food delivered from the Unicorn servants in the central kitchens, this was a serious gesture.

When I told Xavier, he scooped me up in his arms with a whoop. He read the announcement aloud to the trees and flowers, and he made me pretend to go up and accept my award. He played master of ceremonies, and when I accepted, he presented me with an early rose from the garden. "A rose for my Rose," he said, and kissed me sweetly. "I'm so happy for you."

When I got back inside, I was surprised that my parents were already home. Mom poured me a glass of champagne. "Mr. Sommers told me all about it," Mom said the moment I came in the door. "Well done, Rosalinda!"

"Good girl," Daddy said, but he barely looked up from his files. I was used to that, though.

"You're happy?" I asked, surprised. I didn't know why I'd half thought my parents wouldn't be happy. They always approved of me spending my time with, as Daddy put it, my little paint set. They loved me and wanted what was best for me. Of course they were pleased! I grinned broadly.

"It's a wonderful achievement," Mom told me. "I'm very proud of you. Don't you worry about anything, either. I've already taken care of it with your art teacher. I told him you couldn't accept."

My smile died on my face. "What?"

"I took care of it for you. Don't worry."

"What . . . are you talking about? Why couldn't I accept?"

"Well, honey, your art teacher told me you had to accept this award thing in person," Mom said. "You know full well we'll be in Australia that month."

I was flabbergasted. "But . . . but I have to accept. This is the Young Masters Program!" The vacant, inattentive look on Mom's face worried me. She wasn't hearing me. My voice got louder, screechingly strident. "They have art students from all over the planet! I was competing against college students! Mom!"

"Don't you raise your voice to your mother," Daddy said, turning away from his files. This was dangerous ground. To dare distract Daddy from his work . . .

But for once, I didn't even care about Daddy's disapproval. "You don't understand! This is the most prestigious award there is for youth artwork! This is worldwide recognition! I could start selling pieces this year even."

"You're not even sixteen yet, Rose," Mom said. This wasn't true, but she didn't know that. "I don't think that kind of publicity would be good for you at this stage of your life."

"I wouldn't *be* fifteen if you didn't keep locking me up in stasis!" I yelled. I had no idea where that came from.

Mom actually stood up from her chair. She never stood up when she spoke to me. "Don't you dare *ever* raise your voice to me, young lady!" she said in a low, threatening tone.

"Please!" I said, really crying. I was desperate now. "Please, don't take this away from me!"

Mom's face was pinched and she looked over at Daddy. "Do you think she's overstressing?" Mom asked.

No. She wasn't. . . . She was. I could see it in her face. For a moment I just closed my eyes, bowing to the inevitable.

Mr. Sommers's voice echoed in my head. *A full scholarship to the Hiroko Academy of Art.*

"No," I said, banishing my tears, trying to keep my voice calm. I straightened my shoulders, pretended to be adult. "I'm not overstimulated. It is only that this is very important to me."

Daddy frowned. "So important that you have to be rude to your mother, defy your father?" he asked. "We love you. We only want what's best for you. Tell me that you know that, Rose."

I didn't know where the hesitation came from. I knew the answer. It was rote. "I know that, sir," I said, finally finding the words in the torrent of my thoughts.

"You know *what?*" he persisted.

"I know you only want what's best for me, sir," I whispered.

"Good," Daddy said. He sighed. "I think you *are* over-stressing on this, though. Jackie, why don't you tuck her in, calm her down, and you and I will discuss it."

"Good idea. Come along, Rose."

I sighed. I hated it when they did this. They weren't even gone and I was still losing precious hours with Xavier. There would be no gourmet dinner tonight. "How long?" I asked as Mom tucked me into my stass tube.

"Only a day or two, honey," Mom said. "We just need to discuss this. You should keep calm."

"Okay," I said. I lay down quietly and let stass take away all the disappointment. I was fairly sure what they'd decide.

I was not surprised when I opened my eyes and found Åsa

standing over me. Mom and Daddy had left without saying good-bye. It was easier than futilely arguing with them, I supposed. And they couldn't know that Åsa kept letting me out. "Thanks," I said. "How long was I out?"

Åsa's mouth was pursed as she said, "Two weeks. They left last night for Australia."

I nodded. I wasn't surprised. It wasn't the first time they'd simply kept me in stasis until a controversial event was over. A birthday party they didn't want me going to or a school field trip they didn't think I should attend. I was sure they'd planned on simply leaving me in stasis until the Young Masters awards ceremony was over and done with. It was usually something I just accepted.

Not this time.

"Where's Xavier?" I asked.

"At school," Åsa said. "I always wait a few hours after they go, in case they forget something and pop back. It's a good thing I do; they'd have caught us a couple of times."

I smiled, but it was without humor. "That's okay. I should eat something before I talk with him, anyway."

Åsa seemed to catch that there was something more in my tone than wanting to see my boyfriend. "What do you need from Master Xavier?" she asked.

I put my hand on the smooth metal and NeoGlass of my stass tube. "I need the boy who knows how to hack my stass chamber," I said. "I need a boy who can hack my parents' consent for the Young Masters Program."

· · ·

I'd wanted to bring Xavier as my companion to New York, but I couldn't. Through various hacked documents sent over the net, Xavier managed to convince Mr. Sommers that my parents wanted *him* to travel with me to the awards ceremony. Mr. Sommers was thrilled, since he had been planning on trying to go, anyway, and such a trip was no mean feat on a teacher's salary.

It was the cherry on top of the perfect year. I shared a hotel suite with three of the other Masters winners: a college student from the Oriana School of Art; a conceptual computer artist who had grown up on Luna; and Céline, whose presence astounded me. Céline was apprentice to André Lefèvre, a sculptor whose work I had admired since I was six. We discussed art until the wee hours of the morning, and the next day we all took a tour of the New York Metropolitan Museum of Art. I could have stayed there for a year, but when the doors closed, we went back to the hotel and were taken by limousine to the awards banquet. After we ate, all ten of us winners trooped up on stage, and we each received a golden plaque with our name and category and the title of the winning piece below it. ROSALINDA FITZROY, mine read. *UNDERSKY,* OIL ON CANVAS. Then they sat us down as the master of ceremonies patted various employees and volunteers on the back. We were all waiting to see who would win the Masters.

I was hoping Céline would win. Despite her native language being French and our mediums being vastly different, she and I had similar tastes and the same happily sinister feel to our artwork. Besides, she was apprentice to a truly brilliant artist.

So when the name was announced, I was disappointed. I turned to tell Céline I was so sorry for her, when I realized that the name I'd heard that wasn't Céline's had in fact been my own.

I turned my head to the podium and stared at the master of ceremonies, completely unable to move. It took all my roommates pushing me on the back to get me to rise out of my chair.

I was handed the award, a golden pedestal holding a huge round prism, inside of which was the symbol of the medium I'd specialized in — in this case, a paintbrush. The footlights caught in the prism, sending rainbows of light into my eyes.

I was supposed to have had a speech prepared. Céline did. Rachel did. But I had nothing to say. "I've waited for this . . . all my life," I whispered to the microphone, and then the tears poured down my face, and I clutched the award to my chest. Applause roared through the room, and everyone knew that even if I'd had a speech prepared, I couldn't possibly have delivered it. A slide show of my portfolio began to play on a screen above the stage, with a deep cello concerto as the background. When I staggered back to my seat, Céline told me, in her sensuously halting English, that the "elegant and sophisticated speeches" she and the others had written "paled beneath the eloquent purity" of my tears — though I think she was just trying to make me feel better for being utterly unprepared.

When Mr. Sommers and I flew back to the city, Xavier waited for me with his parents' electric car. Mr. Sommers went home, and I climbed in with Xavier.

"I'm so happy for you, I can't begin to tell you," he said as he drove me back to ComUnity.

"I still can't believe it really happened," I said. "I'm only sixteen. That's never happened before. Not in the history of the award."

"Well, you've had more years of experience than any of those others," Xavier said with a laugh. "It was unfair competition."

"Stop it," I said. "I am only sixteen."

"And a brilliant artist," Xavier said.

"I'm not," I said. "I cheat. I won the award for a stass dream. It's all stass dreams. They're what give me the colors."

Xavier looked at me for so long I was afraid he'd run us off the road, but I didn't say anything. "You use the experiences of your life," he said finally. He looked back to the road. "The others did the same, I'm sure."

This was true. The intricate patterns of asteroid collision permeated Rachel's computer pieces, and the circus performers and dancers that André used for his models also influenced Céline. I knew he was right. "I still feel like I'm cheating," I said.

"The stass dreams are dreams," Xavier said. "They come from your head, not the stass tube."

I looked down at the award in my hands. "I still can't believe it's real."

As we stepped into the lift, I handed Xavier the award. "Would you keep it for me?"

Xavier stared from the award back to me. "I couldn't," he said. "You earned it."

"And if my parents see it, what do you think will happen then?" I asked. "Give it back to me in college, when I take that scholarship."

Xavier grinned. "Deal."

He kissed me so long and hard that I began to wonder if the lift was plummeting to the depths. (In actuality, it had stopped and opened its doors, waiting patiently for us to be finished with our business and actually get off at our floor.)

"I love you," I said.

"I love you," Xavier said. "I'm so proud of you." He kissed me on the end of my nose. "I'll see you tomorrow."

We went our separate ways, and I opened the door to my condo and swung myself inside. "Hey, Åsa! I'm back!"

Åsa did not call out with her brusque Swedish, *"Ja!"* so I followed the hall and poked my head into the living room. "Åsa?"

A jolt of cold ran up my spine, leaving the taste of iron in my mouth.

"Åsa isn't here," Mom said, glaring at me.

I licked my lips. Mom and Daddy sat side by side on the living-room sofa, waiting for me. "I . . . I can explain," I said.

"You had better," Mom said. "We came home early, specifically to take you to this . . . thing you so wanted to go to. And what do we find? You're gone. Tube empty. We nearly phoned the police. Do you know what that would have done to your father's standing in the community? Our daughter, kidnapped? Or worse, a runaway ingrate."

"I'm sorry, Mom, it's just—"

"You had better be sorry," Daddy said. "Once we found

out that you weren't waiting for us, we spoke to Åsa. She confessed that she's been taking you out of stasis. No, I thought. Our daughter wouldn't do such a thing. She wouldn't dare lie to my face." Daddy stood up so that his full height bore down on me. "Or *so I thought*."

I shivered, and my stomach dropped. "I'm sorry, Daddy," I whispered.

Mom stood up then and joined him at his side. "She tells us you have a boyfriend. You aren't old enough for a boyfriend."

"Mom, I'm sixteen," I whispered.

Daddy exploded then. I'd never seen him really angry, not that I remembered. It was fear of that anger simmering beneath the surface that always kept me from defying him. "You deceitful little bitch! It's a damned good thing we're here for you, do you know that? Do you know what would have happened to you if you'd been anyone else's daughter? You'd have been diagnosed as crazy! They'd have left you in the streets! You aren't worth anyone's time, let alone ours! You're worthless! A feebleminded, duplicitous, backstabbing little maggot who isn't worthy to lick our feet!"

"I'll handle this, Mark," Mom said, her eyes tight.

"You get that child to behave, or you'll never see her again!" Daddy yelled at her.

"Don't worry, dear," Mom said. "Rose and I can talk this through. She knows what's best."

I swallowed. I suddenly feared Mom's calm more than Daddy's fury.

Two hours later, I went to bed, shaky, exhausted, with my

face stinging from the tears. But Mom was right, just like she'd told me, again and again and again. I knew what was best.

I waited all day in the garden. I could have gone to Xavier's door, knocked, told his parents I wanted to see him. They knew full well what we were to each other, and it had never bothered them.

But I didn't want to pull him from his happiness. I felt like the longer I waited for him, the longer his world would stay complete. I felt like Ophelia. *My lord, I have remembrances of yours that I have longed long to redeliver. . . .* Her confused, clumsy return of Hamlet's gifts and letters, all the time knowing that her father waited behind the arras. Mom and Daddy were nowhere to be seen, and I knew they weren't listening. And yet I knew what I had to do. I wondered if I'd drown myself, wrapped in flowers, in the garden pond after it was over. I wondered if it would even matter.

He saw me the moment he came into the garden. His grin was so broad and happy my heart twisted. I was going to ruin everything for him. But I knew what was best.

He wrapped me in his arms, and I longed to return his embrace. But I didn't. I stood there like a post of wood.

Xavier pulled away and looked down at me, kissing my forehead. "Still in shock from yesterday?"

I took a deep breath. "I . . . I got to know the other artists pretty well while I was over there." I knew this was the only tack I could take. This was the only aspect of my life he had not been present for. "We shared a suite."

"So you said," Xavier said, still smiling. "Did you learn some new techniques?"

"No," I said. "Well, yes, but . . . but mostly I learned about life. They're all lots older than I am."

He tousled my hair. "Must have made quite a pet out of you."

I pulled away. "Stop it."

He finally realized something was really wrong. "Rose? What is it? What's the matter?"

"This," I said. I couldn't prolong it. I had to get it over with quickly. Like slitting my own wrists — if I tried to do it slowly, I'd never get it done. "This isn't working for me anymore."

Xavier's brow furrowed. "What isn't?"

"This," I said, indicating the space between us. "I mean, we're not . . . really the *same*."

Xavier raised an eyebrow. "I should hope not. It would be awfully hard to kiss you if we were."

"I'm serious," I snapped.

Xavier realized that I was. "Come on, what's wrong?"

"Nothing's wrong," I said. "I just can't do this anymore."

"Do what?"

"Be with you," I said.

Xavier froze for a moment. "Why not?" he asked finally.

"It's just . . . I can't."

"No," Xavier said, angry now. "No 'just.' You tell me what is going on."

I'd known it would come to this when I came out the door. I knew that telling him I didn't love him wouldn't work.

He'd know my saying I loved someone else was impossible. I couldn't tell him that my parents disapproved, because then he'd just find a way to see me despite them. Or he'd expect me to disobey them, and I simply couldn't do that. And I couldn't bear to see the hurt in his eyes when he saw, again and again, that I chose them over him. So I did the only thing I could: I told the truth, in the harshest, most dishonest way possible.

"It's too weird, Xavier," I said. "I mean, I . . . I grew up with you. I changed your diapers, for God's sake! It's like . . . like we're brother and sister, or . . . or . . ." I couldn't follow that thought, so I let it go.

"You didn't think it was too weird last night. What's happened between now and then?"

"Nothing!" I said probably too quickly. "Last night I was just so . . . happy and tired; I didn't want to try to change anything. But I knew even then . . ." I was afraid he'd catch the lie in my voice, so I jumped back in. "I've always been so much older than you, tried to look out for you. I mean, you confided to me about your first crush!"

"No, I didn't," he said. "My second, third, yeah. But my first crush was you."

"You see?" I said, leaping on that. "This can't possibly be real. This is . . . this is some kind of adolescent wish fulfillment. It can't be good for either of us."

"Rose, what are you saying?"

I couldn't look at his face. I didn't want to see the stricken look I knew was etched there. But I could hear the strain in his voice, the barely concealed panic. I hoped my own voice wasn't so easy to read. "I'm saying we can't be together anymore," I said. "I'm saying this isn't right."

"Not . . . right?"

I knew what he was thinking. This was the most right thing in the entire world. When the two of us were together, the universe seemed to right itself.

"No." I hoped he couldn't hear me choke on that word. I took a deep breath. I had to get out of there. I couldn't take this one second longer. "Good-bye, Xavier," I whispered. I took a step across the lawn.

The door had never seemed so far away. One step. Two. Three. Four. I got as far as six before Xavier grabbed me from behind, turned me to face him. "No!" He gripped my shoulders and shook me. "No! I don't accept that! Who cares what the world thinks is right or not? We aren't freaks of nature! You and me, this can't be hurting anyone! How could anyone say what we're doing is wrong? We *aren't* brother and sister—we aren't even different ages! It's not your fault it took you this long to grow up!"

"Yes, it is," I whispered.

"Shut up!" he yelled. "Stop doing this to yourself. Stop blaming yourself! I hate those vampires you live with. I hate them! They've sucked you dry of every sense of self-worth and normality! You won't find *anyone* else who understands you but me! There'll be no one, do you understand me? *No one!*"

Now that he had lost his temper, I could use it against him. I hated myself for doing it, but I threw it all back in his face.

"Now who's the one telling me I'm worthless?" I snapped. "I can do anything I want, win anyone I want. Whereas you, you're still stuck in a twelve-year-old's calf love. Grow up! Get over me! I'm worth ten of you!" I pushed him away, and despite the strength in his hands, he actually let me go.

I bolted, running for the door as if the hounds of hell were at my heels. The hounds of hell were already inside me, ravaging my heart, and I could feel their teeth tearing through my chest.

I had to wrestle with the door, as I could barely keep my balance. And in the brief moment of silence before I got the door open, I felt Xavier behind me. "Wait," he said.

"No." I already knew I couldn't take it.

He turned me slowly to look at him. I didn't want to see that face. The heartbreak there was agony to me. "Please, Rose," he whispered. He bent his head to mine and we melted together in one last kiss.

I could taste the pain in him, the fierce, desperate agony that was tearing him apart. I couldn't hold on to myself any longer. I was emptied, and all of me that meant anything flowed through me, fled from me, escaping as if from a burning building, into the sanctuary of this kiss. With one dark, anguished kiss, Xavier took my soul for me, holding it safe. A short eternity hung between us when he had to let it go. His nose touched mine. I could still feel his breath on my lips, as if he couldn't bear to really pull away. I couldn't open my eyes when he left me. I didn't want to see his face again. "Know that I love you, always," was all he said.

I wanted to say it back, but the door behind me opened

under my hand, and I fell through it into utter blackness. I found my way back to the condo in a blind daze of tears. Mom and Daddy had already gone for the day, and Åsa was never coming back. I groped my way into my bed and stayed there as still as if I'd been stassed.

"Mommy, put me in stasis," I whimpered when she came home.

"No, dear," she said, wiping the tears from my face. They'd been coming so long and so hard that they no longer tasted of salt. She gave me a big hug. "You did the right thing, honey. I'm very proud of you."

I didn't know what to say. When Xavier had said that about my artwork, I thanked him. When Mom said it about this, I wanted to die. "Please," I begged. "I don't want to feel like this anymore."

Mom frowned at me, then finally said, "For a day, if you'd like. But you've done the right thing, and I'm not going to let you run away from it."

Things felt better as the stass chemicals washed away the horror of Xavier's anguished face and the torture of my lost soul. But when Mom got me up and forced me to go to school the next day, it all came back, as bad as it had been before—probably worse, with the enhanced memory the stass had left me with.

The next month was nothing but wave upon wave of torment. I would see him, sometimes, in the halls of the condo, and turn away so he wouldn't come up to me. But in the afternoon, when we used to walk in the gardens together, I would go to the window and watch him there, as he wandered the paths alone. He looked so lost. My heart went out to him, as it had when he was five and had lost his stuffed rabbit. When he was seven and had fallen from his bike. When he was thirteen and admitted to having had his heart broken by the girl I had *thought* was his first crush. When the desire to run out to him and apologize got too great, I'd run to Mom instead, and I'd beg her to stass me, if only for a couple of days.

And she complied.

"Until she never woke me up again," I whispered.

—chapter 24—

All of this had poured into Otto's mind. It hadn't taken more than five minutes. Somewhere during the torrent of self-blame, Otto had let go of my hand to wrap his arms around my shoulders instead, his cheek pressed against mine. He was warm and still and his breath was heavy in my ear.

I was surprised that I wasn't getting any thoughts from Otto. I could almost feel something in the corner of my mind, an unfinished thought, quietly not touching anything. I pulled away a bit, but Otto's hand was still around my wrist. "Why aren't you throwing all the platitudes at me: it wasn't your fault, you couldn't have known, your parents forced this on you, no one deserves a slow death through stasis no matter what they've done, all of that?"

Otto's eyes crinkled a bit, and I realized this was his genuine smile — not the forced one he'd cultivated for society. *"You just said it all yourself,"* I thought in someone else's voice.

"I don't believe it."

"Yes, you do," Otto told me, in thoughts that were more than words. *"You've always believed it. You've just hated yourself too much to admit it."*

Otto really didn't lie. I could *feel* how much he meant what he said. He had felt how much I had buried beneath my self-loathing. I would have seen it myself, one day, but with Otto's help, it all came to the surface much faster.

My parents had always been wrong. And they'd molded me in such a way as to force me to believe that they were right. It wasn't Xavier they disapproved of; it was anyone knowing what they'd done to me. That was why I'd tried to protect Guillory by not voicing my suspicions. I was used to it. I'd been protecting Mom and Daddy from everyone, keeping secret every nasty thing they said to me, every demeaning thought they'd forced into my head, every term in stasis when they put me away so they didn't have to deal with their daughter.

When I'd won the Young Masters Award, they'd panicked. I had freedom, just like Otto did when he won his scholarship. They wouldn't have their perfect, brainwashed daughter anymore. So they had to take it from me in a way that made it seem as if I'd rejected it. They made me give up Xavier, so that they could lock me away without him telling anyone.

I wondered if they'd ever planned on waking me up. Maybe. It had been only a year and a half when the Dark Times came, and they could have continued to leave me in for my own safety. Perhaps they'd just forgotten about me for those last nine years, or maybe keeping me in stasis had simply become a habit with them. But I knew without a doubt that they hadn't stassed me for my own good.

They'd kept me a child for as long as they could, for their own selfishness. So that Mom could have her live doll to dress up and play with. So that Daddy could have his little sycophant, always ready to say, "Yes, sir. You know what's best, sir." They'd switched me from school to school to keep me thinking I was stupid. They stassed me regularly to keep me young, and they made me believe it was what I wanted. They let me play with my paints because it was nonthreatening, harmless, and distracting . . . until I'd won the Young Masters Award. Then it became too much for them.

Had they lied? I wondered. Had they really come home to let me go to the awards ceremony? If Otto weren't there in my mind, I might have let myself think that. But with all my self-loathing neatly cleared away, I could see my distrust of them as clear as day. They terrified me. They always had. I loved them with every atom, but they terrified me, and I did not trust them.

"Do you think they loved me?" I thought to the silent presence.

"They probably thought they did," thought the other voice in my head. *"But I don't think they knew how."*

I sighed and tried to pull away. Otto kept firm hold of my wrist. *"I'll love you,"* he thought to me. *"We can be family."* He kissed my temple very tenderly, and I surprised myself with a smile.

He let go of my wrist then, and the silent presence vanished from my mind. "Thanks," I whispered. "Do I still scare you?"

Otto nodded, but his eyes crinkled. He brushed his hand over my cheek and a thought of a wild briar-rose hedge surrounding a beautiful castle flashed into my mind. Sleeping Beauty's castle. Only he didn't see me as the cursed and passive beauty, quietly waiting to be awakened by her Prince Charming. I was the stunning rose hedge, wild and impenetrable and strong enough to withstand a hundred years of people trying to hack their way through it to the vulnerable innocents I would protect. A hedge that knew which person, which people, to let inside.

I frowned. "Who am I protecting?"

His eyes smiled, and he placed his hand over my heart. *You.* Then he touched his own heart. *Me.* He crossed his hands and gestured, indicating the whole world. He playfully touched my nose, and I got one quick flash of thought. *"I trust you."* It wasn't exactly an "I." Nabiki was right; what he thought didn't always translate into language. There was a "we" in it, as his family was part of it. But he was the one who knew me.

There was the sound of a cell beep. Otto reached under his shirt and pulled out his cell. "What do you have a cell for?" I asked.

He looked at me and shook his head. I realized even if he couldn't speak over it, others could speak to him. He made a clicking sound with the side of his mouth, which obviously activated the incoming call. Bren's face materialized in Otto's hand. "Otto, did you get hold of Rose?"

Otto nodded, then handed me his cell.

I felt awkward. "Um, hi," I said.

"Rose, thank God! Are you all right?"

"Yeah, why?"

"Granddad celled me. The Plastine stormed the Uni Building about twenty minutes ago."

I blinked. "It *what*?"

"Took out a wall and started shaking down the security checkpoint. They tried to stop it, but you just can't stop one of those things. It did a lot of damage, and some of the people who tried to stop it are in the hospital now. When it couldn't find you, it drove off again. The police are trying to track it, but it has some kind of stealth mode tuned to UniCorp access points. Even UniCorp's security cameras don't register it. UniCorp computers digitalize it out with an automatic patch. That's how it's been wandering around ComUnity undetected. It is definitely acting under orders from someone inside UniCorp."

"How's Xavier?" I asked, and I couldn't keep the panic from my voice.

"Granddad's fine. He's coming to get you. I'm on my way, too. It should take me five minutes to get across campus. You're with Otto?"

"At the dorms, yeah. Look, I don't think I'm ready . . ."

"We can deal with anything that isn't your imminent demise later! For now, just ignore it!" Bren snapped, and I knew he was right.

"Okay. Has anyone found Guillory?"

Bren's face darkened. "Yeah. We don't think he was the one who set this thing on you."

"Why not?"

"He was found in your hotel room, beaten to death," Bren said. "News didn't get to us until now because he was under the name of Jance."

I didn't buy it. "Then what did he mean when he said it was a shame what was going to happen to me?"

"Probably what he always means," Bren said. "That you're going to get old and not be so pretty. He's said that to Hilary, too. He was drunk."

I felt cold. The man was still an ass, and I still didn't like him, even though he was dead. But if he hadn't been the one who tried to kill me, I wouldn't have wished for his death, no matter how big an ass he was, no matter what atrocious things he said or thought while he was drunk."So who *is* trying to kill me?" I asked, my voice trembling.

"We still don't know. Where's Otto?"

Otto took his cell back.

"Otto, keep her there until I get there. I'll only be a minute."

That was one minute too long. A shadow filled the doorway of the waiting room. The harsh Germanic plastic voice cut through the silence. "You are Rosalinda Samantha Fitzroy. Please remain still for retinal identification."

—chapter 25—

I didn't have time to react. I felt myself tackled twice, first by Otto's body and again by his mind, which was a rampant surge of defensive panic. He knocked me behind the sofa, grunting incoherently.

There were sensible undercurrents to Otto's thoughts as he sorted through everything we knew about this creature. He knew the Plastine was methodical, easily distracted, felt no pain. I caught a very distinct, *"Burn it, no paint!"* as his eyes surveyed the room looking for a possible weapon. He pushed my head down. *"Don't make a sound! It can use your voiceprint to confirm its initial ID. If it thinks you're not you, it might give up. I'll distract it. You head for the door."*

Before I had time to remind him what had happened to Guillory, he was gone, keeping to the corners of the room, out of the Plastine's immediate line of sight. As I scrambled on my stomach behind a chair, Otto shoved an end table between me and the Plastine. The Plastine plowed through it, leaving it in splinters, and grabbed for my ankles.

I shrieked and scrambled behind a second chair. With a sudden blow, the Plastine split the chair over my head. Stuffing spilled out, and the cushion flew halfway across the room. I rolled away, my stass-fatigued heart protesting the exertion. I couldn't catch my breath, but I was able to pull myself to my feet. The Plastine was still between me and the door. I was trapped.

Otto caught my eye as I dodged between more furniture. He had picked something up—the cushion from the demolished chair. He tore it open and pulled out the plastifoam core. He coiled like a cat, then flung himself onto the Plastine's back. The cushion case came down over the Plastine's head and arms, imprisoning him in the fabric. Otto looked directly at me then, jerking his head toward the door.

I didn't need to be told twice. With my heart in my throat, I lunged past the blind assassin. As I passed, I saw his plasticized arm reach up for Otto's.

I was nearly at the door when I heard the crunch. My heart froze. I turned just as the screaming started. It was a sound I never wanted to hear again. It was all too human, but entirely without language. Once, at a country charity banquet with my mother, I'd heard a rabbit scream as it was killed by a dog. It had chilled my blood. But Otto's cry of pain was a hundred times worse. The sound of ripping fabric followed as the Plastine tore the cushion case off its head, and Otto with it. Otto slammed against the wall, his arm twisted at an unnatural angle, then slid down in a weakly moving heap. And Otto was still between me and the Plastine.

I couldn't let it happen. What happened to Guillory had proven the Plastine's lethality. As the Plastine reached down and picked Otto up by his shirt, I lunged forward and squeezed myself between them.

The Plastine's shiny eyes searched my face once and then let Otto go. He fell to the ground with a thump that made my own head ache. The Plastine seized me by the wrist. "You are Rosalinda Samantha Fitzroy. Please remain still for retinal identification."

I remained perfectly still and let him search my eyes with his own dead ones. "Identification confirmed." He lifted up the control collar and wrapped it around my neck. I didn't struggle.

With a screech, Otto surged back up from the floor and tried, with his unbroken arm, to wrestle the collar away before it closed. The Plastine raised its hand to knock him away, likely with lethal force, but my hand was faster.

I grabbed Otto's arm, and I did something intentionally cruel. I took all of the darkest, deepest pain I felt, the blackest and most tangled thorny corner of my psyche, combined it with the memory of the pain and fatigue I had felt getting out of stass, and thought of it so strongly that Otto gasped with shock. He cringed away instinctively, long enough for the Plastine to secure the control collar around my neck with a final click.

The first few seconds under the control collar were a shock.

My mind screamed at me in panic. It was like going into stass without the soothing chemicals. My body refused to work. All of my systems were dependent upon the electrodes that had embedded themselves into my brain. For a split second *everything* stopped, and in that second I was dead. Then things began to start again, but strangely, unnaturally. My heart roared back to life, my lungs stretched, seeking breath, and my muscles contracted, then relaxed as the Plastine acclimatized his processors to my natural system.

Now that he had fulfilled phase one of his programming, he began to initiate phase two.

My legs followed him as the signals from his plasticized programming poured to my brain over the net. I couldn't look to see if Otto was all right. I could barely think. At first all I could do was follow, never mind that I hurt everywhere. The Plastine was moving my legs for me, forcing my lungs to continue breathing, forcing my heart to beat. But he did not know the best way for me to move my muscles, so I kept cramping. He did not know my body's natural pattern, so my heart staggered arrhythmically. Every breath hurt as he sucked too much air into my lungs, and then forced it out again.

He dragged me across campus. He hadn't accounted for my tear ducts and saline production, so my eyes were dry and smarting, and I couldn't even blink. Despite this, I could still see. The Plastine was headed for a skimmer. Not just any skimmer. That was Guillory's luxurious hover yacht.

The door to the hover yacht opened, and the Plastine

climbed inside. My body was forced to bend and follow. Just as I reached the door, a body hit me, hard enough to bruise. I was shocked to see Bren. I only saw what the Plastine directed me toward, so I hadn't seen him coming over the grounds.

Bren's fingers tried to rip the collar from my throat. The Plastine turned. *No!* I thought. *No, Bren, run! Run! Run, run, run!* As my body was twisted into the yacht, and the Plastine ducked my head, the electrodes lost contact with my brain for a millisecond. I was able to cry out—only one syllable, but it was enough.

"Run!"

Bren heard me, and to my surprise, took the warning to heart. He dropped and rolled beneath the hover yacht before the Plastine was fully able to designate him as a target.

For an eternity of a millisecond, the Plastine crouched in the door of the yacht, flipping through options in his processors. Then, the impediment gone, he climbed back into the yacht with me and we took off. I yearned to turn around and be sure Bren was okay, but my body belonged to the Plastine.

But it was a complicated body. A hundred autonomic functions, a thousand nerves containing all my motor control. There were so many systems in my natural programming that he was forced to keep running through his limited processors. It made him slow.

Slow enough that I was able to acclimatize. I tried to figure out which part of my mind was still my own. There was enough of me left to hurt, so I knew there was enough to think with. Otto's manipulation of my own electro impulses was subtle, delicate, and easily breakable. I suspected that if I wanted to force Otto from my mind, I could. The control collar's impulses were a ham-fisted, violent seizure of control, stealing all my autonomic functions and all of my motor control.

But higher brain function was still mine.

Moreover, I wasn't exactly alone. Like with Otto, I could sense the Plastine's presence in the corner of my mind. He was linked to my systems, but—without his being entirely aware of it—I was also linked to his. The control was all his, but my attention could go where I wanted.

Once I tuned in to the Plastine's processors, the echoing presence in my mind was almost overwhelming. It was a deafening roar of information, far too much for my own organic processors to encompass. If I could have shut my eyes and turned away, I would have. But it was inside me, and I couldn't. Panic swelled, and I feared I would go insane. But then the stream of information mercifully ceased.

DATA STREAM 197 SCANNED, came the thought in my head. PRINCIPAL UNAVAILABLE.

What? What did that mean?

BEGIN SCAN DATA STREAM 198: INITIATE.

A further string of incomprehensible information flowed past my consciousness. But I thought I recognized some of it. With a burst of understanding, I realized that the Plastine was searching through the net. Once I knew that the stream of information was from the net, and not from the Plastine himself, I was more able to distance myself from that and focus instead on the Plastine's programming.

At first all I caught was SCANNING . . . SCANNING . . . SCANNING . . .

DATA STREAM 198 SCANNED. PRINCIPAL UNAVAILABLE.

I focused on what he meant by "principal." It was there in his programming, a subfile connected to the word. PRINCIPAL: PRIMARY OPERATION PROGRAMMER. That had to be the one who had programmed him. The one who had sent him after me. I looked more closely. The first file the primary operation program was keyed to was a retinal scan, which meant nothing to me. The second was a voice recognition program, which was nothing but wave patterns. The third was a name.

MARK ANDREW FITZROY.

Daddy.

All the functions that would have made me blanch or sob or feel nauseated were being run through the control stream of the Plastine, so all I could do was feel it burning inside my head. But it all made perfect sense.

Mom and Daddy were highly prestigious, well-known figures. They'd stressed to me a million times the dangers of being kidnapped and held hostage by people who wanted to hurt them. I'd taken the warnings to heart and feared leaving the preset patterns Mom and Daddy had set for me. School to home, home to school, otherwise never leaving Unicorn Estates, certainly never leaving ComUnity. If I wasn't in either of those places, I was always with Mom and Daddy.

If I had been kidnapped, this plasticized horror had been

programmed to rescue me. Guillory died, and Otto and Bren and Zavier were targeted, because the Plastine was programmed to disable or eliminate the kidnappers.

Terrifying, yes. Sad . . . but calculated. Because suppose I hadn't been kidnapped. Suppose I had run away.

Suppose, just suppose, their perfect, delightful little child had decided that she didn't want to live with them anymore. What were they to do? Allow an undisciplined child to ruin their standing in the global community? Let people know that I wasn't the perfect plastic child they'd tried to mold me into? Allow me to possibly tell their secrets, splash to the net all their shortcomings, send all the skeletons buried in the closets on a parade down Main Street? No. That wouldn't do.

Best to pretend, then, that I had been kidnapped. Even if I went of my own free will, the Plastine wouldn't care what I said—he was not programmed to obey me. He was programmed to assume that anyone trying to impede his mission was an accomplice. Anyone who tried to stop him from retrieving me—friend, classmate, official—was designated a hostile target and destroyed accordingly. With no record. No fingerprints. No way of tracing the deaths back to my parents.

DATA STREAM 199 SCANNED. PRINCIPAL UNAVAILABLE.

Of course the principal was unavailable. Daddy was long dead. But I couldn't explain that to the Plastine.

I tried to look at the Plastine's programming as a whole. Just at the top of all of his programming was the file PRIMARY DIRECTIVE. I focused in on that. I saw what I'd expected to see.

-311

PRIMARY DIRECTIVE: RETURN TARGET TO PRINCIPAL. I was the target, and I was to be returned to Daddy.

But then there was that other directive, hidden beneath the first one. SECONDARY DIRECTIVE, PRINCIPAL UNAVAILABLE: TERMINATE TARGET.

When he was completely certain that he could not get me back to my parents, he was programmed to terminate me. The full horror of my parents' plan dawned on me. I had known that the Plastine was an assassin. But that my own parents would rather have had me dead than out of their control? That was not love. That was slavery.

Already suspecting what I'd find, I turned my attention to the date of the implementation of the Plastine's mission. This macabre thing hadn't even been commissioned until after I'd received my Young Masters Award. Daddy, and probably Mom as well, had only decided to set this thing after me after I'd shown that I was no longer theirs. My love for them boiled into hatred as I read the precepts of the Plastine's implanted mission.

But my attention was caught by the TARGET file. To my surprise, I saw more than one subfile there.

The first one, when I looked at it, was what I expected to see. Retinal scan, voiceprint, and my name, ROSALINDA SAMANTHA FITZROY.

The other two files also had retinal scans and voiceprints. And two names.

STEPHANO LUCIUS FITZROY.

SERAPHINA ALEXANDRA FITZROY.

Both files were still active. The people whom those files represented had not been terminated.

Seraphina . . . the name rang a bell. Sarah. My little friend Sarah, back when I was so young. What if she hadn't been the caretaker's daughter? Seraphina Alexandra Fitzroy. Sarah was my sister! My big sister! I wasn't alone. I had family. I had a brother and sister somewhere, probably stassed, as I had been. I had to find them. My purposeless hatred turned into something fierce and protective, and suddenly it didn't even matter that it was impossible.

I forced my attention back to the Plastine's scan of the net. He was going through a systematic check of all possible net screenings. While the net seemed never ending, and was constantly fluid, it was ultimately finite. He'd find and scan his way through all data streams eventually, and when he was unable to find retinal scans, voiceprints, or a current entry for the name MARK FITZROY, he would terminate me. So where the hell was he taking me?

Even having the question provided me with the answer. It was there in his programming. RETURN TO STATION. Great. Where was the station? I looked under that file and found exact latitude and longitude, down to the fiftieth decimal, but that meant nothing to me. I looked more deeply and was able to find a tactical report of his station. It was a chair, probably a recharging station. I backed away and tried to find a log of his movements through the last few days.

He'd been busy. I flipped through it backward. He attacked Uni Prep and managed to fulfill phase one of his programming. Retain. Before that he had been on his way back to his station in Guillory's hover yacht when he caught my retinal scan over the net at Uni Prep.

It was the retinal scan! Every time I was scanned, he was alerted over the net. I'd been saved by the antiquated fingerprint scanner at home and the fact that I never went anywhere but school and my physical therapist's office. If Otto had decided to talk to me in the quad instead of the dorms, we'd all still be there, hale and whole, instead of Otto broken and bruised, and me on my way toward termination.

Before that, he'd been at the Uni Building, ascertaining that I was not on the premises. Lots of security guards and broken glass. I even caught a glimpse of Xavier once, shouting at someone, and my heart leaped.

I flipped through the journey back from Nirvana. I mentally cringed at the backward, flickering image of Guillory's death. No one deserved that fate. And it was even worse—I'd spent all this time hating him, and Guillory had actually been trying to stop the wretched thing. He must have grabbed my arm trying to pull me out of the way, but was too drunk to do it. I went back through the journey in the purloined skimmer. I saw, backward, and from a different perspective, the news program I'd seen on Nirvana, of the Plastine hijacking the skimmer.

Ah, here it was. Finally, I watched the Plastine's log as he traveled across . . . what? It looked like a garden. A secret entrance? I had no idea where he was until I caught a glimpse of the front gates of Unicorn Estates.

The burned thing had been beneath my feet the whole time! The image went backward, and I saw the Plastine pass through the subbasement, past my very stass tube! He must have walked right past me as I huddled there the first night he attacked.

A secret door . . . or probably not so secret. Simply forgotten. A metal panel opened and the Plastine returned, backward, to his station in the corner of the room.

The room his station was in was hauntingly familiar. I recognized the layout. Daddy's office at the Uni Building had been exactly the same, with all the multiple screens hooked up to the net, the rich leather chair by the desk. The screens were dark and dusty now, only one or two of them still throwing off an erratic flash as power trickled inconsistently through cables. The leather chair had cracked, and some kind of rodent had made a nest in the stuffing. But I knew this had been Daddy's second home office: the one where he could organize all the not-quite-legal dealings it had taken to turn UniCorp into the largest commercial company in human history.

I turned my attention away from the replay. I knew where we were going now. And I knew, or thought I knew, how I was going to stop it. It all depended on the crucial second when the Plastine stood me back up and made me exit the hover yacht. The one moment I'd had any control over my body was when he'd twisted my neck to get me into the yacht. If I could exploit that millisecond while the control collar's implants were partially disconnected, I might be able to get out of this.

The Plastine pulled the hover yacht into the courtyard of Unicorn Estates, and he climbed out. My legs moved to follow, my arms lifted to balance, and then my head ducked to move his precious target undamaged out of the yacht.

Even before he moved me, I had been telling my arm to go *up*. *Up*, burn it, and grab my neck. As my head bent, the connection failed, and my arm reacted to the steady impulse I'd been sending it. It shot up as quickly as if I'd been burned. My right hand grabbed the collar. . . .

And the moment had passed. I had moved my hand, but not fast enough. Instead of ripping the control collar from my neck, all I'd succeeded in doing was forcing my fingers underneath it. It was hopeless. If I could have sagged in defeat, I would have. But I was walking now, through the garage, to the subbasement, to my impending demise. My arm hung awkwardly, my fingers hooked beneath the collar.

But something was happening. I could move. Not very much. I could twitch my leg, just a bit, and then it would follow the impulses of the Plastine again. I whimpered with the pain for a split second before such reactions were suppressed. What was going on?

I realized it as the Plastine's overburdened systems hit me with another arrhythmia. As my heart pounded, my fingers found stronger purchase on the collar. It was my pulse. The surging of blood against my fingers was causing the connection on the collar to pull away. It was less than a millimeter for only a millisecond. But that just might be enough.

I wished I could blink so that I could see better. Things had gone hazy through my dry, unlubricated eyes. But as we turned the corner, I saw it sure enough. Right there. My stass tube, the shiny NEOFUSION™ label visible even through the blur.

With every pulse of my minimal control, I leaned my body to the left. I had been walking immediately behind the Plastine, but now I was slowly but steadily altering my course to collide with my stass tube. The activation control was right on the left side, by my knee. With everything Xavier had done to hack the thing, it had an absolute hair trigger. If I could aim myself right, when I collided with my tube I could activate it.

It was a desperate plan. If this failed, I was history—just as my parents had intended.

The Plastine continued onward, oblivious to my slightly altered course. He passed by my stass tube. And I didn't.

With an explosion of fresh pain, my left knee connected with the stass tube, and the quiet hum of gentle music floated from the cushioned bed. It was activated. The momentum from my collision knocked my rag doll body over, and I fell headlong over the tube. The stass system's established program took over. Stass chemicals wafted through my lungs, lulling me into a fearless dream state. The clear lid of the tube automatically began to slide closed. And in my dropped rag doll position, it began to close upon my legs. But more important, on my twisted arm—the arm connected to the hand whose fingers were wrapped around my control collar. As my elbow was forced over my ear, and my shoulder was nearly ripped from its socket, the control collar was pulled off.

I could almost hear the sucking sound as the electrodes

were pulled from my skull. The stass chemicals were already doing their work, and my eyes closed drowsily. I'd always tried to hold on to my stass dreams. Now I fought them off, banishing the peaceful lightning storms of my imagination, forcing my eyes to see the dim blue-gray of the subbasement and not the bright colors of my dreams. I embraced the pain in my knee and the ache in my shoulder and my burning eyes and pulled myself away from the tube. It beeped, recognizing a flaw in the system. Slowly the lid began to slide open again.

With the chemicals flowing through me, I felt no fear as I saw the Plastine, already turned, having recognized the disruption to his programmed procedure. He paused, his systems resetting, as his original plan was thwarted. He'd be after me in a moment, his program adapting. I could have run then, but I wouldn't have gotten far. I hurt too much, and my nanos weren't working, and he'd have cut me off before I got halfway to the lift. But there was an alternative to flight.

Having no fear always granted a peaceful kind of clarity. I think that was why I always tried to hold on to stass, even when I didn't have to. The clarity made me see that there was only one way to defeat a heartless plastic foe.

Heat.

With the edge of the control collar, I gouged at the soft, pink satin-of-silk cushions inside my tube. The sharp electrodes caught on the fabric, and the strong edges of the collar ripped up whole chunks of padding. I knew what I was looking for, and I knew where it was.

With shreds of satin-of-silk clinging to my hands, I found

the connections to the NeoFusion battery that powered my stass tube. I followed them down, ripping up the secondary safety panel, and there it was. The battery, a large cylindrical canister as long as my forearm, as big around as my head. Adrenaline gave me the strength to rip it from its housing. It was heavy, but not impossible.

With an angry whine, my stass tube died, its lights and chemical dispensers blinking off. The Plastine had started moving again and was less than five meters from me. I shook up the battery, with its huge UniCorp logo, exciting the neutrinos and reversing its natural polarity. I mentally cursed my father for making me believe I was too stupid to understand. I could have run UniCorp with no trouble. I'd picked up enough knowledge about UniCorp's most impressive product, hadn't I? Can't use NeoFusion batteries in skimmers or anything that might have a collision. Too volatile.

And so was I.

I threw the battery at the Plastine, hoping it would explode on contact. The Plastine caught it deftly, and my heart sank. I fell into my ruined tube, hoping for residual chemicals, hoping my last moments would be without fear. I was dead. Good-bye, Xavier. Good-bye Bren, Otto, Mina, Sun, Moon, stars, love, pain, regret, happiness, art, beauty.

But I'd forgotten the Plastine's strength, and I had forgotten its programming. Stop anything that tries to impede retrieval. With a quick flick of his hands, the Plastine crushed the battery casing, and raw power surged.

I reached forward and grabbed the lid of my tube, forcing

it to close over my head. I wasn't quite fast enough. The first surge of heat blasted me with pain, and my entire body turned bright red, like a sunburn. My fingertips, which were the last to enter the tube, received blisters. But the tube had been designed to withstand fires and deep space and nuclear holocaust. It could more than protect me from a single mild explosion of NeoFusion.

I squeezed my eyes shut through the worst of the blast. When I opened them again, a flickering light was flashing and I dared to look up through the NeoGlass of my tube lid. The sudden burst of heat had passed—it could last only a few seconds once the casing was compromised—but in those few seconds of intense heat, the Plastine had combusted.

The creature was melting, flames leaping from his plasticized body, yet he continued slowly toward my tube. His system had no recognition of pain. He continued to burn, fire scorching the ceiling of the subbasement. A fire alarm went off, but the heat from the initial explosion was so volatile that the fire-suppression system above our heads was already damaged. Shelves filled with antiquated junk burned behind and around him. One of his legs collapsed beneath him, melting into liquid. An arm dripped like a burning candle.

I slid my tube lid open and watched as my enemy, my father's tool, collapsed into a burning puddle. With his head on fire, half of his face melted away, I heard one last statement, mushy with melted plastic. "Mission, aborted. Damage report . . . 11 . . . percent . . . capacity . . . 10 . . . percent . . . 6 . . . per . . ." The voice melted along with the rest of it.

I wished I felt triumph. All I felt was immensely tired.

Belatedly, the redundancy program of the fire-suppression system took effect, and I was splashed by a sudden shower of rain. For some reason, it made me laugh. The cool wetness soothed the pain of my burn. I held my face up to it and lifted my arms. Against all odds, I was still alive. The last remnant of my parents' control was melted at my feet, tangled in a web of thorns it could not escape. I was the rose. I was the briar patch.

—chapter 26—

The water didn't do much good for the plastic fire, and the fumes in the room were something lethal, I'm sure. I must have looked an absolute witch when Bren, Otto, and Xavier pelted across the subbasement to my rescue. I was standing in the rubble of my slaughtered stass tube, arms spread, laughing somewhat hysterically in the artificial rain, with the still-burning remains of the Plastine flaring behind me. I dropped my hands when I saw them, grinning rather sheepishly. Their belated rescue had been thwarted. I almost felt bad about that.

Xavier was the one who spoke. Gingerly, as if afraid I'd lunge for his face, he asked, "Rose? Are you all right?"

I giggled, then coughed, shuddering. The cold water and the fumes from the burning plastic were wreaking havoc on my stass-fatigued body. "Yeah," I said. "What are you all doing here? Why didn't you cell the police? Otto, your arm!" His arm was hung in a makeshift sling. I recognized the fabric of the ruined cushion back at the dorm.

Xavier looked completely lost, wet and frail and ancient. It was Otto who came to me, putting his good arm around my shoulder and leading me gently (very gently once his thumb touched my neck and I told him exactly how much I hurt) back toward the lift. *"I'll be fine,"* he told me. *"I've had worse. We did cell the police, but Bren's grandfather knew we'd get here faster. He was pretty sure where it was going, and the Plastine was still in stealth mode. Hard for the police to track."*

"I'm sorry you got hurt."

Otto flashed me a burst of thought, of how he would have felt if he'd just stood back and let it all happen. I cringed. He was right. It would have been worse.

"I'm sorry for what I thought at you."

"I know why you did." The image of the guardian briar-rose hedge came again into my mind.

"You were right," I told him silently. *"And I know who I have to protect."*

The look of horror in his yellow eyes when I thought of Seraphina and Stephano mirrored my own thoughts. *"Anything I can do,"* he offered.

Bren had gone ahead of us and was waiting at the lift. He'd stopped the water. "I'll take care of the fire," he told me, pulling a fire extinguisher from a red cabinet on the wall.

"You tell Xavier I expect to see him upstairs," I called after him.

Bren threw half a laugh back at me, and then I let Otto pull me into the lift and up to my apartment.

"Are you sure you're all right?" I asked once we'd gotten inside. "Your arm."

"I'll go to my doctor. Penny's going to want to hear about this, anyway. She loves adventure stories."

"Your doctor's at the lab?"

"Of course. Who else could figure out how I work? I don't even heal the same way. Besides, you're the one who really needs a doctor. You're as red as a rose."

"But a live one!"

Otto's eyes crinkled. *"Where are your parents?"* He wasn't really thinking the word *parents,* but that was a close translation.

"Knowing Barry and Patty, playing golf or something," I said. "No, that's ungenerous of me. Probably at work."

"I only ask because the police were going to cell them. You might want to be able to guess when they'll get here."

I nodded. "Right," I said. I slipped into my room and pulled a fresh uniform off a hanger. It was more difficult getting dressed with my burned fingers than I might have thought. They still felt on fire. "Ow!" I muttered, pulling the soft cotton over my heat-burned flesh. My wrenched shoulder hurt, too, and my knee throbbed, and my eyes still stung a bit, and all my muscles ached, and Bren had really bruised me trying to get the collar off. And to top it off, my elbow was still swollen from hitting the Plastine on Nirvana. It was hard to dress. I only slipped on a shirt and skirt, abandoning most of the rest of the uniform.

When I limped back out to the living room, I saw Otto had pulled the first aid kit from above the refrigerator. Rather deftly, with his one good arm, he managed to put Icestrip™ bandages on my fingers, which made me feel cold, but also made my fingers stop hurting so much. He made me swallow a painkiller, and he was just spraying my lightly burned face with a cooling salve when Barry and Patty came home.

"What are you doing here?" Barry said.

"What trouble have you gotten into this time?" Patty asked.

"Why did the police cell us?"

"Who or what is that?" Patty added, pointing at Otto, who rolled his eyes.

I ignored their questions. "You're fired."

"What?" Barry and Patty both looked at me in shock, and Otto made a strange, choked sound. He was laughing. I took strength from that.

"I said you're fired. Get out of my apartment."

Patty's face turned incredulous. "I don't know what you're thinking, young lady, but we are your appointed guardians. . . ."

"No, you're not," I said, without ire. "Guillory hired you to keep an eye on me. You were never designated my guardians. Everything had to go through him. Well, Guillory's dead. And until someone reorganizes the company, that means *I'm* the one who employs *you*. And you're fired. From this job, anyway; go back to Florida and pick up where Reggie made you leave off."

They protested until Xavier strode, damp and elegant, into the foyer. "Listen to your boss," he told them quietly. "If it isn't her, it's me. If she doesn't want you, that's it."

Unable to decide which of us to look at, Barry asked, "Did you mean it when you said we could go back to our jobs at Uni Florida?"

"Yup," I said.

"I guarantee it," Xavier added.

Barry nodded. "All right, then." He turned to his wife. "Let's pack."

And they both disappeared into the master bedroom.

Xavier shook his head at their retreating forms. "I'll find you someone better," he said to me. I stared at him. He looked away, backing toward the door. "Someone has to cell the police; tell them the worst is over."

"Done it," Bren said, popping up from behind him. "On the way to turn off the fire system."

"We'll need a paramedic."

"Done. Celled Mom, too. They're on the way."

Xavier nodded. "Yes. Well, I'll go wait for the ambulance."

"No," I said to Xavier. "You stay."

Xavier gazed at me. "I think someone should show them to the scene."

"Bren can do that, or Annie," I said. "We have to talk."

Xavier bowed his head. "Now might not be the best time," he said.

"Now might be the only time I ever get you in a room with me again," I said. "You've been avoiding me since I came out."

Xavier swallowed. "You're right. I have."

I glanced at Otto. Otto, who knew the whole story. He took my hand. *"I'll take Bren out to the garden, wait for the police."*

"Thanks," I said. I watched the two of them go, then turned back to Xavier.

He was wet and rumpled, and he obviously hadn't slept for days. He looked very much like he didn't want to have this conversation. I went to the bathroom to get him a towel, so he could at least dry his hair.

Zavier had been locked up in the bathroom with a bowl of dog food and a chew toy. He jumped up when I opened the door, and he nearly made me scream as he promptly put paw and nose on all my most tender spots. "Ow! Sit! Stay, Zavier!"

He sat down, panting, clearly glad to see me again. I grabbed a fresh towel and let Zavier follow me back to the living room. "Here," I said, throwing the towel to Xavier.

He caught it quite deftly, for an old man, and dried his face and shoulders with military efficiency. "Do you like Dizzy?" he asked almost absently.

I turned to Zavier. "You answer to Dizzy?" I asked him. He looked confused for a moment, then wagged his tail placatingly. I patted his blond head. "I call him Zavier," I said. "With a Z."

Xavier froze. "Oh," he said. He covered his face with the towel again. I suspect he did it more for something to do than because his face was still wet.

I stared at Xavier, forcing myself to see the boy I knew. It wasn't hard. I couldn't believe I hadn't noticed it right away. But then, he'd barely spent five minutes in the same room with me until last night. And I probably hadn't wanted to see. I petted my dog's head. "I needed to ask you something."

"I know," Xavier said, and his voice fell like a lead weight.

I took a deep breath. "How could you leave me like that? For so long?" I asked. I said it without malice.

Xavier let loose a deep sigh and slowly lowered himself to

one of his chairs. "You've no idea how it's tortured me," he said, refusing to meet my eyes. "I've been asking myself the same question every hour since Bren found you. I've barely slept. I . . ." He sighed again, then forced himself to look at me. "I truly didn't know."

"How could you not know?"

Xavier moved his head the way he had as a child, when he thought I didn't understand something. "Rose." He paused. "You broke up with me."

I nodded, trying to understand. I curled up on the couch. "So, you thought . . . it wasn't your role anymore?"

"No," he said.

"Please, I'm trying to understand this, Xavier. Either you absolved yourself of responsibility for me, or you felt I deserved to lose my life. And I refuse to believe that. Despite . . ." It was remarkably hard to pull the next words out of the pain. "Despite your staying away even when I came back."

"No, damn—" He hesitated, unable to find words. "There *is* no absolution! Do you *know* how long it's been? I've been looking back through fifty, sixty years, through every moment of my life, trying to see how I let this happen, and there is no excuse that can absolve me of this . . . neglect. How could I let you know, now? How could I . . . torture you with the knowledge of me? Better let you believe I had died, along with everyone else."

I looked at him. This really wasn't my Xavier. My Xavier's eyes used to laugh. My eyes caught on the sketchbook on the coffee table, the one I'd abandoned when I grabbed the new one for my trip with Reggie. I pulled it over and found a blank sheet. "Did you ever try to find me?" I asked, tugging the charcoal pencil out from the spiral binding.

"Yes," he said, surprising me. "Not hard enough, apparently."

"Tell me," I said. I sat back and watched him, letting my hands begin another sketch of him.

"I didn't realize what had happened, at first," he said. "After you said good-bye. I saw you in the corridors, but you avoided me. You'd disappear on and off, and I'd start to get nervous. But you always came back, and you still avoided me. I believed you really didn't want to be with me. And then, when you finally disappeared for so long, I was glad. I didn't want to see you. It . . . Everything always matters so much at that age. It hurt, seeing you—and not being with you."

I smiled ruefully. I was still that age.

"But then . . . a year went by. Åsa was gone, and I began to wonder if maybe . . . maybe Mark and Jacqueline had forced you to break up with me. And because you weren't being the perfect child they'd created, they'd stassed you, just to get rid of you. It was just a little suspicion. But it ate at me and ate at me until I was about to head for college." I sketched a study of Xavier's wrinkled hands as he moved them, emphasizing his speech.

"I mean, I'd be gone. And there'd be no one else who even knew you were there. So I waited until your parents went off to one of your mother's charity galas, and I broke into your apartment."

I could just picture him, sneaking to the Unicorn central computer, hacking into the key codes until he could sneak into my apartment.

"I didn't know if you'd be glad to see me or not. But I was eighteen, and I already had a place of my own at Princeton. And no matter what you thought of me, a year in stass for no reason was beyond ridiculous. I'd already come to the conclusion that it was abusive."

He sighed. "I thought I'd give you the option . . . not of being with me, but just of . . . getting out of there. No more stass, no more playing dress up as Mommy's little 'live doll,' no more, 'Yes, Daddy, of course, Daddy.' Just you. Just Rose."

With my burns still smarting from the Plastine's attack, I could just imagine if he'd succeeded. The Plastine would have caught up with us at Princeton, new, fresh, not suffering sixty-two years of neglect. Programmed to kill any who tried to stop it.

That thought gave me pause. If I'd been given the choice, back before I was stassed, of giving up my love for him or letting him die, I knew what I would have chosen. I would have gladly sacrificed sixty-two years of my life for his. Fate had always been against us, no matter how much I loved him.

Xavier took a deep breath. "And, yes, if you'd wanted, just you and me. As we'd always been. I missed you."

I closed my eyes at that. I felt a stir in my chest that I hadn't felt since waking up. Not nervous flutterings and giddy uncertain hopes, but a tiny sparkle of real joy.

"I crept to your closet, but your tube wasn't there," Xavier said. "Your room was still there, all your things, but you were gone. I stood there, not knowing what to do. Then, apparently, it turned out my hacking skills weren't up to the challenge. I'd set off an alarm and the police burst in and arrested me. They put me in a jail cell for the night and tried to contact Mark and Jacqueline to charge me with breaking and entering." He took a deep breath. "The arraignment didn't get very far. Before dawn, almost everyone in the police station was dead."

I looked up from my sketchbook, horrified. "No," I whispered.

He nodded. "My timing could have been better, I guess. But then, if I had let you out right then, you'd likely have gotten sick, too. The plague hit ComUnity that very day." He took a deep breath. "I was there, alone in my jail cell. Charges hadn't yet been drawn up. And as I waited, suddenly I saw people through the bars, sweating and coughing and clutching their chests and then screaming and screaming. . . ." He shook his head. "I huddled in the corner, staying as far away from the death as I could. I was . . . scared. I was so glad I hadn't found you. I could hear the screaming from the streets, and sirens wailing from the ambulances. And then they stopped, and I realized their silence was more frightening still." More than his hand was trembling now. "I had no food, no water for two days. And then I started to get sick."

"No!"

He pursed his lips at me, trying to tell me it was all right. "I was far away from the general population, and I hadn't touched anyone, so the disease didn't catch me until it became airborne. I started to cough, just at the end, as the bodies started to decay. By that time, I wasn't scared any longer. I was almost relieved. I didn't want to be there anymore. And just then, as I was preparing to die, UniCorp security dressed in biohazard suits pushed open the doors against the piles of dead and shoved antibiotics into my veins."

He shrugged. "Mom and Dad were dead. Princeton was a ghost town. Mark and Jacqueline had disappeared, headed, I found out later, to one of their off-world colonies. By miraculous chance, they hadn't brought the plague along. I was drafted into the civil service, and I spent the next five years treating plague victims, quelling riots, and distributing supplies." He looked at me. "I won't say you weren't in my thoughts, because you were. You had to be. You were part of my life for so long, you became an imprint on my psyche. But there was death all around me. I knew you were in one of two places: either safely in stasis or already peacefully dead. Either way, there was nothing I could do for you."

In my sketch I shaded his eyes. Yes, I could see the horror there. The stern lines that so much tragedy had etched onto his face.

"When I finished my stint in the CS, I applied for an internship at UniCorp. Ordinary college education had gone by the wayside, but my bout in the CS counted in my résumé. I was surprised they took me in, but my name was known. Mom and Dad had worked for Mark, and your parents still remembered me. Apparently, in all the chaos, it had never filtered back to them that I'd broken into their home." He took a deep breath. "I only joined UniCorp for one reason. To get close to them, to ask them about you."

That startled me. I looked up from my sketch. "Really?"

He stared at me. "You were always in the back of my mind, Rose. I'd never been able to forget you. I frequently wished I could have. I'd have dreams about you. They would spring up from out of nowhere, with no warning. I wouldn't even have been consciously thinking about you, and there you'd be again. And every time you showed up, I'd spend the whole dream trying to tell you how much I missed you. I'd wake up and spend the morning pounding my head, muttering, 'Stupid psyche!' It seemed I was built around the mold of you. You were my measuring stick. Every person I ever talked to, every friend I ever had, every woman who ever glanced my way was held up in measurement to my memory of you."

I wanted to smile, and I wanted to cry. It was tragic. I settled for finishing my sketch.

"When I got close to them, finally, I asked them about you. They grew so angry; your father nearly hit me. 'Leave the past in the past,' he said. 'We don't unbury our dead.' And I believed him." Xavier's voice faded almost to a whisper. "Like a damned fool." He shook his head. "I was twenty-four. I should have tried harder." The self-loathing was clear in his voice.

Twenty-four. He would have been only eight years older than me. I cringed as I realized that.

He sat up a little straighter. "I know they debated firing me after that, but healthy, whole people with half a brain were scarce during the Dark Times. They couldn't afford to lose me. So I ended up staying. Working for the devil. I debated leaving, but about that time the true tragedy of the Global Food Initiative came out. And I'd been poisoned, too, along with the millions of others. No children. Ever. Or so I thought—reliable countermeasures hadn't been developed at that time. And I *hated* them so much. I knew UniCorp had so much *power.* I thought if I stayed, I might be able to undo some of the worst evils.

"I started by trying to sabotage the corporation, make the whole thing go under, and then I realized I could work tangentially and use the corporation to actually do *good.* It's a slow process, and I keep a lot of it very quiet. I didn't want power; I wanted to defuse it from men like your father and Reggie. It was really all there was left to do."

"You realize you're president now," I said.

"Unfortunately, yes. I've been trying to avoid that. I actually have more control when people aren't looking directly at me."

"Elevate Bren's dad," I said. "Delegate to him. He's a good man, and he likes the work. You're"—I tried to think of a word that wasn't *old*—"near retirement. The board would understand."

Xavier frowned. "That's an idea. You're right; he could do it. Annie had good taste."

"I like her," I told him.

"She likes you," Xavier said. "She told me."

I couldn't help but ask. "Why did you call her Roseanna?"

Xavier looked down. "My wife's sister was among the dead. She was called Hannah. We put them together."

"You wife knew about me?"

"Of course. We loved each other."

I wanted to feel jealous, but all I felt was curious. "What was she like?"

He smiled. "Like you," he said. "Compassionate. Dutiful. Artistic. I told you that you were my measuring stick. She was a bit tougher than you, but Dark Time survivors tended to be. She was a designer in the graphics department. She made up a game for herself, to get me to smile whenever she saw me. I'm surprised she saw anything human left in me in the first place. And she put up with my surliness. And with all the invasive procedures it took to get Ted and Annie."

"I'm glad," I whispered. "I'm so glad." I didn't need to elaborate. "You miss her?"

"Actually, not so much. Not that I don't wish she were still here, because I do. But I feel like part of her *is* still here." He gestured around the apartment. "Her soul, maybe. Waiting for me." He shrugged. "Of course, what do I know? I rather thought yours was, too."

"It was," I said. "I gave it to you to hold, like my Young Masters Award."

"I still have that," Xavier whispered.

"Well, you had my soul, too. I gave it to you with that last kiss."

"I never wanted to take your soul," Xavier said.

"I wanted you to have it. Keep it," I said with a laugh. "I grew a new one."

I glanced at the grandfather clock against the wall. The

paramedics should have been here by now. Otto. He must have been keeping them at bay. It was a good thing, too. Xavier seemed to have relaxed, but I wasn't done with the hard questions yet. "Why didn't you tell me who you were?"

He shook his head. "How could I? Sixty years thinking you were dead, and then my grandson cells me up from out of the blue and tells me he's discovered Rosalinda Fitzroy in the subbasement, and the entire structure of the universe has changed." He rubbed his temple, as if he had a headache. "All that time came rushing at me. I split in two inside. As though I'd failed to take the life I was meant to have, and someone else's life came and stole all those years. There was the me I knew: father, grandfather, businessman. And then this angry, wounded teenage boy surged up from out of nowhere, and you can't believe how he hated me. He would scream at me. Sometimes half the night. *'All the time she's been right there, literally under your feet! How could you not go and get her?'*" Xavier sighed. "He blamed me entirely."

He sniffed and closed his eyes. "You were so pitiful, nothing but bones. And so painfully *young.*"

I thought about that. He'd had a wife. He'd raised two children. His grandson was the same age as me. I must seem an utter child to him. How ironic. I'd helped teach Xavier to walk.

"I thought about telling you, right at the beginning, while you were still in the hospital. But when you didn't even recognize me, I thought . . . maybe that's for the best. How could you not blame me for leaving you there? When I was the only one who *knew.*"

My sketch was finished. There he was. A careworn, tormented old man, with a broken heart behind his eyes. I always understood things better when I drew them. Xavier's smile had died during the Dark Times. It was my job to resurrect it, to take it out of stasis and put it back where it belonged. I stood up.

Xavier looked at me, his milky-green eyes curious. I grinned. "You've grown so *tall!*" I said.

He stared at me in confusion. "What?"

"I always say that," I said. "It's tradition."

Xavier took a deep breath and looked down at his knees. "I'm not sure it's true this time. Age tends to wear on one."

"As does guilt," I said. I laid my hand on his shoulder. "Stop hating yourself. It wasn't your fault. It wasn't mine, either. It just happened."

He lifted his hand and placed it on mine for a moment, then let it fall again. "I missed you," he whispered.

Tears stabbed my eyes then. "I missed you," I said. "I missed everything."

We were silent for a moment. I sank to my knees and leaned my head against the arm of his easy chair. "Well," I said, "at least now you can have your apartment back."

Xavier shook his head. "No. It's yours."

I shook my head back at him. "I didn't say I was leaving it."

"What do you mean?"

I squared my shoulders and looked him dead in the face. "I mean, I've finally learned to make decisions all on my own. No more passive lying down and letting others tell me what to do. I know what I want, and I want you. I want you to be my guardian."

Xavier shook his hoary head adamantly. "I can't do that, Rose. It wouldn't be right."

"Says who? Xavier, when has our being together ever been wrong? I'm not stupid," I added, cutting off whatever he'd been about to say. "I know what can and can't be between us. We lost something. That blazing, all-encompassing inferno of first love. And that isn't fair." I couldn't quite keep the tears out of my voice, but I held them back. I had to make him see. "That will never be fair. And I will always grieve for it, as much as you have. My parents stole you from me as surely as they stole my life. But that isn't all we had. That was the least of what we had together. We had something more real, something time and age difference simply can't kill. I *know* you, Xavier! We were always together. It wasn't always romantic. You started as my little brother, then became my best friend. Why can't we go on? Become something else? I'm all alone. I *need* you now. I need my family." Damn it, now I *was* crying.

And his frail arms were around me. "Shh, shhh. Hush, now." He kissed my forehead with as much tenderness as I used to kiss his, back when he was barely more than a baby.

I pulled away and looked at him. "Xavier, from the very beginning, you've been doing everything in your power to show me you still loved me. My studio, my schedule, Desert Roads." I smiled. "The prism. It was *your* hand I felt stroke my hair, in this very room, after I was attacked."

His eyes lowered and I saw that I was right.

"I know you want to be with me. You want to be my family. The only reason you don't is because you think people will think it's wrong. Well, burn them! They don't know what we are to each other. I know you're probably horrified by the idea of what we once were to each other, as horrified as I would have been by the idea if you'd suddenly turned three again when I was sixteen. But that's over. That girl died. And *I'm* here now." I looked to the ground for a moment, willing the strength from all my thorny inner briars. "Are you really going to deny me the only love I've ever known?"

Xavier looked at me for a long moment, and then he frowned. "Are you and Bren . . . ?" he asked.

I laughed, which fortunately banished my tears. I knew I'd be blushing bright pink if I weren't already red from the burns. "Why do you ask?"

Xavier looked away, and I realized he was afraid that I expected something impossible from him, that I wasn't ready to let that part of my life move on without him. "I don't know," I said, as reassuringly as I could. "Maybe one day. I scare him right now."

"You're scaring *me*," Xavier said. "I've never seen you be anything but passive."

I shrugged. "Hasn't done me much good. So," I said, "do I get you as my family, or do I have to get my board to fire you?"

Xavier laughed.

"I'm serious," I said. "Now that I've found you, I'm not letting you go again."

Xavier blinked at me. "I thought that was my line."

My face broke into a grin. "You mean I get to keep you?"

He sighed. "Why not? You have me already, anyway."

I jumped up and hugged him. He smelled old, and of that cologne I noticed in his office, and he didn't feel like my Xavier when I held him anymore. And I loved him as much as I ever had. Brother. Best friend. Grandfather. What did it matter? He was my Xavier.

—epilogue—

I will try to hold on to my dreams for the future as long as I can. I'm past the game of marking time, holding on to fantasies, denying what's in my heart and what is before my eyes. I try to keep myself active, keep my heart open, refuse to sink into despair when I find myself crying for no reason in the middle of the night.

I often have dinner at Bren's house, and Bren good-naturedly tries and fails to teach me tennis. I don't know how I feel about him anymore. He's my gorgeous, sexy friend who could have been my grandson. It's all a tangle of confusion and awkwardness, but it's good. We're fond of each other—almost family, almost not. It'll do for now.

I link up with Otto's screen every evening, and we try to find new reasons to laugh. I don't know how I feel about him, either. I know how he feels about me, though I think he thinks he's keeping it a secret. He has my sympathy and my love . . . but what kind of love I'm not even trying to figure out yet. What we have is what it is, and that's all I want it to be. For now.

As for Xavier, he is very formal with me, and I don't blame him. This is a somewhat disturbing situation I have forced upon him. He will hug me (with only one arm) if it seems necessary—like if I'm crying. Otherwise he won't touch me. I respect his distance. He's teaching me how to cook, and he still sits down with me to help me study. That part of our relationship hasn't changed in sixty years. My grades are improving. I'm not as dumb as I once thought I was.

I don't know where my brother and sister are. Xavier helped me to track down their existence—my parents couldn't manage to erase every hint of their birth, and physical records were filed in the local archives. If Sarah is alive, she's been in stasis now for nearly eighty years. Stephano would have been stassed for more than ninety. Even the thought of it fills my throat with bile.

I dream that one day I'll find them. I dream that one day I'll truly believe in my place in this world. I dream that I am strong. And I have three best friends who dream with me.

My name is Rosalinda Samantha Fitzroy. I am one hundred years old. I am free. I am haunted. But if nothing else, I am wide awake.